LIEUTENANT

Governor Trilogy
Book 2

Lesli Richardson

Dear Copper,

Thanks fr readig!

Lesl. Richardson /

Tymbr Dolton

Lieutenant
Governor Trilogy Book 2

Copyright © 2018 by Lesli Richardson
First Print Publication: September 2018

www.LesliRichardson.com

DEDICATION

For Hubby, for my bestie, Trish; for my Tymber's Trybe group, and for Sir—He knows why.

AUTHOR'S NOTE

Florida politics are messy, nasty, sexy, brutal, funny, insane, impossibly complex, and a lot of fun to write about. (Mostly because they're messy, nasty, sexy, brutal, funny, insane, and impossibly complex.)

Since the focus of this trilogy isn't the politics so much as it is the people, I've taken certain liberties and simplified a few things here and there.

The kinky shit, however, is absolutely realistic.

Also, in this world, Covid-19 isn't a thing, so it's not mentioned.

Events in this book reference events from *Governor* (Governor Trilogy 1). The series continues with *Chief* (Book 3), *Yes, Governor* (Book 4), and *Pet* (Book 5). The books in this series are best read in order.

CHAPTER ONE

Now

I never knew what I was getting into when I first met Owen and Carter.

Maybe it's better I didn't know.

Maybe I would've run away if I had.

But now I've been sworn in as the lieutenant governor of the great state of Florida, working with Governor Owen Taylor.

Publicly, it might seem that I serve at the governor's pleasure, but that's nothing close to the truth.

He serves *me* at *mine*. Especially the pleasure part.

We both serve my husband, Carter Wilson. My Master and Owner.

Also Owen's best friend and chief of staff.

And, as Owen dubbed him long ago, a bastard extraordinaire.

Boy, how I love him. *Both* of them.

Not many women are lucky enough to have two men who love them as much as Owen and Carter love me.

I grew up in a political family. My father likes to "joke" that me changing my party affiliation from GOP to Independent contributed to the massive heart attack that forced him out of running for higher public offices and into semi-retirement.

Except, here's the thing—I never wanted to be known as Benchley Evans' little girl. I *always* wanted to make my own name.

If anyone's to blame it's my father, because he's the one who taught me how to be ruthless.

Brutal.

Never come in second.

There's only one winner.

Joke's on him. We came in first, all right. By a damned landslide.

Without running under the banner of his precious GOP. And without the help of being a Democrat, either.

Both parties have good points, but both parties have increasingly fatal flaws that mean neither is doing their constituents any favors in this state. Tribal politics run rampant. No one's interested in actually governing, only scoring poll results and sound bites. Florida's a major swing state, and party candidates are frequently too busy tonguing the taints of national-level pols, trying to curry favor with them to help their own careers, instead of focusing on what's important to the people of *our* state.

I wasn't Florida's first female lieutenant governor, so that wasn't a glass ceiling I could shatter. But I damn sure plan on being Florida's next governor, provided Owen is re-elected.

There's no reason to think he won't. Carter won't let him lose.

If there's someone who wants to win even more than my father and I do, it's Carter. Which is one of the reasons why Daddy hates Carter so much.

If only Daddy knew what else Carter does, he'd *really* hate him. Him and Owen both.

But I love them, and no way in hell will I give them up.

Not for Daddy, and not for anyone else, either.

* * *

Right now, I'm leaving Owen's office and returning to my own before I finish for the day. At my husband's earlier summons, I'd left my chief of staff, Draymond, while we were going over tomorrow's schedule.

As I stand waiting for the elevator, I feel a draft up my skirt and Owen's cum threatening to slide down the insides of my thighs where Carter had him fuck me over Owen's new desk just minutes earlier.

That's one way to break in an office.

Except I screwed up.

Well, not screwed up, really.

I was counting on Carter being so damned busy today, between the swearing in ceremony and it being Owen's first day as governor, that Carter wouldn't think to do a panty check.

I should have known better. Of course he would figure out a way for the three of us to privately celebrate the inauguration.

Carter ripped them off me, and now they're in his pocket.

Which is why I have to squeeze my thighs together and pray the elevator hurries the hell up and gets here.

Of course, squeezing my thighs together reminds me that I'm going to have bite marks and bruises all inside my thighs from where Carter pinched and bit me only minutes earlier, because there were too many people in the outer office for him to spank me.

Worse, the bastard extraordinaire didn't get me off.

Ohhh, I'm sure I'll get a proper punishment later tonight at home, after the inauguration ball, but…

Yeah.

I know I'm smiling right now over that thought. Because it's not like I'm dreading it or anything.

Just like I'm not dreading the fact that Carter gave Owen carte blanche permission to bend me over and fuck me anytime we can safely do so without risk of discovery.

* * *

I make it back to my office and hold up a finger to stall Draymond as I duck into my personal bathroom. I take a quick moment to clean up—breathing a massive sigh of relief that I haven't left a damp spot on the back of my skirt—and then return to hear what my COS was saying.

I really like the guy, Draymond Garcia. He's a talented attorney who worked on several of Owen's campaigns for us, and a friend of Carter's. Carter took care of me, the way he always has, and hired Dray to be my chief of staff shortly after we won the election.

Carter is the power behind the power, and don't think I don't know that.

Daddy always says that time is never your friend, and it's never on your side. But my Nana always told me to take time to make time, or else I'd regret it.

Those two contradictory pieces of advice are both correct.

Dray helps me in both ways—keeping track of my time for me and helping me make time where I need to. He is as hungry for power as Carter and I are. Another good reason he's here—he wants to be here for the long-haul. Dray is focused on spending the next sixteen years in Tallahassee with us.

With me.

The only full-time woman in his life, outside his family and the occasional friend.

No, seriously. He's gay. Hot as hell, and his long-term live-in boyfriend, Gregory, is just as gorgeous.

Draymond's fashion sense is on fleek, too. Another reason Carter wanted him working for me—to make sure if he isn't around to personally approve how I look, he knows Dray will step in and fix me up. He's a handsome mixed Latinx with impeccable style, getting his six-five height and flawless dark brown skin from his tall father, and his gorgeous green eyes from his Puerto Rican mother.

If I had to worry about Carter and Owen's fidelity, maybe I'd be a little jealous of Dray and the time he gets to spend with my husbands.

But more importantly, Carter trusts Dray with our secrets. He'll be not only my body man but also my point man in terms of making sure I look like I'm where I'm supposed to be, even if I'm sneaking away for a few private moments with Owen.

One of the three men Carter saved from the car bomb that fateful day in the desert by throwing his body over theirs was Dray's older brother, Samuel. That means we *literally* don't have to worry about his loyalties. If Carter called Dray and told him he had a body he needed help hiding, Dray wouldn't waste time asking stupid questions.

He'd show up with shovels. Or maybe even a wood chipper.

And I can guarantee you he'd look good doing it, too.

Carter helps pair Dray with discreet beards for family functions involving his grandparents. His parents and brother know about him being gay, but they all pretend around both sets of grandparents, just to keep the peace.

Dray's boyfriend goes, too. They've told the grandparents Gregory's an orphan—which is technically true, since his asshole family disowned him when he came out—and that he's Dray's roommate—again, *technically* true—so they welcome him as another grandchild and are none the wiser.

Once both sets of Dray's grandparents have passed, the two of them plan to get married.

Dray finishes going over this week's schedule with me. I don't miss the playful smirk he's wearing.

"What?" I ask.

"Nothing, ma'am." Unlike when Owen calls me that, the *m* is lower-case.

"Just say it."

He shrugs. "Your husband called me right before you returned. He told me that, in the future, I'm to snitch on you if I see you wearing panties, unless he's specifically told me ahead of time he's cleared it."

I glare. "Snitches get stitches."

He grins. "I'm more afraid of *him* than I am *you*, ma'am."

I prop my elbows on my desk, my head cradled in my hands. "Dammit."

He snorts. "Sorry, ma'am, but he outranks you."

"*I'm* the lieutenant governor."

"Yes, ma'am."

"And you know damn well I'm running for governor in eight years."

"Yes, ma'am."

I lift my head. "And as my chief of staff, you'll still squeal on me even then, won't you?"

He grins and shrugs. "Sorry, ma'am. Sarge outranks you."

I slump back in my chair. "You're not sorry one damn bit. I think you're a sadist, too."

"You might not be wrong, ma'am. Now, let's firm up Monday's schedule, please?"

*   *   *

When I'm ready to leave and head to our townhouse here in Tallahassee, the FHP officer assigned as one of my permanent security detail is sitting at his desk in my outer office, along with my administrative assistant, Andrea. He goes ahead to get the car.

I personally don't want a security detail, but Carter—and Owen—have insisted. Yes, it's customary for the lieutenant governor to have security, but I was hoping to avoid it. They worry with Carter being Owen's COS, and with me being Senator Benchley Evans' daughter, that that it might paint a larger target on me.

And, as Carter informed me, if he wasn't Owen's COS, *he* would be my personal security detail.

Our townhouse isn't far from the Florida Governor's Mansion, not even two blocks, but it might as well be miles away for me. I won't be able to sneak back and forth very easily. It's a quick walk for Carter, however, which is one of the reasons he selected it.

The other reason is that it's a center unit. Owen owns the one to the left of ours, and Daddy owns the one on the right. Daddy's sits mostly vacant, unless he needs to travel to Tallahassee for meetings or events. They used to have a house here, but sold it and bought the townhouse after Daddy's heart attack. Once his term in the Florida Senate ended, they started living in their house in Brandon again full-time. Now, he and Momma are talking about buying another house here, since I'll be here most of the time. If they do that, at least it means I won't have to worry about them being right next door anymore.

Meaning we'll have nearly guaranteed privacy.

We first invested in the townhouses when Owen was elected to the Florida Senate, which turned out to be a doubly good choice once I was elected to the Florida House of Representatives not long after. Just like with our two homes in Brandon, just outside Tampa, we're usually using only one. Owen's townhouse is for show. There is, in fact, a hidden door that connects our unit to Owen's.

We pass the Florida Governor's Mansion as the trooper drives me through the chilly January afternoon, and I stare at the place as we ride by. I can't tell you how many times I've driven past that mansion in my life, or how many times I've been inside it as Representative or Senator Benchley Evans' daughter.

I can't tell you how long I've wanted to live there. Not as the wife or daughter of the governor, either.

Eight years.

Eight years, and I'll officially be living there.

I hope.

I'm already trying to think of how we could explain Owen living there with us, even though I know Owen himself, and Carter, will nix that plan.

I'm already missing our house in Tampa, our bedroom, our large bed, falling asleep in a warm, naked pile of jumbled limbs and unhampered love.

This is going to be a major sacrifice for all three of us, but I think it's worth it.

Our state suffered greatly under several terms of GOP governors who were beholden not only to the state and national parties, but also to the NRA, Big Sugar, and other dark-money lobbyists. A party that spent too much time and money trying to court hard-right Evangelicals instead of returning to its fiscally conservative roots. It's difficult to spot it if you're merely a tourist in our state, enjoying the beaches or theme parks. Nothing feels wrong in those fantasy lands.

It's in the plummeting graduation rates and increased pollution statistics where the truth begins to emerge. Toxic algae blooms, increasing sinkholes, more dangerous tropical storms and hurricanes hitting our shores more frequently, the rising sea levels threatening our coastal regions.

I'm no longer sure if, after sixteen years of running our state, I'll still want a national office. I'm beginning to think no. I know Owen doesn't want to pursue a US Senate or House seat. He wants to help get me elected and then return to private practice, this time in Tallahassee, so he can remain with us.

Except...if I run for the US Senate, my time will be split between Florida and DC, and I'm not sure I can handle being away from my guys for that long, or if I'll still have a taste for being a politician by then.

The trooper walks me to my front door and waits to leave until I'm locked inside and have reset the alarm. I'm not going anywhere until it's time for me to depart for the inauguration ball, and a limo will be sent for me then.

One of the few times the three of us will be able to ride together without any questions being asked. It won't be unexpected that we'd share a limo tonight. Our public victory celebration.

It's saving money that way.

One more excuse Carter will ruthlessly use to explain some of the choices he'll make over the next sixteen years to give us as much time together as possible. It's less money to protect several people in one place, versus two groups of people in different locales.

Daddy wanted to hire me a personal assistant, at his expense, to accompany me to Tallahassee. To help ensure my privacy and to do things for me like run errands, shopping, so there was no risk of spending taxpayer dollars on a state employee doing those kinds of things.

Carter shut that down in record time, reasonably explaining that we couldn't start our first term in office appearing to take largesse from someone so intrinsically tied to the GOP, my daddy or not.

Fortunately, Daddy is a reasonable man and understood that.

Unfortunately, Senator Benchley Evans is also a sneak. Carter soon caught wind of him setting up a blind trust, through which Daddy thinks he's going to hire someone.

I'm leaving that fight up to Carter. I don't have time to deal with it.

Right now, I need to get ready for tonight.

I strip and examine my new marks in the bathroom mirror.

Yep, those will show nicely for a few days, at least. Carter was careful not to mark me on my shoulders or neck or upper arms over the past couple of weeks, so they wouldn't be exposed by the gown he and Owen chose for me to wear tonight.

I take my shower and fix my hair, my makeup, and go through

my work e-mail as I await the limo's arrival. Carter had his tux sent to the mansion. He'll take his shower and get ready with Owen, working to keep Owen calm and prep him for facing the crowd tonight.

That's one way Carter knows he doesn't have to worry about me. I am my daddy's daughter, and I was raised on these kinds of events. I can just about walk through them in my sleep.

Even the ball is a relatively sedate affair when compared to the lavish, political party- and lobbyist-funded galas of past administrations. We've deliberately kept it low-cost—as low-cost as one of these things can be—and have invited people not just from our campaign staff, but lawmakers from both parties, as well as some private citizens worthy of recognition for their volunteerism, or their efforts for our campaign.

Other than Daddy and three of his closest friends, who were more like adopted uncles to me growing up, there are no "lobbyists" on the invite list.

Instead of spending money on A-list celebrity entertainment, Carter's enlisted bands and choirs from a local high school and from FSU, which is located in Tallahassee. The cost of bringing them all in is still far cheaper than we'd pay for an hour of time for some well-known Top 40 band. Plus it highlights state talent. And had we accepted offers by celebrities for donated performances, it would have been labeled cronyism in the works by our opponents.

What are they going to do, complain that talented high school and college students are being spotlighted? That will make any complaints look bad no matter how they try to spin it later.

Carter hopes some of them *will* try so he can have Comms viciously lance their griping as sour grapes and petty, partisan politics. Also something we can point to as proof that it was time for a change in how things are done in our state.

Our food tonight is being prepared by people who work for several non-profits in the Tallahassee area and which receive state funds to provide services to the homeless and needy. Meaning the fees they earn tonight are going to help charities while spotlighting them and giving them well-deserved media coverage.

Our campaign is also paying for the decorations and facility fees. Carter is still weighing what to do with the remainder of cash left in our campaign coffers. Whatever its final destination, it'll be a worthy recipient and that will be "leaked" to the press when it happens.

Carter is ruthlessly protecting our infant administration. We'll face so many outside threats as it is that any self-inflicted scandals we can prevent aren't a bad thing.

Right now, we're still surfing a wave of both major parties' desperation over our landslide victory numbers. Lawmakers are trying to jockey for position to appear to their constituents to be the most reasonable at working with us.

That has to continue for as long as possible for us to achieve a fraction of our agenda. Giving either party a toehold to exploit scandal will torpedo us. But the fact that we ran as Independent— and won by such a huge margin—has already opened the floodgates of candidates deserting both parties to switch their affiliation to *I*.

It's also why I know we'll have to make such excruciating personal sacrifices, and we'll all face some lonely nights ahead of us.

I'm used to that. I was raised in a family where that was the norm, not the exception. I know I'll be okay.

And it's why I desperately worry about what the stress of that will do not only to Carter without Owen sharing a bed with us, but especially to Owen.

I consider Owen every bit as much my husband as Carter. So does Carter.

Dray knows, because he works for us, but he's also a trusted family friend and has signed an NDA. We just can't tell anyone else.

Yet.

Owen completes both of us in ways I never imagined possible. Which is why this works for all three of us.

One day, we'll be able to openly express our love and our relationship.

Unfortunately, today is not that day.

CHAPTER TWO

Logistically, it's easier for the limo to pick me up first, then swing by the mansion and get Owen and Carter. Normally, the governor doesn't get a huge security detail on a scale like you see for POTUS or other dignitaries. But on a normal workday, when going to the office and back to the mansion, Owen will usually have an officer assigned as a driver, as well as a shadow car. I'll normally have one officer, who is also my driver.

Unless we're making an appearance somewhere. That's when the head of security will evaluate every situation on a case-by-case basis. Our daily security detail officers, and security for any work-related events, are paid for by the state. Tonight, we'll have a car ahead of and behind the limo, since we're all together.

Extra officers that Carter was careful to make sure were paid for—as was the limo—from our campaign funds. This isn't an expense the taxpayers are footing. We are going to be extremely careful with how we spend funds.

I'm ready to go when an FHP officer in full dress uniform rings our doorbell.

"Good evening, Mrs. Evans."

"Good evening, Officer."

He offers me his arm to hold after I've set the alarm and locked the front door behind me.

I smile. "Thank you, Officer."

I hook arms with him and let him escort me down the front walk, to where the limo is waiting, even though my heart is aching that it's not Owen or even Carter who's walking with me. There aren't many opportunities now where I get to walk with Owen and can hold his hand or his arm without it raising suspicions.

Tonight is one such night.

Ironically, it's a very high-profile night, too.

The driver is holding my door open for me, and the officer waits until I'm safely inside and the door's closed to return to his marked car idling in front of the limo.

And away we go.

Carter's already planned our arrival at the ball. He told us that he'll help me out of the limo, but make a very public point of handing me off to Owen for the walk inside, and he wants us to have the first dance together tonight. He wants there to be no whispers or innuendo, wants people to see that he has no problems with Owen having that kind of contact with me.

We're Governor Taylor and Lieutenant-Governor Evans. We've earned the right to celebrate tonight.

My sweet boy. He did it, just like Carter and I knew he could.

It's a short ride to the mansion. Carter and Owen are standing on the front porch and waiting for me when the limo pulls up. They look gorgeous, the two of them together and dressed to the nines in their tuxes, both of them in black ties. I'd been looking at my phone, and I snap a quick picture of them, for my eyes only, before I drop my phone in my purse.

My boys clean up well. Not that I had any doubt of that. They both look gorgeous on a daily basis in their suits and ties.

I keep myself planted in the middle of the limo's backseat as the driver opens the door for the men.

Tonight, despite our previous rules, Owen has to go first. He'll be walking ahead of both of us for the next four to eight years.

At least, he will in public.

I know our boy will hate it every time, feeling it's not right, wanting us to walk ahead of him. But he'll still do it, because he's our good boy.

"Governor Taylor," the driver says.

"Thank you."

My boy ducks inside the limo. His smile lights fires in me after his gaze sweeps over me, taking in the sight of me wearing this gorgeous shimmering blue gown, a gown which he helped pick out.

"Mrs. Evans," he says, smiling.

I wink. "Governor Taylor."

He moves out of the way so Carter can get past him and sit on my far side. Owen will exit the limo first and needs to sit on the passenger side. With the door closed, Owen settles in on my right.

"Here we go," Carter murmurs. "Public faces."

I don't care. My hands sneak out, to either side, and my fingers curl around their hands. Inside the limo's darkened interior, the gesture can't be seen. Even if someone's planted a secret IR camera or something, it can be explained away as simply feeling nervous and wanting to hold their hands.

We're friends, for crying out loud.

Even if I wish we could publicly come out to the world as more.

* * *

I know the "rules" that Carter has put in place to protect *us*, the three of us. I was raised on a variation of them, my father taking me to many political events over the years as I was growing up. Especially as Momma grew to hate them and I usually ended up being Daddy's plus-one for RSVPs. Giving my daddy all due credit, however, he wasn't mean or even particularly strict when teaching me about the "public rules" he gave me. He led by action, treating me in many ways like an adult, even when I was still a little kid.

Assume we are always being watched and recorded.

Assume anyone can hear what we're saying—and that they are recording it.

If saying something in a whisper, always cover your mouth so your lips can't be read—but assume it's not safe to talk in public.

Assume all mics are hot, and treat them accordingly.

Never let down your guard until safely behind a locked door with the curtains drawn and you have double-checked you're alone in the space.

And even then, assume the walls are paper-thin, and that there are people standing outside with their ears pressed against the door, unless it's a situation like you're safely at home.

Even in a car, assume people can see and hear you.

No public displays of affection with each other, beyond the occasional hug.

Remember the long game and our goals.

Never lose our cool in public.

Although Owen did break that last one during the campaign, when that stupid fucking Kevin Markos from Full News Broadcasting interviewed him the Sunday after the school shooting.

But even Carter gave Owen a mulligan on that one, because Owen still handled it professionally, and it is likely no coincidence that Owen's poll numbers gained another five points after the live interview aired.

Other networks replayed Owen's on-air takedown of Kevin Markos for several days. Both Rachel Maddow and Anderson Cooper—as well as all the late-night talk show comedians—had a field day with it at Markos' expense. Hell, even Fox News' morning crew zinged Markos over it on Monday morning.

When Carter gently squeezes my left hand and doesn't pull away, I know he's not going to ding me for this, either. I also feel badly, because there are things I can get away with around Owen that Carter can't. Like dancing together tonight.

I wish I could put Owen's hand in Carter's and send the two of them out to the middle of the dance floor together, because Carter has certainly earned that. He loves Owen beyond depth and reason, and I don't begrudge it in the slightest.

Carter fell in love with Owen.

Owen fell in love with me.

I fell in love with Carter.

Somewhere, along the way, we all fell in love with each other, held on tightly, and didn't let go.

But the world at large is incapable of understanding that, how that works.

Especially the world of politics. They'd eat us alive, looking down on Owen for choosing to kneel before us, and looking down on me for having two men. Carter would likely come out okay, except some would criticize him for "sharing" his wife.

Carter, however, would literally throw himself on a sword before exposing Owen to a scandal of our own making. He would, without hesitation, take any blame and direct all criticism onto himself to protect our boy.

It's why he's ruthlessly protected our administration from the day we filed primary paperwork, hiring an attorney dedicated to doing nothing but making sure we didn't violate a single campaign finance law or break any election laws. It's why, if in doubt, we paid from our own pockets and then the campaign reimbursed us later, if it was a valid and allowed expense. It nearly always was valid and allowed.

But we were *careful*.

Nothing got paid out of the campaign accounts unless there was a receipt. *Period*. Every donation was documented, and yes, we refused several large and questionable donations. It was better to err on the side of caution.

Now, here we are. We have allies on both sides of the aisle because we were courageous enough to take a stand and fight the good fight. It's given good people in both parties the courage to take stands of their own to help us accomplish our agenda. It inspired several lawmakers to change their party affiliation from Dem or GOP to Independent.

Make no mistake, it's also made us a few enemies. Though our three worst enemies, who we were most concerned about derailing our agenda, lost their re-election bids. Three state senators—two Republicans and a Democrat.

Turfed out by the voters. One of the Republicans actually got thoroughly trounced in his primary by a moderate first-time candidate who was only twenty-two and had just graduated college with a poli sci degree.

Granted, we have term limits in Florida, but it's hard to get turfed out after one term once you win the general the first time. Especially in a primary.

You *really* have to be doing something wrong.

Or, you've really had to run afoul of the father of a candidate for lieutenant governor, said father who then anonymously drops some interesting documents about shady real estate dealings you've conducted in another state into the inbox of a reporter for the *Miami Herald*.

Thanks, Daddy. I owe you yet another one.

* * *

Owen's fingers stay curled around my right hand until a block before the hotel where the inaugural ball is being held. Then I give his hand another squeeze and pull mine away.

It's showtime.

Owen is so much better at these events now than when we first started this journey. Carter and I had to deprogram a childhood's worth of bullshit, courtesy of his narcissistic bitch of a mother. He was always nervous, sort of stiff, and terrified to talk too much.

Whereas Daddy always encouraged me at these events, even when I was literally a kid, to talk to people, to ask questions, taught me how to converse.

Owen's mother used him as a prop for her own purposes.

Okay, in a completely unhealthy and nonconsensual way, compared to how *I'm* admittedly using him. As Carter himself said, we broke Owen down, with love, to first deprogram him and remove all the bullshit he'd been taught. Then we built him back up stronger, better, healthier. Owen is the man he is now because of the hard and unconventional choices we all made back then. The Owen we know and love was reborn over sixteen years ago, his second year of college, when he and Carter became roommates in the dorm and then they met me the first day of school.

We were all reborn.

We are all better people now.

We are stronger, and we *are* going to make our state a better place.

The limo pulls to a stop in front of the hotel and a uniformed trooper immediately steps in to open the door for us. Owen emerges first, followed by me, Carter right behind me. Normally I'd follow Carter, too, except I'm the lieutenant governor.

Carter's "just" Owen's chief of staff.

If only everyone knew the truth.

Fortunately, there's not a huge crowd outside the hotel, but Owen does want to work the rope line.

I go with him. I can't help but notice that Carter's gaze is as intense and watchful as any of the troopers or county deputies in the security detail, studying the crowd, watchful for potential threats as he stays close to both of us. Once we reach the door, Carter rests his right hand in the small of my back, pats Owen's shoulder with his left, and obviously guides me into position to take Owen's arm before Carter falls in a step behind us.

Owen smiles down at me. "Shall we, Ma'am?"

One small capitulation Carter allows, because no one but the three of us knows that Owen means that with a capital *M*.

I smile back. "Let's do this, Governor Taylor."

Dray is waiting for us inside the lobby. Normally, it's easier—and safer logistically—to take a VIP in through a service entrance. But tonight is a celebration, and we've earned this little bit of pomp.

When we enter the lobby, the people inside erupt in cheers and applause, and both Owen and I smile and wave, looking great for the cameras, I'm sure.

I know Carter is still shadowing us, watching. This is the other reason he wanted me walking with Owen, so he could be more watchful, more ready.

Since the day of the school shooting, I've seen a far darker side of my husband emerge. More nightmares, more sullen moods from time to time. The wary, combat-hardened sergeant instead of the polished attorney.

What happened that day at the school a couple of months ago reminds Carter too much of his time in the Army, when he was on deployment, and the day he almost died.

But even more importantly, Owen still has no idea how close he *really* came to death that day in the school. It's a lesson Carter will not forget, and refuses to stop beating himself up over. He'd let his guard down that day, thought they were safe. Had he not shoved Owen to the floor and dragged him around behind the counter in the school's office, it could have been Owen who got shot next. He'd been standing in front of the counter, but directly in line with the opening to the hallway where the deputy was shot.

The shot that killed the deputy would have, no doubt, hit Owen first.

Sure, one can make a lot of arguments against that line of thinking. Except *Carter's* convinced of it, and that's all that matters. It's *his* mind that frantically races, worried about Owen, about me.

It's why Carter insists I *will* have a security detail.

I know it's also why, when last Friday night I tried asking him one more time to loosen that requirement, he grabbed me by the arm, dragged me into our bedroom, and paddled my ass red without speaking a single word. He didn't stop until I tearfully apologized and promised to never again ask for him to cancel my security detail.

Then he pulled me into his arms, tightly holding me, silent sobs wracking him as his waking and sleeping nightmares fought for control of his soul, until I was the one holding him and he fell asleep in my arms.

His first halfway decent night's sleep in weeks.

He never sleeps well when the two of us aren't in bed with him, but especially when Owen isn't, and Owen had to be in Tampa for interviews that night and stayed over in the Brandon house.

I'm afraid what might happen to Carter if there's ever another close call. I don't honestly think he could handle losing either of us. I think it would completely snap his sanity.

But that's fair, because I don't think I could handle losing either of them. From the first day I met them, I sensed we were all meant to be together, even though, at the time, I didn't realize that was going to be *literally*.

All because of Carter and his master plan.

Or maybe I should call that his *Master* plan.

CHAPTER THREE

Then

I think I fell in love with Carter first. But he was older, off-limits.

Or, he should've been.

And then I fell in love with Owen. How could I ever choose between them?

That's when Carter made me a promise—that I wouldn't have to choose.

Ever.

All I had to do was trust him.

When I look at the bigger picture, I honestly think I got the best deal. Owen likely never would have run for office—*any* office—if it hadn't been for Carter. What we've accomplished was never part of Carter's original plan that he secretly formulated before they met me.

Not really.

Carter never would have plunged into the world of Florida politics the way he did if it hadn't been for *me*.

Yes, Owen had a wishful-thinking kind of dream about maybe being governor, one day. But even he'll tell you he considered it a pipe dream. That he didn't have the drive or determination to go for it, even though he longed to help people.

Carter, however, saw through him, and realized he absolutely could get Owen elected, once they met me.

I *wanted* to be governor, and Carter saw that immediately. Not like I hid it. But he also knew it would be easier to get Owen elected first.

Carter sacrificed *everything* for that goal, for *me*. He sacrificed being able to love his boy and his pet in relative obscurity. All because he knew Owen's biggest wish was to make *me* happy.

Could we *not* have pushed Owen to run, and ended up staying in the private sector? Sure.

Except Carter also knew I'd never be happy settling for a simpler life like that, even though, had Carter asked it of me, I probably would have agreed to it by the time I realized how much I loved these two men.

Owen was content to be carried along in my current, following me and Carter in our wakes. As a result he's now governor, but he's lost all privacy, lost the ability to flop into bed with us at the end of a long day, or to curl up with us on the couch and unplug, with his head in my lap and his feet in Carter's and simply...be.

Lost the peace of mind coming home every day gave him.

He's lost the freedom to be Carter's boy—and mine— whenever he wants.

Lost the ability to speak or even live freely, in that he now has to worry if someone's got a cell phone camera pointed at him any time he's outside the confines of his private residence, or ours.

No more runs to our favorite tap house in Hyde Park to have flights of craft beers, drinking to the point we're all giggling and laughing before we take an Uber home, pawing at each other in the backseat the whole way, Carter pulling each of us in for long, deep kisses without a care who sees us.

No more intimate dinners for three at our favorite steakhouse, tucked in the corner booth we love and able to play footsies with each other.

No more casual strolls through the grocery store together with us laughing and joking about nonstandard uses for phallic-shaped foods.

They've done all of this for *me*, with no guarantee we'll be able to make it all the way. I have no illusions, either. If I don't get elected the first time I run for governor, I'm not going to make some pitiful repeat attempt in four years. That's just pathetic. I'll have already moved on to bigger and better things by then.

These two men love me, and love each other. Maybe some people would rightfully criticize Carter for how and why he brought the three of us together, but you'll never hear me or Owen complain about that.

What we have is perfect, perfectly *us*, and perfect *for* us.

But back then we were kids, and we laughed and loved and planned.

And I remember the day I first laid eyes on the two of them as if it were yesterday.

* * *

When I wake up that Monday morning for my first day of college, I'm filled with excitement. I have a load of classes I'm eager to dig in to, starting with Florida Politics & Government. Daddy warned me over the phone last night to try to keep an open mind, listen, and learn, even when I know more than an instructor.

In some of these classes I'm already sure, based upon the curriculum and syllabus, that I know more than the instructor.

I start my first year at USF Tampa a year and a half ahead with credits earned through dual-enrollment. The only reason I don't already have a two-year college degree is that I spent my freshman year of high school in Tallahassee, working as an intern to state senator Marlene Samuels. The sixty-two-year-old—at that time—

had energy and enthusiasm to spare, and she ran my ass into the ground.

I learned so much from her. It was her last year in office, and she was the reason I knew *I* could run for office. It wouldn't surprise me if her daughter, ShaeLynn—who's only two years older than me and who was, at that time, already in her third year of college and studying to be an attorney—one day ends up as President. ShaeLynn's a force of nature, someone even more driven than I am.

I know that I'm lucky with my lot in life. Blessed, even.

Doesn't mean I won't still work my ass off.

Daddy might have money but, as he cautioned me countless times, it doesn't mean *I* can be lazy. I fully understand why he snagged me the internship with Senator Samuels. It was well worth having to take classes remotely, doing schoolwork in the evenings and on the weekends, so I could spend my weekdays studying at the feet of Marlene Samuels.

You cannot pay for that kind of education.

Even though Senator Samuels is a Democrat, Daddy highly respects her and has always spoken well of her, and cautioned me to work my ass off to impress her.

I did, and she wrote me a glowing letter of recommendation for my college application packet.

I'm determined to make straight *A*s and make a name for myself so I don't spend the rest of my life known as Benchley Evans' daughter.

I'm Susa Evans, and I'm going to make sure people know who I am because of what *I've* done, *not* because of who Daddy is.

Momma had felt nervous about me living in Tampa by myself this year and not staying at their home in Brandon, but Daddy knows I can handle myself. I'm my father's daughter in more than one way.

Driving to campus every day will be annoying. I'd wanted to

live in a dorm this year, but Daddy nixed that. The politician-to-be knows he's right, but I'm still mad at him for overruling me. Buying me a house was his way of trying to compromise and soothe my anger over him putting his foot down about me not living in a dorm.

I'm also annoyed because it means I'll have to figure out how to deal with my ex-boyfriend, Kendall. That storm will no doubt blow up tonight, if the increasingly desperate and pleading tone of his multiple e-mails are any indication. I broke up with him right before he departed on a trip to France with his family, and he's due back in town tonight. If I was living in a dorm, I'd have all the backup I could handle.

Douchey timing on my part, I know, but it was calculated. I knew had I done it sooner, I never would have gotten rid of him. He would have been whiny and clingy and apologizing, maybe even cancelled going on the trip, and I needed a few weeks away from him to gain some extra perspective.

Because while he was good in the sack, that was about all he was good for. He damn sure wasn't someone good for my future. Especially not with the load of debt his family's carrying, something I didn't know about until I ran a full background check on him just before I broke up with him. Having him out of my hair has been a relief, meaning I definitely don't want him back.

The last thing I want to do is call Daddy and ask him to talk to Kendall's parents for me, to get Kendall to leave me alone.

That would be like admitting I can't adult.

Scratch that. Calling Daddy is the second-to-last thing I want to do. Calling the *cops* is the *last* thing I want to do, because I know damn well it'd get back to Daddy anyway.

I'm still mulling all this over when I walk in that classroom Monday morning, where I immediately spot the two hotties sitting in the far back corner. Hard to miss them, from how they've moved their desks. The one guy looks a little older, intense brown eyes with smoky depths and a watchful gaze that sees everything. Brown hair, gorgeous. He's literally backed his desk into the corner, angled out toward the room.

The first thought that flits through my mind when I look at him is *former military.*

He has the same look on his face worn by some of the law enforcement officers I met in Tallahassee who work security for the capitol building. Officers who were former military, and who saw active combat during their in-country deployments.

They didn't like having their backs to a room or a door, either.

I'm immediately drawn to the guy and hope I've just found the answer to my Kendall problem. With my luck, this guy's probably got a clingy, whiny girlfriend who will stomp her feet and refuse to let him do what I ask of him tonight.

But it's either take a chance and ask, or sac up and face Kendall on my own. Otherwise, I'm going to have to hang around the damn library until about midnight and hope Kendall hasn't parked himself at my front door. I refuse to call law enforcement except as a last resort, because I know damn well it'll get back to Daddy.

Then good-bye living on my own. I know I'm nineteen, but he and Momma would basically move in with me at that point. Or, at least Momma would.

That would mean good-bye any sex life I might hope to have.

The guy seated next to Brown Eyes appears to be a little taller, most likely a little younger, too, from the lack of lines on his face and around his eyes. Gorgeous green eyes and blond hair, super hot. He's angled his desk, too, and sits to the right of Brown Eyes.

Still, it's Brown Eyes I want to get to know better.

A *lot* better.

I decide to go for broke, since I don't see a ring on either of their hands. I walk over, smiling as I do. "Mind if I sit here?" I point to the desk that technically now sits to Brown Eyes' left.

Brown Eyes might think he's looking pretty casual when he shrugs, but I've already spotted the flash of resentment, gone almost before it's there.

Green Eyes is practically drooling, bless his heart. He's adorable.

I wonder if Brown Eyes is gay and lusting after Green Eyes.

"Thanks," I say. Then I proceed to move my desk, too, to match how they arranged theirs, and I sit and focus on my textbook.

Or, I pretend to.

As I listen to them resume their discussion about cooking, of all things, I give thanks. It sounds like they're both single, probably dorm roommates, and Brown Eyes is going to teach Green Eyes how to prepare a Greek dish tonight, one that I can cook in my sleep.

I finally make my move a few minutes later. Greek food is something I can cook the *hell* out of, fortunately, and I offer to let them come cook at my house tonight, I'll provide the kitchen and groceries, and all they have to do is scare Kendall off.

Thankfully, they accept.

It's not until the end of the class when I actually learn their names. I'm even more convinced by Carter's mannerisms that he's former military, even though he hasn't specifically said that. It's painfully obvious Owen is already smitten with me, which is adorable and not exactly a bad thing.

But it's Carter I'm really drawn to. He wears a dark air of danger—and I know that sounds stupid, but it's *him*.

Sure, I suppose if Carter turns out to be gay or something, I'd definitely love to give Owen a chance. I might have turned nineteen just last week, but it's not my first rodeo. I've had a couple of boyfriends besides Kendall.

I'm positive one of the reasons I'm having trouble getting rid of Kendall isn't his love of me so much as it's his love of my money.

Carter strikes me as exactly the kind of guy I need to scare Kendall off for good.

As I head to my next class, I'm finally feeling relaxed about the confrontation with Kendall that I'm certain is coming tonight.

I also didn't realize until much later that my world had literally shifted on its axis, setting me on my course for the future.

* * *

I almost feel sorry for Kendall when he shows up and Carter handles him.

Almost.

I can tell Owen isn't great with physical confrontations, but he's doing a fantastic job standing there behind Carter and looking downright imposing.

Owen's also big enough for me to hide behind while Carter damn near breaks Kendall's arm in the door when the dumbass tries to force his way inside.

At least tonight I don't sense the resentment I thought I spotted in Carter's expression earlier. Tonight, when I hug Carter after Kendall's departure, Carter returns my strong hug with one of his own that lasts even longer than I hoped it might.

It leaves me feeling gooey all over.

This man is a warrior. I mean, I know now, from our conversations, that my earlier guess about him being former military was correct.

But then when I hug Owen...

Sigh. Perfection.

Thank god Daddy and Momma never scrolled through my Kindle. It's full of e-books featuring a heroine with two—or more—guys who are strong enough to take care of her and keep her safe.

This would be a ready-made dream come true, with the two of

them.

When we sit down together to eat dinner at my tiny IKEA table that only seats four—the men are my first real guests, because Daddy and Momma have been up in Tallahassee—it feels perfect then, too.

Being friends with them feels comfortable in a way nothing has ever felt before. Carter is twenty-eight, almost ten years older than me. Owen's only two years older than me.

Doesn't matter. Not to me.

After dinner, once the kitchen is cleaned up and we've returned to the living room, as we continue discussing politics it strikes me that Carter is a far deeper man than most people likely realize. He's got a way of grasping the larger picture you don't usually see in someone so new to the jungle that is Florida politics.

While I'm studying Owen, an idea comes to mind.

I can imagine Owen being sworn in as governor, with me as his lieutenant. Because Carter's put forth an interesting proposition of a third-party run, and I can see it all laid out.

It'd piss Daddy off something fierce, but it's workable.

Really workable.

And it'll ensure everyone knows *my* name without the parenthetical statement of who my father is as the sub-lede.

I want that.

Really, *really* want that.

It's amusing to learn Carter has an eidetic memory. When I quiz him, he literally can recite nearly verbatim what both I and the teacher said on the subject. From the shock on Owen's face, I can see this is news to him, too.

My mind races, miles and years ahead of where we are right here tonight. Someone like Carter, who can remember *everything*?

He's a weapon in more ways than one. Especially in the political world. Maybe he doesn't realize that.

Or, perhaps he does.

At the end of the evening, Owen excuses himself to use the bathroom before they prepare to return to their dorm. Once I hear the bathroom door close behind Owen, I turn, and Carter's now standing *right* behind me.

I mean, he moves like a damn cat. He'd been sitting on the couch and I never heard him move.

My clit's throbbing as I stare up at him, at the intensity in his gaze as he studies me.

"You *really* want to be governor?" he whispers.

I nod. "I do."

"I want Owen to be governor. He wants it, but he'd never go for it on his own." He studies me for a long moment, his gaze sweeping my body before settling on my eyes again. "I don't want to hurt him," he says.

How bad is it that I know *exactly* what he means?

And that we're going to do it anyway.

"Me, either," I say.

"I mean, there's a *lot* of stuff you don't know about him, or me. We do this, *together*, but we do this *my* way, and you don't argue with me or deviate from the plan. *I'm* in charge. That means keeping this a secret from him, for now. You fuck the plan, or you lie to me, and we're *done*. No second chances. Understand?"

This is the second moment my world seriously shifts, although this one I vaguely recognize, at the time.

"Yes, Sir," I whisper, because no other answer feels right.

The long, slow, sexy smile he gives me sets my clit throbbing in ways it never has before, no matter how great the sex, no matter how hot the book, no matter how fantastic the vibrator.

Never have I ever felt like this before.

I viscerally recognize that not only does this man completely understand me, he is in many ways a twin to me when it comes to politics, and the opposite side of the coin to me in personality in the ways that count.

He leans in, cups the back of my neck, and slants a world-shattering, possessive, hungry kiss across my lips that I try to chase when he pulls back. He stops me with a finger to my lips and *that* smirk.

"My *very* good girl," he whispers. "We're going to do great things, the *three* of us."

I turn when I hear the bathroom door open down the hall. When I turn back, Carter's now sitting on the couch as if he never moved in the first place. He drops me a wink, which convinces me no, I didn't imagine the whole thing.

Shivers. *Literal* damn *shivers* race through me, and I don't mean the spooky-house kind, either.

I mean the *I really want to fuck him* kind of shivers.

Because I *know* as we stare into each other's eyes that this man before me is going to be the man I marry. He'd *just* claimed me.

Believe it or not, I'm damn good with that.

CHAPTER FOUR

Now

Owen and I walk into the massive ballroom to thunderous applause, a literal standing ovation. Dray and Carter have put together an amazing event for us tonight, one that's personally meaningful to us as a campaign, as the people taking office, as an administration, and one that's meaningful to our state as a whole.

We want to heal divides and put our best foot forward while showcasing our state's talents in multiple areas.

There will be a light dinner first, buffet-style, before the actual dancing. And cake. We have a table near the stage where the bands will play. Momma and Daddy are seated nearby, along with Owen's dad and step-mother. Other tables close to us seat Carter's parents and some of his brothers and their significant others, Owen's brothers and sisters, and other close friends and family.

We juggled the seating around a little to put Dray on Owen's other side, since Carter was seated next to me. I jealously didn't want any women seated next to Owen. I joked we could say I hogged Owen's COS for the evening, so Owen hogged mine.

But bless their hearts, my guys made it so.

When I see that, I drop Dray a knowing wink, which he returns with a smile of his own. Gregory's on Dray's far side, and that's the end of the table.

Carter and Dray also played around with the seating chart so that a larger and much more visible table holds quite a few dignitaries, such as the members of the Executive Cabinet—the Attorney General, Chief Financial Officer, and Commissioner of Ag, who are all elected, not appointed—along with the Secretary of Education and the Secretary of State—who are appointed. That table's occupants also include US Senator ShaeLynn Samuels.

It's close to our smaller table, which unlike all the other tables is straight instead of round. It's also much more visible than our own, which is positioned in the front left corner of the ballroom, and at an angle to the stage. An emergency door is located directly behind us, so it's not merely to make Carter comfortable. It's also a legitimate security issue. An armed deputy stands guard by the door to keep anyone from coming in, but Owen and I can easily rush out that way, if necessary.

More importantly, the dignitary table is placed so it's easier for them to see and *be* seen, especially by the press. Makes them feel important and spotlighted, and everyone has to pass by them to reach our table.

Meaning they're getting a lot of attention, and people are hung up talking to them before they ever reach us. The dignitaries' egos are stroked, and they're happy.

Carter and Dray are geniuses. We're not bogged down with as many people as we would be, because they're stopping at the dignitary table first.

Brilliant!

Plus, Carter's no dummy. Senator Samuels is a huge boon to have in attendance tonight. Rumors are flying she's eyeing a run for POTUS in a few years, just like I imagined she would all those years ago when I interned for her mother.

Despite the fact that she's a Democrat, a sophomore Senator, and only thirty-seven, we want her on our side for many reasons. She stumped for us during this election, and she'll be an important endorsement for Owen's re-election, as well as for my own run in eight years.

I learned so much from Daddy over the years by attending events with him, listening to his talks with other politicians and party officials. But I learned a few valuable lessons from Senator Marlene Samuels, ShaeLynn's mother.

The first thing I learned was to never be ashamed of your goals, never apologize for them.

Own them.

Carter and I are involved in a discussion with Daddy about— what else—a bill that will be hitting committee, when I realize Owen's left the table. I never saw him leave, and I don't have time to look around for him. But when he returns a few minutes later, he's carrying two plates of food.

One for himself, and one for me.

It's perfect, too, because he knows exactly what I like and would want to eat from the offered selections.

I somehow manage to blink back tears while I give him a friendly smile and poke his shoulder. "Thank you, O." It's our public-safe code when I don't dare call him *boy*. His first name's Owen, *duh*, and we're friends.

He smiles, my sweet boy. "You're welcome, Ma'am." He tucks his napkin into his lap and glances my way.

I give him a quick nod, knowing what he wants.

He starts eating.

We won't always be able to do this, so I want to give him what I can, when I can. Carter long ago lifted his requirements for Owen to ask permission to start eating, or before leaving our sides when we're in public, rules Owen loved and thrived on for years.

That he made a point of doing this for me tonight means the world to me. It's one small way he can also let me know he still considers himself mine, even if he's now my boss.

Carter leans in to peck me on the cheek. "I see someone's on the ball tonight. Excellent. I'll be right back." He crosses behind Owen when he leaves, giving Owen's shoulder a brief squeeze when he passes.

This is something else I know kills Owen a little inside. The fact that Owen watches Carter head for the buffet line is just more proof.

Owen wanted to get *both* our plates, but getting one for me, his friend and lieutenant governor, is being a gentleman.

Getting one for his chief of staff?

If anyone noticed and decided to ask about it, it would mean uncomfortable questions, at best.

Insinuations at worst.

Insinuations we can*not* risk. Especially right now.

* * *

Once Owen and I have eaten, we each set out to work the room, greeting people, thanking them for their attendance, taking pictures, selfies, all of that. Carter shadows Owen and Dray shadows me, both of them periodically making notes on their phones as necessary.

This is a celebration, but it's a working one.

Before the cake is served, a series of people stand on stage and give brief comments, congratulations, prepared remarks, including Senator Samuels.

Then I take the stage. I normally would have prepared remarks to read from, but not tonight. Tonight, the spotlight rightfully belongs on Owen, not me. I want it to be my boy's words they remember.

A trooper from the security detail, who is standing in front of the stage, holds my hand as I climb the steps and take center stage to thunderous applause, a standing *O*. I'm handed a cordless mic.

I glance first at Carter and Owen, then at Daddy and Momma. Daddy looks proud of me, and for a brief moment I feel badly that I now hold a higher office than he ever did.

That feeling vanishes when I realize he himself would chide me for feeling like that.

Daddy's proud of me, of that I have no doubt.

But Senator Benchley Evans is even prouder, even if his soul is likely a shade of pure green right now.

"Thank you, everyone, for coming tonight. We'll be getting to the dancing here shortly, but first, I wanted to say a few words. Tonight is about all of you as much as it is about what we've accomplished. We never could have done this without you. I, for one, am very grateful."

I let the applause settle before I continue. "My husband and I have known Owen Taylor since college. We were roommates with the man for years and didn't kill him."

I smile, pausing for the laughter. "He's not just our best friend—he's adopted family to both of us. He's a *good* man, which is why I didn't hesitate to say yes when he asked me to run as his lieutenant governor. And I can*not* begin to tell you how proud I am to stand here before you tonight and be the one with the honor and privilege of introducing to you the governor of our great state of Florida...*Governor* Owen Taylor."

I have no words to express how powerfully that hits me, saying it like that.

I blink back unexpected tears.

Owen's eyes are fixed only on me through the applause. He stands, waving as he approaches and steps up on the stage to take the microphone from me, pecking me on the cheek as he does.

"*Thank you, Ma'am,*" he silently mouths to me with his back turned to the room. I step out of the spotlight and return to the table to stand next to Carter, clapping with the rest of the audience.

I know Owen's a little choked up, but he's got this. He's

rehearsed this speech dozens of times with me and Carter and Dray, and he knows it by heart.

"Thank you, everyone. Thank you. Before I say anything, I want to thank my best friend, Carter Wilson, for his years of love, friendship, and support." He smiles down at Carter, who's wearing *that* smirk. Carter tips his head in a nod that both Owen and I know has silent meaning.

Love you, boy.

I'm so proud of you.

You did good.

"I'd also like to thank Carter for letting me borrow my other best friend, Susa, for the next four to eight years. I couldn't have done this without her, either. Or without all of you. Dad, Mom."

That means his step-mom, Katie, and is a deliberate dig at Owen's mother, who isn't here tonight because Owen has no contact with her anymore.

"Senator and Doctor Evans. Lieutenant Colonel and Mrs. Wilson. Our family and friends. Everyone stepped in to support me and help me and encourage me, and that humbles me.

"I never want to forget why we're here, or what we're here to do, or the fact that I'm not a governor only to the people who checked the box by my name. I'm the governor of *Florida*, of *all* its residents, regardless of how they voted or what party they're registered under.

"Tonight is truly the start of the next stage of my life. I'd be lying if I said I'm not nervous. I'm not going to let that stop me, though. I'm going to remember this feeling and use it to make sure I weigh every action I take, every decision I make as governor, so I know that it's what's in the best interest of our state. Even if it's an unpopular decision.

"I'm not going to pander to some mythical 'base' that doesn't exist. I think the fact that we got elected as Independents means that there are voters on both sides of the aisle who are as tired of politics as usual as we were when we decided to run. I'm looking forward to working with lawmakers from both parties—and the growing number of Independents who are choosing to run outside the usual party lines—to make our state even better. Thank you, and let's dance!"

Thunderous applause fills the room. Someone takes the mic from Owen. As our boy descends from the stage, Carter leads me out from behind the table, holding my hand. When we meet Owen at the bottom of the steps and the orchestra starts playing, Carter makes a point of handing me over to Owen with a smile and a flourish, bowing from the waist and making both of us laugh.

I step into Owen's arms, and we're dancing to the orchestra playing *Next to Me* by Imagine Dragons as a girl from the choir sings the opening lyrics before the rest of the choir chimes in.

Owen picked this song. It was one of the details they held back from me, Owen wanting it to be a surprise. It's one of his favorites, one of Carter's favorites. Somehow, I manage *not* to cry. I also force myself not to press my body against his like we've danced in private countless times. He's wearing a smile and silently singing along with the words as we slowly sway in time with the music.

I stare up into his gorgeous green eyes and smile. "I'm proud of you, O."

He smiles. "Thank you, Ma'am."

As we dance, I'm aware that Carter has started dancing with his mother. Daddy and Momma, as well as Gerard and Katie, are dancing, too. Carter hands his mother off to one of his older brothers, because his father can barely walk due to his arthritis and begged off dancing. Then Carter walks over to us to cut in, as was planned. Owen's supposed to dance with Katie next.

But instead of handing me off to Carter, Owen grins, grabs Carter, and leaves me standing there wide-eyed and laughing as he spins off across the floor with Carter in his arms to a chorus of laughter and applause from everyone who's actually paying attention. It looks like nothing more than a couple of old buddies screwing around. They make their way back to me, Owen giving Carter a long, strong hug and the two of them clapping each other on the back before Owen hands him off to me with a flourish and a deep bow from the waist, just to earn more laughter from the audience.

Our boy.

As Carter and I dance, he's still smirking and glancing over at Owen, who's now talking to Senator Samuels.

"Did you know he was going to do that?" I softly ask, keeping my lips as still as possible.

"No." He chuckles. "I should have known he'd do something." From the playful gleam in Carter's eyes, I can tell Owen didn't earn any punishment strokes for that stunt.

The bastard extraordinaire is happy Owen got to share that little bit of joy with him, right out in the open in front of everyone.

Owen got to dance with *both* of us.

I'll happily take the win, and, apparently, so will Carter.

Personally, we get so few public chances like that, it means we savor and treasure them when they do happen.

We dance and talk, and I take a break to make the rounds again, as does Owen. At one point, I get a moment to hug Rebecca Soliz Martin, who, with her husband and father, were special guests of ours tonight. Her father is an old, dear friend of Daddy's, and a good friend of the family.

Of course I wasn't going to cut them out of this celebration. She's given us valuable advice through the years, especially for Owen's first run for office, for a seat on the Hillsborough County Commission. Years ago, when we were both kids, Rebecca and I used to share a tent together during camping trips with our fathers and their friends. She's only a few years older than I am. I suspect it's no coincidence we both ended up in politics, she as a consultant and strategist, me as a politician.

When I eventually rejoin Carter at our table, I lean in. "Thank you for making sure Rebecca and her father were invited," I whisper behind my hand.

Carter smiles and leans in so he can speak in my ear. "Don't worry, pet. I'll never forget those who helped us get where we are now."

But as he leans back, I almost think…

No, I must be wrong.

Carter has different expressions—smiles, smirks, frowns. Over the years, Owen and I have grown adept at reading those expressions as if Carter were holding up signs telegraphing what he's thinking. The three of us can hold entire silent conversations and understand everything.

There's one expression in particular I've seen the bastard extraordinaire wear plenty of times when he's pleased about something especially devious he's achieved, whether privately with myself or when with Owen, or something having to do with our law careers, such as delivering a devastating point against opposing counsel at trial. Or even something to do with the campaign, such as Owen scoring a powerful blow during a debate.

Carter wore one such look when Owen took down Kevin Markos in that interview the Sunday after the school shooting.

Or, maybe it's just nerves on my part, and I'm seeing things that aren't there. I opt to let it go. Because I know my husband, and even if there *was* something behind that smile, there's something else I *do* know for certain—

He'd never admit it to me anyway.

Plausible deniability.

CHAPTER FIVE

Then

When I was a kid, I learned about partisan politics before I learned my *ABC*s. When I played sports, I was never picked last. Not because I was good, but because I could play the game.

The game of politics.

I got *As* even when I didn't have the best grades, because I could sweet-talk the teachers and they'd overlook my shortcomings, or give me extra chances to improve my grade.

I learned.

Boy, did I learn.

I knew two things about myself before I reached high school— that I hated my father, and that I would make my own name for myself in this world.

Don't get me wrong, I love *Daddy*, the man who sang me to sleep, who taught me how to fish, who took me camping. Adore *him*.

Rarely saw him, though, once he started advancing through the ranks politically. The higher the office he achieved, the less I saw of Daddy.

If I wanted to spend time with my father, that meant I needed to become acquainted with and spend most of my time with Benchley Evans.

It was Benchley Evans, politician and political operator, who I saw most often. The skilled lawyer who taught me everything I know about the game of politics.

Daddy hoped I'd marry a nice guy from his party, settle down, have grandbabies.

Daddy is highly disappointed.

But Benchley Evans is not-so-secretly proud of me for setting myself up to be governor.

Both men despise my husband, Carter. Mostly because, professionally, Carter is everything they aren't...and *everything* Benchley Evans *is*, and more.

My father would have much preferred I married Owen. Owen reminds me so much of Daddy.

How little does he know.

Owen owns my heart as much as I own him and his.

They say girls marry their fathers. Except my father is two distinctly different men.

I guess, in a way, that's exactly what I did.

* * *

One of my early memories is of going on a particular camping trip with Daddy and some of his friends. I didn't understand until I was older that many of them were involved in politics in some way, either politicians, or lobbyists, or lawyers who had an interest in political doings, or even county or city employees.

Momma wasn't into camping, at *all*, but I loved everything to do with it. I also loved the attention I got from Daddy. He taught me how to take care of myself, how to set up my own tent, how to build and tend a fire—all of that. He'd been an Eagle Scout when he was a boy, and since he didn't have a son...

Well, he had *me*.

There was an older girl, Rebecca Soliz, who frequently went camping with us...until she didn't. There was a gap of several years before I saw her again, and at some point, she'd had a baby.

Although that was something no one talked about.

Rebecca's father, Edward Soliz, was one of Daddy's best friends. Rebecca and I used to share a tent, which I always thought was fun. I was seven, and she seemed so much older than me, even though she was probably thirteen or fourteen, at the time.

Daddy bought a new, larger tent, one that had a privacy divider inside it. Once Rebecca stopped going camping with us, I shared a tent with Daddy. It was almost as good as being in my own tent, except Daddy snores like a chainsaw.

At the time, Daddy was working for Hillsborough County as the county administrator. Back then, I didn't know for sure what that meant, but I knew he was important. I loved going to visit him at work and talking to people. Even at that age, politics and government excited me.

About three months after Rebecca stopped going camping with us, we went camping in the Withlacoochee State Forest. We'd never camped there before, but we were supposed to go canoeing the next day, and I was really looking forward to that, because I'd never been canoeing before. Ever.

Friday night, after camp was set up, we had dinner. It was well past dark by then. Daddy sent me to bed in our tent while he stayed up drinking beer with his friends.

"SusieJo," he said—a nickname I only tolerated because he was my Daddy and he seemed to love calling me that—"do *not* leave that tent before daylight, no matter what, without me. Understand?"

I chafed a little at that restriction. He'd never told me that before. "What if I have to go to the bathroom?"

He pointed at our tent from where he sat in a camp chair by the fire. "You can see me from here. If I'm not in the tent, you call for me. I'll hear you. If I'm asleep, you wake me up. It's dark, and it's a new campground you've never been to before, and I don't want you getting lost out there. Plus, it's hunting season. You wander off and get lost, you could end up shot accidentally. Understand?"

"Yes, Daddy." I didn't question it further, because he was my Daddy. And I had heard a few gunshots that evening, but none close to our campground. So his reasons did make sense.

I still thought it was kind of silly, but I was a fairly fearless kid and, again, he was my Daddy. Although we were kind of a ways from the campground bathrooms. Usually we camped closer to the bathrooms than we did this time, and it wasn't like there weren't other available campsites closer. Daddy and the men had picked a site at the edge of the campground, bordering thick woods.

There were maybe only four other groups in the campground that night, and none of them were close to us. There also weren't any lights in the campground, so admittedly I wasn't thrilled about the idea of traipsing around a strange campground in the dark and possibly getting lost.

I remember it was me, Daddy, Chris Norman—who was Daddy's very best friend—another man named Morgan Wheedon—who frequently camped with us but who I didn't like very much—and Chris Norman's older brother, David. David was also a friend of Daddy's, but he wasn't in politics. He ran a chain of tire stores in and around Tampa. But David's wife, Doris, worked for Daddy. She was his receptionist when he was the county administrator. Later, she would go on to work for him when he was elected to the county commission.

At the time, I didn't think about the fact that Morgan Wheedon hadn't been camping with us since the time Rebecca stopped coming. And also that weekend, Rebecca's father, Edward Soliz, wasn't with us, either. It was the first camping trip he'd missed in a while.

Morgan Wheedon had light blue eyes, red hair, and pale skin

with lots of freckles. He had to use a lot of sunscreen or he quickly ended up sunburned. He always wore a really big straw hat, too. I remember he wasn't married because he'd gotten divorced recently. It seemed like my parents had discussed his divorce in hushed tones, always growing quiet or changing the subject around me, so I suspected it wasn't a good thing.

I fell asleep pretty quickly that night. It was a little on the cool side, meaning sleeping was easy and the bugs were practically nonexistent. A particularly close gunshot woke me up at some point in the night, but I didn't hear anything else and ended up going back to sleep.

When I awoke early the next morning, Daddy was snoring like crazy and I hated waking him up. It was just past dawn, but thick shadows and damp mist lay low to the ground.

I crept around the divider and poked him in the shoulder. "Daddy, I need to go to the bathroom."

He rolled over, glanced at his watch, then sighed. "Is it daylight?"

"Sort of."

"Go on. Take your whistle. Blow it if you get lost or have a problem."

"Yes, sir." I wore it on an orange lanyard around my neck. It was one of Daddy's rules, in case I ever got lost. So far, the only time I'd needed it was when a spider crawled out of hiding from behind the handle on the door after I was already in a campground latrine stall, and I'd been too afraid to try to get out.

I wasn't sure if I'd ever live that story down, but my Daddy had rescued me from the evil spider, laughing once he'd recovered from his initial fear that I was being attacked or something. He'd shoved a stick under the door for me and I used that to unlatch the door so he could yank it open and get rid of the spider.

My hero to the rescue.

I made my way through the quiet morning without incident,

found the latrine, washed my hands really well, and made it back to find Daddy and the Normans starting to build a fire.

The men acted tired, but that was normal for Daddy before coffee. Once that had brewed, and they all got a mug in them, they perked up.

It was only once we started cooking breakfast that I realized what was wrong.

"Where's Mr. Wheedon?" I asked.

Daddy and the Norman brothers shared a glance and then looked around.

"Morgan!" Daddy called out. "You want coffee and breakfast?"

"Or did you drink too many beers last night?" Chris Norman called out, laughing. But it sounded kind of...tight.

David Norman smiled, but his expression looked nervous.

"Do you feel okay, Mr. D?" I called him that to differentiate him from Chris Norman, who was Mr. N. They couldn't both be Mr. N.

"Just a little headache, SusieJo," he said. "We drank too many beers last night."

Daddy was on his feet now. "Morgan? You gonna sleep all day?" He walked over to Mr. Wheedon's tent and peeked in. "He's not in here."

Chris Norman looked around. "Car's here. Did he hit the bathroom?"

"I didn't hear anyone else when I was over there," I said.

"Morgan?" David Norman called out.

Now all three men were up and moving, leaving me to cook breakfast while they started searching and calling for him.

An hour later, we were gathered around a park ranger and a deputy, while Daddy and the Norman brothers gave them a description of Mr. Wheedon and their activities the night before. We ate dinner, then I went to bed. The men sat up and talked and drank beer, then they all returned to their respective tents—Daddy to ours, the Norman brothers to the tent they shared, and they all saw Morgan return to his tent.

The deputy knelt and smiled at me. "How old are you, Susannah?"

I didn't feel any fear talking to the man because I was used to how friendly the bailiffs were who worked at the county building where Daddy worked. They always had smiles for me.

"I'm seven, sir."

"Do you like camping?"

"I love it. I want to be in the Boy Scouts, but I can't. Our Brownie troop is lame. We just do crafts and stuff. Daddy takes me camping."

"Did you hear anything or see anything last night?"

I started to say no, when I really thought about it. "I heard a gunshot last night that sounded close by."

All the men exchanged a look. "Do you know what time?" the deputy asked.

"No, sir. I went back to sleep."

"Was your dad in the tent with you?"

I solemnly nodded. "Yes, sir. Daddy snores."

The deputy and the park ranger stepped off to the side. Then the park ranger used the radio in his truck to call someone, said some codes.

An hour later, the search party, led by a dog, found Morgan Wheedon's body. He was sitting at the base of an oak tree about three hundred yards from our campsite, and had shot himself in the head.

He'd left a note. At the time, I was too young to hear the gory details.

It wasn't until after we returned home Saturday evening, having packed and left the campground, including packing Mr. Wheedon's things after the team of deputies finished going through all his stuff, that I thought about something I kept to myself.

When the gunshot awakened me, I didn't remember hearing Daddy snoring in the other side of the tent, and I never got up to check to see if he was there. I simply went back to sleep.

CHAPTER SIX

Then

It's funny, in a sad kind of way, that Owen can't accept how easily he won a spot on our HOA board, or how easily he won his primary while running for a seat on the Hillsborough County Commission.

Daddy's old seat, as a matter of fact.

Owen is incapable of seeing himself the way others see him—smart, funny, articulate, and hot.

Haaawwwt.

He wouldn't be our adorable boy if he hadn't been raised by a raging narcissist, I suppose.

And now…the general election. Running for a seat on the county commission is the first big step in his political journey. Because there isn't a minimum age to hold the office, Carter wants to start him there, as soon as possible. It's a four-year term. Owen's twenty-six now, will be twenty-seven when he takes office.

Carter keeps gently reminding me "if" Owen wins, except I know the truth—there is no doubt in my mind we'll get him elected. He already made it through the primaries with Daddy's endorsement. Now he just needs to take out his blue and red competition.

That's why we find ourselves driving over to Momma and Daddy's house in Brandon on the Sunday after the primary election. We're picking them up to go visit an old family friend. Daddy and Momma will be heading back to Tallahassee tomorrow morning, so it needs to happen today.

Rebecca Soliz Martin is now a cut-throat GOP strategist who's already made a legit name for herself in state politics. The three candidates she worked for during the primaries over in the Orlando area all won their various primaries. She's literally taking only a couple of days off before hitting the campaign trail again, and if her candidates knew she was talking to us today, they'd all probably fire her immediately.

We're not the competition in terms of the office Owen's running for, because none of her current candidates are running in or near Hillsborough County.

But we're not GOP, and her clients are.

We last ran into her a few months ago at Daddy and Momma's house in Brandon, when he threw a Super Bowl watch party. She and her husband, John, and their three sons, had all been in attendance.

I can barely remember the girl who went on camping trips with us when we were kids, the girl I shared a tent with, and I haven't seen her father, Edward, in years. He was supposed attend to the Super Bowl party, too, but ended up staying home because he was sick.

This is a huge favor Daddy's called in for us, for Owen, and I know it. When we arrive at Momma and Daddy's house to pick them up and I hug Daddy hello, I whisper in his ear.

"I owe you big-time, Daddy."

He chuckles. "Sweetheart, you have *no* idea, but that's okay. Hands wash hands."

I catch Carter watching—Carter misses nothing. Owen is busy hugging Momma. I swear she wishes I'd married Owen instead of Carter, but they're just going to have to deal with it. This magic we have, the three of us, wouldn't happen any other way, even if we can't tell people the truth.

Carter is driving, and Daddy gets in the front seat with him. Owen volunteers to sit in the middle of the backseat, between me and Momma, even though I offer to take the spot.

Owen won't let me.

Our good boy, always thinking of me. Even though he's likely going to be our state's future governor and, at six-four, he's way taller than me. Sitting scrunched in the middle has to be uncomfortable for him.

Edward Soliz is widowed now and lives with his daughter and son-in-law in a house fifteen minutes from Daddy and Momma in Brandon. Rebecca Soliz Martin, her father, Edward, her husband, John Martin, and their three kids are all there when we arrive. Their oldest son, Eddie, named after his grandfather, looks nothing like his mother, father, or his two much younger brothers. He's got light blue eyes, red hair, and pale skin and freckles. So pale that he looks like he'd explode in the sunlight. Reminds me of one of the Weasley kids from the *Harry Potter* movies.

A little more thinking on it, and it itches my brain that he reminds me of someone from real life, someone I haven't thought about in years. It triggers a memory of a camping trip when I was a little kid.

I shove that memory away because, today, we're focused on *this*.

Getting Owen elected.

I don't have time for trips down memory lane with old friends right now. We're here for work.

Rebecca warmly greets us. Once we're gathered in the living room, she tips her head as she studies Owen. "I have to admit, I was a little surprised when Benchley called me. I wouldn't be taking this meeting with you all today if it wasn't for how close he is to my father."

"We appreciate this," Carter says. "But Owen is a candidate worth backing."

"I'll be honest that I didn't pay much attention to this race," she says. "So I looked at his results. Impressive numbers, especially for a first-time third-party candidate. I'm guessing there's a bigger picture?"

"Governor," Carter says. "In ten years."

Her perfectly shaped eyebrows slowly arch. "*Wow.* Not sure any candidate can take two county terms all the way to Tallahassee that soon in this political climate. Much less a third-party candidate."

"One term county, one term Florida Senate. Then governor."

Now she can't hide her shock. "Benchley's seat?"

"I'm endorsing him," Daddy says, and I don't miss the way he glances at Carter. "For this race, and for my Senate seat, when he runs."

Rebecca frowns. "You're going to endorse an Independent candidate over a GOP candidate for your *Senate* seat? Very likely over a GOP *incumbent*, at that point?"

Daddy shrugs. "I believe in Owen."

"I mean, it's easy for you to get away with that for a county commission race, especially for your old seat, don't get me wrong. People are writing that off as you doing a favor for your daughter's friend. Besides, no one likes the GOP candidate. Carlisle was turfed out in the primary, but Buchanan is fucking dirty, and everyone knows it. I know damn well the local GOP won't take his loss very personally or hold it against you too much. No one wanted him to run in the first place. Won't take much to make him look like a lost cause. But you do that for a *Senate* race? It's political suicide."

Daddy shrugs again.

She lets out a low whistle. "Benchley, with all due respect, if you do that, you're going to have a screaming pack of rabid demons—and rabid PACs—coming after you when you run for governor. You *do* realize that, right?"

He nods. "I'm not concerned. I have the support for that, too, where it'll really count."

She snorts. "How many ratfucks is *that* going to cost you?"

Daddy simply smiles.

"Here's the plan," I say. As is usual in these situations, Carter lets me take the lead, going over polling numbers, districts, trends—all the minutiae and data that Owen and I thrive on consuming. Carter is more a big-picture kind of guy. Give him the results once we crunch numbers so he can go from there. Our tactician, the mobile response, seeing the overall trends.

He's the one who doesn't panic or rejoice over a jog in poll numbers a point or two in either direction.

I include the long-term plan of getting me elected for a state office, too, then running for governor following Owen's incumbency. Once I finish my part of the presentation and hand it off to Carter, he settles in chatting with Rebecca while I sit back to listen. Owen is intently absorbing everything, asking smart questions. From the way Daddy nods on occasion, I can tell he understands why I want to back Owen as a candidate.

Once we go through all that, she sits back and needs a moment to digest everything. Then she looks at Daddy. "Maybe this isn't as crazy a plan as I first thought," she admits as she slowly nods. "Father-daughter governors. There's a nice bit of symmetry in that." She sighs. "If I didn't think it'd get me drummed out of the GOP, I'd offer to come on board for Owen's state Senate run. But I already have two different GOP hopefuls with their sights on it. Different districts, but still."

Carter grins. "You could still come work for us."

"Yeah, but I'd never get hired by another GOP candidate, and the Dems don't pay worth shit in this state." She smiles. "But before I sign an employment contract, maybe I can look over some info for you and give you a few pointers. Unofficially, of course."

"Of course," Carter agrees. "For now, tell us how to best guarantee Owen a general election win in *this* race."

We spend the next two hours discussing tactics she is certain will give Owen a leg up. She also shares deep background info she has on Buchanan, and on Fleming, the Democratic candidate. Combined with Daddy's endorsement, Owen should be a shoo-in.

The afternoon, as far as I'm concerned, is a success.

We finally break for dinner—pizza that we've ordered, since neither Daddy, Rebecca, nor Carter want all of us spotted out and about in public together—plus her father, her husband, and the kids join us.

I know that Rebecca's husband isn't Eddie's biological father, but I've never really heard the story about all of that, either. It was something Daddy and Momma never openly talked about around me. Obviously, I'm not so tactless that I'd ask that here, but in the car on the way back to Daddy's, I broach the subject.

"Whatever happened to Eddie's biological father?" I ask. I have a suspicion who the boy's father might be, but have never heard that spoken aloud.

I think it's my imagination that Daddy and Carter share a glance. It's probably more Carter being Carter, and him watching my father to see his reaction. Carter loves to pick up stray nuggets of information here and there, especially anything he thinks he might be able to put to good use later.

"What do you mean?" Daddy asks.

"I mean, was he her boyfriend in high school or something?" I fudge. "I know John's definitely *not* that boy's father. He was born before they got together. Besides, he looks nothing like John."

"I don't know, SusieJo," Daddy says, even though he knows

how much I hate that nickname as an adult. "Never thought it was my place to ask. She ended up living in Orlando, for a while, when she had him."

My bullshit meter goes off but I know better than to pry. Daddy's dancing around the issue. No way in hell will he tell me now. Besides, I'm deep enough in his debt as it is for him arranging this meeting for us today.

I do the smart thing and let it drop.

Although I am a little surprised Momma doesn't chime in. A conversation like this, usually she'd be shushing one or both of us, telling us it was impolite. Right now, she's staring out the window with a tense set to her neck. I only see this because I look around Owen when I realize she's not saying anything.

"Are you all right, Momma?"

"I'm fine," she lies. "Just a little headache."

I'm desperate to smooth this over. I know she still hates Carter for how we got married, and spending several hours with him today has probably been about as much as she can handle.

"Thank you both for doing this today," I say. "I love both of you so much. I wouldn't be doing this if I didn't believe in Owen as a qualified candidate."

"Not too late for you to change your party affiliation back," Daddy says as he stares out the passenger window. "You don't need to work this hard, SusieJo."

I ignore the nickname. "You always told me to be my own person, Daddy. That I *need* to work hard to make a name for myself." I decide to address the elephant—sort of literally and metaphorically—in the car with us. "Momma's a Democrat, and you never hounded her to change parties."

"Because she's my wife, and she's not running for office."

And because it suited him, I'm sure, having a "liberal" wife. Made him look more centrist and appealing to socially liberal Republican voters.

Believe me, I know my Daddy.

"You just don't want to admit you were wrong about Carter," I hear myself say, horrified that I actually said it aloud. It takes everything I have not to clap my hand over my mouth like a little kid.

Carter's wearing sunglasses, but I see him glance in the rearview mirror, and I know I just earned strokes.

"*Hmph*," Momma says.

Fuck it. I opened this closet, might as well clean it out for good. "*Six* years," I say.

"You've barely been out of law school *two* years," Daddy shoots back. "You went and eloped."

Carter remains silent. I drew this incoming fire—I know I need to be the one to return it. "You taught me to go after what I wanted, Daddy. To be ruthless. Brutal, even. I wanted Carter. I'd think you'd be happy I married someone who not only celebrates the fact that I'm a strong woman, he doesn't try to tear me down. He *wants* to help me make my dreams come true. If it was up to Carter, we'd be practicing law and settling in to a quiet life. *I'm* the politician. *Me*. And Owen," I quickly add. "You always told me to marry a man who'd value who I was and not try to change me, and *that's* what I did. I married *exactly* that man. And you know what? He reminds me a lot of *you*."

"Touché," Momma quietly says.

At the same time, Owen softly mutters, "Yikes."

And Carter says, "Ouch."

But Daddy laughs. "Fuck me, hard to argue against that, I suppose." I know from the sound of his laugh he's genuinely amused. I'm not sure which part he thought was funny, but at least the tension in the car has eased.

Unfortunately, I can't leave things well enough alone. "Besides," I clumsily add, "Owen wouldn't have let me go through with it if he didn't believe in Carter, too. Would you?"

I know I've put our boy on the spot and I'll owe him a massive apology later.

But he's our good boy, and he lies for me.

Sort of. "I trust Carter," Owen quietly says. "And I trust Susa. They took me in and became my family. I wouldn't have reconciled with Dad the way I have if it wasn't for them helping me. They taught me it was okay to trust people again, after my mother ruined my trust. I don't think I'm out of line to say that you and your wife raised an amazing woman, Senator Evans. I'm proud to call her and Carter my best friends, and even my adopted family. I have never had the feeling that Susa didn't know exactly what she wanted or how to go about getting it. She's an old soul, and she's going to be an amazing governor, one day. I'm simply glad I get to be a part of it."

Daddy sighs, and Momma finally looks at Owen, then me.

"Just don't go getting her pregnant yet, Carter," Daddy admonishes.

"That's not going to be a problem, Daddy," I say, feeling mixed emotions about *that* truth. "You don't have to worry about it."

* * *

To Carter's credit, he waits until it's just the three of us again and we're almost home to finally bring it up.

"I don't think that was the best way to approach things, pet."

"I know, I know. I'm sorry."

He points over the back of the seat at Owen, who's now sitting behind me, on the passenger side.

Carter's message is clear—it's not *him* I owe an apology to. It's Owen.

I turn. "I'm sorry, sweetie."

He's looking out the window. "It's all right, Ma'am."

"No, it's not. I shouldn't have asked you to lie for me."

"I didn't lie, Ma'am." He's still looking out the window.

Technically, he lied by implying he was at our wedding, when he knows damn well he wasn't. He didn't find out about that until well after the fact.

And I forced him to make that implication by dragging him into the discussion.

"I mean, I shouldn't have put you in that position. I'm *really* sorry."

"It's all right, Ma'am."

I feel even worse now. It's bad enough that I can never openly admit who he is to us. He will forever be playing the third wheel, so to speak. We have to pretend he's just a really good friend, not a third of our love. Meanwhile, he gets his face inadvertently rubbed in that fact every time we're all out together somewhere, especially with my parents, or in any kind of professional situation.

I glance Carter's way. He removes his sunglasses when he has to slow and wait for the gate to our development to open for us.

He shoots me an angry glare.

That's the kind of glare that means *I'd* damn well better fix this before *he* has to, because if *he* has to fix it, *I* won't be sitting down for a week.

At least.

CHAPTER SEVEN

We arrive home moments later, and Carter pulls the car into the garage. Even though I know Owen wants to open my car door for me, I get out first, before he can, and stand there with my hand out, waiting. The garage door is already rolling down behind us, meaning we are safely concealed. He finally reaches out and takes my hand and lets me lead him inside after I disarm the alarm.

This house is our refuge. Owen's house is next door, but he essentially lives here, with us. If he drove separately to work, he parks his car in his garage, lets the door roll shut behind him, changes into a T-shirt and shorts, and then walks through his side door and into our home, concealed by a tall privacy fence that spans the side-yard gap between our homes. In the morning, he reverses the procedure, usually showering with Carter after their morning run or work-out, then pulling on shorts and a tee to go get dressed at his house. If he rides in with Carter, he gets dressed over there and returns to our house.

Most of his clothes and his personal items are there, but only what he doesn't need on an immediate basis. Everything else is here.

This is *our* home, the *three* of us, and where we sleep nearly every night—together. There are plenty of pictures of all three of us on the walls, so Owen isn't some faceless ghost in our marriage whose presence isn't noted except when he's physically here.

He's all around us, *part* of us.

He *is* us. There would be no *us* if it wasn't for Owen, and don't think I don't recognize that.

I love him every bit as much as I love Carter, and I need to remind him of that right now after my thoughtless words earlier. It's instances like this, where I make time to center him in my world, that will live in his heart and sustain him through the lonelier times ahead of us.

When he starts to pause in the hallway just inside the garage door so he can strip, as per the rules, I don't let him. I tug his hand and make him follow, leaving him snatching his chain collar from on top of the shelf there and carrying it with him.

My good boy.

He's always been my good boy.

Could I have settled for Owen instead of marrying Carter? Probably. I know we would have been reasonably happy together, Owen letting me do my political thing, following me around, the dutiful husband.

I wouldn't have cheated on him, because that's fucking douchey.

We probably would have had a couple of kids, at least. I can envision Owen being an amazing dad, and it makes me sad in some ways to know he'll never realize that dream.

It's one of the few things I regret about all of this.

He wears a stainless steel necklace as his day collar, something innocent and unrecognizable to the average person as anything other than jewelry. I have a matching one, as well as a bracelet, that are my day collars. I can wear either—or both, if I choose. When I wear the bracelet, I do so on my right wrist. Carter also wears a matching bracelet, on his left, as our Master and Owner.

It's a subtle reminder for me and Owen.

This is in addition to the matching tattoos we all have, Carter's on the inside of his left wrist, and Owen's and mine inside our right wrists, a small symbol for infinity. Carter's is usually concealed by his dress shirts or blazer, Owen's by his shirt, or a watch, when he's wearing short sleeves, and mine I don't bother hiding.

I don't care who sees it.

When in our home, Owen usually wears the stainless choker chain collar that was his first day collar, and it's locked around his neck with a small padlock.

I take that collar from him now and set it on the dresser before I grab his tie and pull him in for a kiss. I want to do this as Owen and Susa, not as Ma'am and boy.

I need to remind him he means far more to me than merely being my property, even though that's all he wants to be.

I need to remind him he's part of my heart, part of our marriage. That I consider him my husband every bit as much as Carter is.

His arms slide around me as I press my body against his, releasing his tie so I can drape my arms around his neck. At six-four, he's a good six inches taller than Carter, but Owen's body is every bit as familiar to me as Carter's is.

Finally, his hands slide down my back, to my ass, and squeeze as I feel his cock harden against me in his slacks. Carter always rescinds the no-underwear rule when we have to deal with my parents. Today, I chose panties.

Owen, however, is always our good boy, and did not. I grind against him, feeling his kiss intensify, the hunger growing there as I rock my hips against him. Not until I hear the soft, needy sounds he's making, borderline whines, do I reach down and unfasten his belt and slacks. My gaze, however, remains fixed on his sweet green eyes. When we're like this they always get darker, hints of steamy jungle colors coming to mind, fertile and verdant.

I almost think he's not going to release his grip on my ass so I can sink to my knees, but he finally does. When I go down on him, swallowing him all the way to the root, I never break my gaze with him.

Now he's *gone*. His hands tangle in my hair, finding and unfastening the barrette holding my hair in a loose bun. He tosses it onto the dresser with his collar and runs his fingers through my tresses, fisting my hair as his hips begin to rock in time with my movements. I slide his slacks down his thighs and cup that firm, gorgeous ass of his and hold on tight.

Sometimes, it's difficult to coax Owen to take control. He's always happy to be the bottom, to be *on* bottom, or to default to doing what he's told.

Today I want him to remember he's not a passive piece of furniture—he's *mine*.

Ours.

The fact that Carter hasn't joined us yet is further proof the bastard extraordinaire is completely right.

Owen *needs* me like this, right now.

I hear his breathing become more ragged even while his taste begins to spill over my tongue as he grows closer.

"I love you, Susa," he grits out. I sense him trying to hold back, wanting to make this last, and I don't rush him. I don't know if he's going to finish like this, or bend me over the bed, but it's his choice right now and he knows it.

When he slows his thrusts moments later, my heart races because I know what he's chosen.

He grabs my arm and pulls me to my feet, immediately pushing me back and onto the bed, where he shoves the hem of my dress up.

Off come the panties, discarded on the floor. I think he's going to plow me hard and deep but he surprises me. He trails sweet, gentle kisses from the inside of my right ankle, all the way up my leg, to my inner thighs. Then he skips completely over my pussy and down the inside of my left leg, to that ankle.

My shoes stay on as he drops to his knees and pulls me forward so he can bury his face between my thighs.

I'm...*undone* is the only word to describe it. My boy's technique has come a long way since the first time he ate me out back in college. While Carter might still be better at sucking Owen's cock than I am, Owen is better at eating my pussy than Carter.

Not that I have complaints about Carter's technique, it's just a subtle difference in the motivation, perhaps? I don't know.

What I *do* know is that with my legs over his shoulders and his hands clamped around my thighs to keep me from squirming free, Owen's sweet mouth quickly sends me to heaven time and again. No vibrator can compare to the wet heat of this man's oral skills.

Twenty minutes later, when *he's* satisfied he's made me come enough, only *then* does he pause to toe off his loafers before he climbs onto the bed and shoves my legs back. My legs are still draped over his shoulders, and now my thighs are pressed against my chest while his cock slides inside me, filling me. He cages me with his body and his fingers lace with mine. I'm practically bent into a pretzel—thank you, yoga classes—and he slowly starts grinding.

Wow. A sweet, sexy smile fills his face. In this position he can last a long time, and I can't exactly complain because he *just* gave me joy.

Like this, Owen knows he can eventually fuck one more orgasm out of me, because his body rubs against my swollen, throbbing clit with every stroke.

In this way, too, my men are different. Carter has his favorite position that he enjoys grinding on me like this, on our sides, facing each other and with our legs scissored together, one of his arms wrapped around my waist.

I taste myself when Owen slants his mouth over mine. I *love* kissing him. In the early days, I loved sitting on his lap, facing him, fucking him and kissing him. I could kiss him for hours.

Although there were times I sat on his lap like that and kissed him for hours with us both fully dressed, just to tease and torment him.

Hey, he admits he's a masochist in several different ways. We both are, or we wouldn't be with Carter.

Speaking of, he still hasn't joined us. Usually by now he's made his way in, at least to lie on the bed and watch us, reach out and touch us, or kiss us.

That he's still not joining us means he really feels Owen needs this time with me right now, and even greater shame fills me.

Our boy isn't complicated. He's really not. I quickly learned from Carter not to take Owen for granted, or carelessly let words fly. To immediately recognize and take ownership of any unintended and stinging verbal barbs, and to apologize, love the hurt away.

I'm sure I'll be punished by Carter at some future point for this.

Not right now.

Not around Owen.

He never punishes me for these kinds of infractions in front of Owen, and rightfully so. Whenever Carter feels I've done something against Owen worthy of punishment, he makes sure I make it right with Owen *first*, and later evens the score in private with me. Otherwise, Owen will feel guilty for me incurring punishment on his behalf.

We also never tell Owen about those times. That is completely between me and Carter. Owen doesn't even know about that particularly strict set of rules I agreed to.

There is no converse to that, either—no consequences for

Owen for violating any rules against me in that way.

Owen never does, never has.

He *truly* is our good boy.

Even if he did, one of the secret rules I agreed to back then, before Carter married me, was that there are some permanent inequalities in our relationship.

Owen *always* comes first, for *both* of us, because he doesn't get legal recognition the way we do as a married couple.

Because his mother was a fucking cunt and abused him.

Because he's a sweet, gentle soul who doesn't have the stable foundation Carter and I did growing up.

I wouldn't be here if I thought it was unfair—it's completely fair and voluntary, on my part.

Sure, we've "funished" Owen countless times. Not to mention he's endured the sadist's amusement ever since we started doing this. But Carter was adamant about that with me at the start. One of his ironclad rules for me was that Owen could never be "punished."

Ever.

Talked to, gentle corrections, sure. And Owen does have rules and consequences. But they're *set* rules with *set* consequences that Owen not only expects but in his own way welcomes, because he knows it means we're paying attention. They're also consequences he *agrees* to.

If today had been reversed and Owen let loose with an outburst and drew me in like that? No way would Carter have punished him for it, even though Carter and I both know Owen would expect punishment.

Owen trusts us, because Carter was careful and smart in the beginning. Carter took the time to learn our boy inside and out, including the bullshit Owen's mother put him through as a kid.

The first time I accidentally ran afoul of that rule, Carter nearly called an end to our relationship as a whole and walked out with

Owen right there, although Owen will never know that.

Again, that's between me and Carter. It was the first time I truly realized how much Carter loves Owen and has devoted his life to him.

It's one of the reasons I fell so hard for Carter and knew I could spend the rest of my life with him. Because devotion like that doesn't come cheap.

It's only wrenched from the bottom of a person's soul, and is sometimes carved out of their flesh.

And Carter has already survived both extremes more than once.

CHAPTER EIGHT

Even when making love, my men have different "feels." They could both do the exact same thing to me, and a different emotional painting takes shape.

If it's only Carter and me making love like this, as equals and without any sadism involved, Carter stills wears a thick shell with me. He can't help it. I'm not even sure if he realizes he does it. It's a shell I've seen disappear when he makes loves to Owen, though. Maybe he feels Owen is physically stronger than me and better able to hold Carter's demons in check, I don't know.

It's not a feeling of a *lack* of love when Carter's with me, though. It's like there's an openness and vulnerability in the way he makes love to Owen that's not present with me. I'm positive it's an indescribable, intangible artifact left over from trauma Carter suffered long before we met, one which he refuses to discuss in anything but vague hints.

The most I could force him to confess to was that it had to do with whatever happened to him in Germany, when he was in the Army, and that it involved the woman he got a vasectomy for—a relationship that didn't work out, in the end.

A bitch whose name I don't even know but who I wouldn't piss on if she was on fire.

A woman I'd love to hand a gasoline cocktail…and then toss her a lit match.

Because of what she did, Carter and I can't have kids. I know he would love to have kids. I thought about Owen fathering them for us, able to co-parent with us, because Owen also wants to be a father.

Until Carter gently pointed out to me during one of our private conversations that we ask enough of our boy already when it comes to publicly denying who he is to us, and that we will be asking even more of him throughout the years. That it would be cruel to add this sacrifice on top of that pile, to force him to watch his children be publicly claimed as Carter's.

And he's right.

I don't want to put Owen through that, either. Because then the issue is compounded—how do you explain to the kids not to call Owen "Daddy" around others? How do you ask children to keep their entire lives a lie?

Or how do Carter and I even pretend Owen isn't the father of all our children when all either of us want is to include him in all ways as our husband?

We can't. *I* can't. I won't ask Owen to endure that, either. It also means I won't pick IVF or other methods of parenthood, because then it's like we're rejecting Owen, and Carter agreed he'd already thought of that, too.

Carter did give me a choice—kids, or politics. That he'd toss my birth control pills himself and we'd settle down together, the three of us, as an openly poly triad.

Except…

I want what I want. I wouldn't be happy leaving politics this early in my life, before I even have a chance to make a run of my own for any office.

Carter permanently closes that discussion with one caveat—

that unless I change my mind about kids versus politics, I won't discuss the subject of having children with him or Owen again, unless Carter brings it up to me first.

It's the only time I think I really felt a crisis of conscience regarding our chosen path.

There's a seductive emotional pull when I imagine a houseful of kids, and the three of us sitting by the pool while watching them splash around together. Of carpools and PTO meetings, kicking back at the end of a day, or on a Friday after leaving work for a weekend with our family, and just *being* a family together.

I know Owen would be an amazing dad, and so would Carter.

Unfortunately, I was seduced a long time ago by my first love—politics.

Its siren song is far stronger and more hypnotic than any what-if thoughts about the three of us playing house together.

While I have no doubts about my husbands' ability to be great parents, I'm not so sure about my own.

I was an only child of doting parents who raised me well, if I do say so myself. Unconventionally in some ways, but that's because they were rich and because of Daddy's chosen career path. I learned to work hard to get what I wanted, and that drive has always been there.

But it also means I'm not used to giving up my dreams for others. Stepping aside and being magnanimous and sacrificing myself. I can drop to my knees for Carter when I *feel* like it, but he's the only man I'd ever think about kneeling for.

And he knows when to back off.

Owen, however, has a pure slave's heart, if you could ever categorize such a thing. He lives to serve us. He truly is happiest living in ways beneath myself and Carter that would make me miserable if I had to live like that all the time.

Add to that the fact that Owen wants to be governor and never thought he could make that dream come true, until he met us.

I'd be taking away his dream of higher offices, not just my own, if I asked for us to switch course now. No, we haven't talked about this with Owen. It's a "command decision," as Carter calls it. Owen wouldn't complain, I'm sure, but Owen *literally* will not complain about anything that doesn't make him violate Carter's most unbreakable rule—Owen will always protect himself first and foremost, in all ways, even if that means protecting himself from me or Carter.

Right now, with the two of us alone in bed together, Owen is relaxed and focused on *me*, on *us*. I feel it when he settles into his rhythm as he fucks me, one he can maintain for as long as he needs to. Every driving thrust he takes makes his cock and his body hit every perfect place inside and outside me and mine. My climb starts again, too.

With his forehead pressed against mine he makes love to me, kissing me, sucking my lips, nuzzling my nose. When Carter and Owen *kiss*—meaning more than just a quick, gentle peck—for any length of time, it looks like they've barely survived an orgy, both of them ending up with swollen lips and reddened cheeks. I love watching them *kiss*.

When Owen *kisses* me, even at his most passionate, it's sweet, gentle sunshowers, hot chocolate on cozy winter nights, the whisper of lace and satin across skin.

When Carter *kisses* me, it's straight bourbon and the dirty growl of an electric guitar while a tropical storm roars outside.

Like this, completely corralled and pinned down by Owen's body, I know I can come. Years with Carter have taught me I need the bite, or the restraint, the same way Owen does, in his own way.

He's still being of service and giving me what I need, even if what he's giving me is himself.

My sweet, gentle boy.

I rub my cheek against his, the slight scratch of his afternoon stubble rasping against my flesh. He nips my earlobe, tugging. It's the deliciously desperate edge to his breath filling my ear that trips me over unexpectedly. Carter's trained me too well in too many ways, including my own sadism. I love having my boy needy and wanting me.

I arch my back as his lips close over mine again. He pounds into me, wanting to catch up, to fall with me. It's something we don't get very often like this, and it's so much sweeter when we do. I'm swirling around that funnel, heading down, when I hear his deep, desperate gasp, and I know he's *there*.

My hands squeeze his as my body lets go and pleasure rolls through me once more, not as intense as his mouth on me, but lasting longer. Every stroke prolongs it, until he finally falls still inside me and we're both lying there nuzzling each other once more.

"Love you, Susa," he whispers.

I wait until he's looking me in the eyes. "Love you, too, Owen. Are we okay?"

He nods, kissing me again. He's not allowed to lie to either of us, even if it's an uncomfortable truth, so I know we're okay.

The rest remains unspoken. I have promised him that, once we are both out of politics, we will reveal the truth and live openly. It won't be a secret to some by then, I'm sure, but that goal lays unseen years in the future.

That is my vow to my boy, and I damn sure will keep it.

* * *

Owen's still inside me. He's released my hands and is resting on his elbows when I feel the mattress dip next to us.

I don't break eye contact with Owen. "Did you enjoy the show?"

The bastard extraordinaire chuckles. "Beautiful, as always, pet." Carter kisses Owen first, then me.

Always Owen first, like this.

I never mind, because there will be countless future times where it's just me and Carter, or where Carter won't be able to kiss Owen in front of others. I will never begrudge our boy being first whenever we can put him there.

Like now.

Carter reaches over and strokes Owen's head, rubbing his scalp in that playful, tender way that immediately drops Owen into subspace.

Like now. I smile as I watch Owen's eyes fall closed, his body relaxing even more on top of mine.

The bastard extraordinaire might be many things good and evil, but I cannot deny he knows our bodies even better than we do, sometimes.

"Although you both have too many clothes on," Carter pretend gripes.

Owen's eyes are still closed. When I look at Carter, his gaze is fixed on me.

"We got distracted."

"So I see, pet." I can also see Carter's fly is tented. I'm sure he stood in the doorway and watched, squeezing himself through his slacks as he did, the handsome perv.

He loves to watch.

I love putting on a show for him with Owen.

But now we've also fired him up, so I wonder which one of us he'll choose to slake his lust with, and how. Unless he specifically asks for one of us to volunteer, I've given up trying to outguess him, in that regard. I'm never right, it seems.

Sometimes, I think he does it just to fuck with me.

Damn, I love the sadist.

He stretches out alongside us and kisses Owen again. I see the way Carter's arm tenses and I know he's just fisted Owen's hair. A soft, sexy moan from Owen a second later confirms that for me.

Carter holds Owen in place and kisses me, then tips his face to bring Owen in so we're all kissing each other.

Hey, don't knock it.

"I think I want you both to stay right there," Carter finally says before he releases Owen and sits up.

Oh, I *know* what he's decided.

Seconds later, Carter shucks his slacks and kneels next to us, his cock sliding between our mouths as he holds his shirt out of the way. Owen and I automatically start licking, sucking, as Carter rests a hand on Owen's back and begins fucking the space between our mouths. Together, we take turns deep-throating him before he's back to using our lips pressed together to stroke his cock. His cock is already leaking pre-cum and is that kind of steely-hard engorged that tells me he was *way* more than just turned on by watching us—he was halfway to coming.

When he finally unleashes a deep, sexy groan I know means he's hit the point of no return, instead of burying himself inside my mouth or Owen's, he opts for one of his favorites—painting both our faces with his cum as he starts furiously stroking his cock with his hand. He smears it all over me, over Owen, our foreheads and cheeks and chins, making both of us take turns sucking every last drop from the head.

Then he sits back and watches, smiling as we lick each other clean, both of us now giggling, laughing, kissing, our usual balance restored.

The bastard in charge.

Believe me, we wouldn't be here if we didn't love it, and Carter, or weren't certain how much he loves both of us.

CHAPTER NINE

Now

It's a great inauguration ball. I eat too much, dance too much, talk waaaay too much. I'm stuffed, my feet freaking hurt, and I'm going to be hoarse tomorrow.

And I'm sure I still have a panty violation caning to endure at some point tonight.

It's just past midnight when the remaining guests start getting a gentle hint from the waitstaff that they don't have to go home, but they can't stay here, when they start clearing the tables, removing tablecloths from empty tables, and quietly stack chairs. At midnight we switched over to piped-in music from the hotel so the bands can pack up and go home. Some of the FSU students have classes tomorrow, although the high school students have excused absences.

Literally. Notes personally signed by Owen, although we've already cleared it with the principal.

Still, that'll be a neat keepsake for the kids.

My parents, Carter's family, and Owen's family are staying at the hotel. At eleven thirty, Carter escorted his mom and dad upstairs, but he hasn't returned yet. Owen's family left a little after ten, because they're departing early in the morning to drive back to Tampa. Daddy and Momma have already left and headed to their hotel room.

I plop down in my chair next to Owen after ShaeLynn Samuels says her good-byes for the night.

"Can we blow this party yet?" I mutter as I lean forward to take my shoes off under the table.

I know Owen's watching me. It's probably killing my poor boy that he can't drop to his knees, help me do it, and then massage my aching feet for me.

"Soon," he says. "*Someone's* not back yet."

I personally think he likes torturing himself a little. When he can't refer to Carter as "Sir," he'll frequently call him "Someone" instead.

Still gets that *S*-sound in there.

I glance around, catch Dray's eye, and tap my left wrist, where a watch would be if I wore one tonight.

He nods and starts looking around, quickly excusing himself from the people he's talking with, and heads out of the ballroom.

He's on it. Carter chose well hiring him to be my chief of staff, and I'm looking forward to him working with me for the next sixteen years, if I'm lucky.

I grab my shoes, set them on Carter's empty chair next to me, and sit back in mine. "This was a good night. I've been to several of these things, or ones like them, and they're usually sucky. I think we did great."

Owen nods, but he's staring at his left thumbnail as he sort of picks at it with his right index finger.

Our boy is exhausted. *Done.*

And damned if I can do a single thing about it right now. I'm kicking myself in the ass we didn't get a hotel suite of our own, but Carter nixed that idea. Said even if we are paying for it out of our own pockets, and paid the security detail ourselves, it'd still look bad because only half the story would get out.

Better to do this the right way.

He's right, I know he is, but that doesn't mean I like it.

I hate that I'm not going to be able to let our boy curl up with me tonight and rub his head while he goes to sleep.

As I watch Owen, I think about last night, the conversation Carter and I had.

Seeing Owen like this, at the end of his emotional tether, I wonder if in eight years I'm really going to want to run for governor after all.

* * *

Last night, while I'm standing at the end of our bed and staring down at the two different outfits I have laying on it, and I'm trying to decide which one to wear to the swearing in ceremony, Carter walks in the room and sits on the edge of our bed.

A bed that's going to be empty by one far too soon. Owen is over at the capitol tonight, and will be home at some point. I thought Carter was going to be with him, but he surprises me by returning early.

"I want to talk, Suse."

When he calls me that he gets my full attention, because not only are we talking as equals, it's something serious and personal he wants to discuss. It's kind of our conversational safeword.

I call him *Carter Edward Wilson* to achieve the same effect, because he says it reminds him of his mom yelling at him with his full name as a kid, and is a guaranteed chub-killer if ever there was one.

If I call him *Mr. Wilson* it just turns him the fuck on.

Kind of turns me on, too.

"What's wrong?" I ask.

He meets my gaze from where he's lounging on the bed. He's still fully dressed, another reason I know he's about to delve in to something serious. We can't do these talks semi- or fully naked, because, inevitably, we end up fucking.

"I want to revisit a discussion," he says.

"About?"

"Children."

I actually need a second to process what he said. We had that talk years ago, before Owen ran for the Hillsborough County Commission. We haven't talked about it again, because Carter told me not to bring it up unless I was ready to give up politics.

Carter told me he gave Owen a similar admonishment years ago.

It's been the untouchable topic for all of us since then.

"Um." I swallow because my throat's gone dry. "Ooookaaaay?"

"You and I both know Owen wants kids."

I nod. That's a given. He's a great adopted uncle to Carter's nieces and nephews, and to children of friends of ours.

He'd be an amazing father.

"And so do I," he says.

I stare at him, unsure how to process this.

"Yes or no answer only, Suse. No qualifiers. Do you still want kids?"

"Yes," I whisper. I can't help it. I do, even though I'd pretty much given up on the thought of having them.

He nods. "Okay." He stands and turns to go.

"Wait, *what*?"

He's heading toward our bathroom. "What?" he calls back without turning.

I follow him. "That's *all* the conversation we're having about this?"

"It was a yes or no question, *pet*. Is your answer still yes?"

"Well, yes, but—"

He turns, his expression now full of dark thunder. "*Devotion*," he snaps.

I can't help it—I drop into the formal bow right where I stand on the bathroom floor. My heart's pounding in my chest even as my forehead presses against the cool tile.

I hear him moving around, the sound of him opening the medicine cabinet, taking something out.

The sound of something landing in the garbage can.

The bastard extraordinaire's fist grabs my hair and wrenches my head back. In his other hand is the bathroom garbage can.

He tips it so that I can see inside it are my packages of birth control pills.

"When I flip you back to pet," he softly growls, "and you don't safeword, you do *not* fucking get to question me or forget to 'yes, Sir' me." His tone sounds low, deliberate, threatening, and *very* fucking sexy. "Do you *understand* me?"

"Yes, Sir."

I'm...*wet*. I mean, I can feel my juices running down the insides of my thighs right there, and my clit is throbbing something crazy. We haven't had any playtime in the past couple of weeks, and I know tonight all we'll do is collapse in exhaustion.

But right now, if he wants to bend me over and fuck me...*yeah*. I'll happily do it.

I forget how fucking hot it is when he forces me let go to him.

How much I want and *need* this from him sometimes. I *need* the bastard extraordinaire, and I'd be lying if I denied it.

This is what I can't get with Owen, because Owen doesn't have a bastardly cell in his body, much less a bastardly bone.

Although the bone he does have is very, very nice.

"*I* will handle Owen," Carter says. "If you're changing your answer to no, then tell me now."

"I..." I swallow, trying to figure out how to phrase it. "Not changing my answer, Sir, but I'm not giving up my current office or my career."

"I'm not asking you to give up politics, pet." He chuckles. "We're *here*. We've done it. But when I sat down and thought about it this morning, I realized how much time has passed, and how old we're getting."

His grip in my hair gentles and he sets the garbage can aside to sit on the floor with me with a soft, pained grunt. "If we're going to have kids, we should probably have them sooner rather than later." With his free hand, he brushes the hair away from my face. "At Ease," he softly says.

I rise into the position. Like this, I'm looking into his eyes.

"I'll talk to Owen," he says. "I'll handle it *my* way. We're not kids just starting out now. We'll figure it out, how to juggle everything. If he's okay with me being listed as their father on their birth certificates, then we'll do it. I really think he will. Back then, I honestly don't think he could have handled it. But we're all older and tougher now."

"Time is never our friend, and it's never on our side," I say. It's one of Daddy's favorite sayings, and Carter knows that. "And take time to make time, or we'll regret it." That was one of Nana's favorite sayings.

He knows that, too.

Carter slowly nods as he smiles. "Exactly."

I study him for a moment. "Is this about what happened at the school, Sir?"

I don't have to clarify. He damn well knows what I mean.

The shoot-out.

He doesn't answer me, at first. I was beginning to think he wouldn't when he finally sighs. "Yeah. I can't say no to him, Suse. I know he wants kids. He's never asked since our conversation years ago, but I...I can see it in his face every time the subject is brought up. Every time you and I dodge the question of kids from others and he's standing *right* there listening and trying to pretend it doesn't impact him, too. Someone was joking with me about it today in front of him, and…I could see it fucking *kills* him.

"I'm sure Owen's not going to care who's on the birth certificate as long as he gets to help raise them. In four to eight years, he'll get to step back from this life. You know as well as I do that he doesn't want to run for anything else. I want him to have a greater purpose once that happens, and it would make him so damn happy to be a dad. And if you run for the US Senate, all the better. He can stay home with the kids while I help you on the campaign trail."

I snort. "You won't be able to stay away from him that long. You big softy."

He finally smiles and touches a finger to his lips. "Don't tell him that. Don't want to lose my bastard label."

He holds his hands out to me, wiggling his fingers, and I stand to help him up from the floor. "Also, don't be shocked if I mindfuck him a little," he adds. "Go with whatever he says I said, huh? I might have some fun with this. He's so tightly wound right now, I need to work some secret kink into his routine."

I smirk. "Yes, Sir. Whatever you say, Sir."

"Smart-ass." He smacks my ass, then rubs the sting away and kisses me.

"Is that why you're home early?"

"Yeah. He'll be along shortly. Security detail will bring him. I wanted him to try to get used to *not* having me there sometimes."

About that time, we hear a tell-tale beep next door, the sound of the alarm being disarmed at Owen's townhouse. Moments later, the sound of him walking upstairs, then the beep as the door between his bedroom and ours is unlocked with the keypad and opened.

Carter drops me a wink and tips his head for me to go to our boy.

Owen's…exhausted. I can see it in his face before he drops to his knees in front of me in greeting. I immediately sit in front of him on the floor, much like Carter sat with me, and I rub his scalp. This will be the last time we get to do this for a while. Tomorrow night, he'll officially belong to the people of the great state of Florida, he'll officially be living in the mansion, and it'll be Carter who mostly gets to do this with him.

"My *very* good boy," I coo. "You made me *so* proud today." I pull him into my lap so he can curl up there with his head against my thighs.

* * *

As I sit in the hotel ballroom tonight and watch my boy, I think about last night's conversation with my husband before Owen returned home.

Combined with this afternoon's earlier desk fucking in Owen's office, I know it means Carter likely had the conversation with Owen right before I was called in. Maybe just after.

Carter sometimes has a flair for the dramatic, when it suits him.

It's also likely why he took the risk of stripping Owen there in the office, because better that than risk Owen accidentally getting suspicious stains on his suit.

Owen had a shitty childhood with a viciously narcissistic mother. Ironically, I know it's one of the reasons Owen wants to have kids. A chance to right his own wronged childhood by having kids to bestow the kind of unconditional love on them that he didn't receive until he met Carter and me. A way to finish healing the thin spots that still exist in his soul and heart.

I want to pull Owen into my arms and hold him right now. I want to make love to him—all three of us—and pick out baby names together.

Make no mistake about it—I'm going to let Owen name our children. And they will all have Taylor as their middle name.

And, meanwhile, I will look to see what can legally be done to have both men's names on the birth certificate. California has added some interesting workarounds to take IVF parentage into account when it's an open arrangement between all three people, the "parents" and the "donor," if the donor is going to be an active part of the child's life.

The easiest solution would be the simplest, most straightforward, and the honest one—my husband can't father children, and we asked our single and unpartnered best friend to do so. Our best friend who also happens to want children. It's not something we could have risked, politically, years ago.

We can now.

I hate myself.

I hate that I'm already working the angle in my head, spinning the narrative out in such a way as to gain us sympathy and votes. A personal triumph for non-traditional parenting. Overcoming infertility in a creative way.

I grow more excited as I think about it further. We wouldn't even have to mention anything about our personal lives. In fact, it would solve *all* our problems. The public's assumption would be Owen is always with us because, duh, he's our children's biological father, and we *want* him to be there, with us and them, because he's a part of their lives.

We imply we used IVF, a fertility clinic, all while asking people to respect our privacy.

It's utterly perfect! It's...

I inwardly groan.

It's likely aspects of the whole situation that Carter's already taken into account and researched himself.

Fucking bastard.

I smile and shake my head.

Damn, I love that man. He keeps us on our toes, that's for sure.

I can't help it—my hand goes to my tummy. I know there's no logical way I could be pregnant right now. Hell, I'm just barely due for my next pill.

But wouldn't it be…cool?

Dray returns a few minutes later as Owen and I are talking to a couple of people who are heading out. From behind them, Dray catches my eye, nods, and holds up five fingers.

We're back on the clock.

Fuck it, my feet hurt, and I'll carry my damn shoes. I grab my purse and my wrap and stand, patting Owen's shoulder to give him the signal. He stands and we're fully "on" again as we make our way out of the ballroom, my arm hooked through his and us pausing near the main doorway where Dray has us hold for a moment.

Carter returns three minutes later, offering me a smile. "Sorry." He leans in and pecks my cheek before giving Owen's shoulder a friendly squeeze. "Got to talking with Jace and Gene and lost track of time." Those are two of his older brothers, whom he hasn't seen since two Christmases ago.

We spent last Christmas Eve and Christmas locked up at home, the three of us alone, because Owen asked for that the night he won the election.

He'd needed it.

We *all* needed it.

The limo is ready and the security detail escorts us out. This time, Owen insists I get in first, and I'm too tired to argue. There's no one outside now behind the barricade lines.

Moments later, we're on our way. Both of them loosen their ties and sit back with nearly identical exhausted sighs.

At the mansion, I grab Owen's hand and hold him back, pecking him on the cheek and smiling as I rub the lipstick off. "*Good boy*," I mouth, and he smiles.

Tired, but he smiles.

Then I kiss Carter on the lips before he gets out, and I whisper in his ear. "Give him that for me please."

"I will, pet," he whispers back, dropping me a wink.

Then they're gone, heading inside the front door as we pull out of the driveway.

I sit back for the short ride home, somehow keeping my tears at bay. I want to curl up in bed with both my men tonight and celebrate what we've achieved, and I can't.

I shiver as the officer escorts me up the walk, because I've left my shoes off and the concrete feels cold against my bare feet on this relatively mild Florida January night. Once I'm inside with the alarm reset...

I'm alone.

I head upstairs, missing our big soaking tub at the Brandon house.

The hot tub.

The pool.

Our bed.

My men.

But *this* is what I wanted, and I know it's the exhaustion talking. A full night of sleep under my belt will help immensely.

I strip and stand in the shower, scrub the makeup off my face.

Think about the bite marks and bruises inside my thighs.

And I smile.

Yeah, the way Carter's setting this up...

That's freaking haaawwt. Being called up to Owen's office could mean a simple budget confab...

Or me being ordered to lock his office door behind me as he stares at me with that sweetly hungry look in his eyes as he unfastens his belt.

Holy...fuuuuuck.

Note to self, remind Carter to have Owen keep a spare change of clothes at the office, just in case we accidentally spooge whatever he's wearing.

I love my life and what we have, but leave it to Carter to amp things up after we've *just* taken office.

As if we didn't have enough excitement, and he manages to shake things up even more.

After my shower, I dry off and don't bother putting on clothes as I head for bed. I suspect my panty infraction caning won't happen tonight after all. Owen will need Carter for a while.

Clean sheets.

It's the little things, sometimes. Right now, with our lives a whirlwind, sometimes they're the only pleasures we get.

But this is what we signed up for, so I can't bitch too much.

Especially since it was what I wanted in the first place.

I finish pulling back the duvet cover, to the end of the bed, until it's spilling off of it like a blue and white cotton waterfall.

I miss our bed in Tampa, the king-sized mattress we spent weeks shopping for, the three of us raising eyebrows when we'd all climb onto the floor models, giggling and laughing like little kids as we tested them out.

But how else were we to know if someone rolling over would make it dip? Or jostle someone? Sometimes, Carter has nightmares that only Owen can really soothe him through.

And that was before Owen's first election. On a third-party ticket.

You can bet I playfully rub my father's face in *that*.

Every damn chance I get.

He smiles and takes it, too, because it's not bragging if you've actually done it. As Daddy always taught me, there's only one winner, and it's not second place.

I know he's proud of me, proud of what we've done, and what we're going to do next, even if he does hate Carter's guts and wishes I'd married Owen.

I saw the pride in his gaze tonight. I did what he couldn't do.

One last thing before I can really decide to call it quits, and then we can just be people, and that's run for governor myself.

As exhausted as I am, it still takes me a little while to fall asleep. It's weird being totally alone in bed, and I realize how much I don't like that feeling.

But I do finally fall asleep. At some point, the feel of someone climbing under the covers with me awakens me. I don't need to see him to know it's Carter from the way he moves.

He spoons his body around mine and I wiggle against him, getting comfy.

"It's only four," he says, brushing his lips against my shoulder. "Go back to sleep, pet."

"Is he okay?"

"He'll be okay." He nuzzles the back of my neck. "I gave him your kiss. And a little more."

"Did you fuck him or blow him?"

I feel him smile against the nape of my neck. "Both. He was a good boy tonight. He earned it."

"Yes, he did."

I pull Carter's arm more tightly around me, our hands pressed against my flat belly, and send up the closest thing I have to prayers that we get what we want and what Owen so desperately needs, because there's only so much our love and our shared past can do to heal him.

CHAPTER TEN

Then

That first week of classes, Carter and I get very little time alone together.

Neither do Owen and I. That's simply how this works—it's the *three* of us. That's not a complaint, though, because if I was ever forced to choose between the two men, there's no way in hell I could.

Am I lusting after Carter in my fantasies when alone?

Absolutely. Especially because when we're at my house in the evenings, every time Owen leaves the room, Carter's either kissing me, or grinding against me, or shoving a hand between my legs to tease me, or shoving my hand between his legs to show me how hard—and hung—he is.

I love every second of it.

And the things he texts me are even filthier.

I lust after Owen, too, only for different reasons.

I would love to see the man naked on his knees for me, serving me, taking care of me.

Just like I'd love to be naked and kneeling in front of Carter and serving him.

Yes, I'd love to be wedged between them in bed. I know it would be hot, because it's a fantasy that Carter relishes teasing me with, and promises me he can and will make happen.

As long as I follow his plan.

It's filthy and selfish to wish for *both* of them, though, no matter what romance novels might insist.

Isn't it?

Besides, the public face of Susannah Evans recoils in horror at the thought of getting on my knees for anyone, even though the part of me that's been strong for as long as I can remember longs to let go and just *be* for once in my life.

With someone I trust.

I trust both men, but it's Carter I'm quickly coming to trust in a different way, the way I damn well know Owen already trusts him. Don't get me wrong, it's not like everything between Carter and I has to do with sexy teasing. The man's wicked smart and quickly grasps even the most convoluted of political situations with a spooky and enviable ease.

I lust after the man's brain as much as I do his cock.

And even with his scars, his body is hotter than hell. Maybe the scars make him even hotter, I don't know.

But watching the way he can move, even just walking through a room, can make me weak.

Finally, the next Monday, Carter privately arranges for the two of us to meet for lunch at my house. I arrive first and leave the door unlocked for him. When I hear a noise, I turn, startled to find he's standing right there behind me, not even feet away.

He shoves me against the wall and takes my mouth in a bruising kiss that leaves me whimpering and wet and ready to be fucked. I know I have a safeword with him—saying his full name, Carter Edward Wilson.

But I don't *want* to say it.

I know if I don't say it, he won't stop until he's ready to.

That was the deal.

A deal I really want.

A deal I *need*.

"Ask me like a good pet," he mumbles against my lips.

"*Please*, Sir," I beg.

We've already agreed to this in text, even though I didn't know the specifics of when or how or what would happen.

I didn't *want* to know.

That makes it even hotter.

He grabs me by the hair with one hand and forces me to my knees, another fantasy made real. With his other hand, he yanks open his shorts and shoves them down far enough he can pull his cock out. My first look at it up close and in person. He's hard, ready, and even though I've already opened my mouth, he smacks my face with it, leaving a trail of pre-cum.

"*Say* it, pet."

"I'm yours, Sir. I'm your toy and I belong to you. I promise to put Owen first, and follow your rules about this and him, and keep this a secret, for now."

His positively evil smile makes me even wetter. "Good girl. Now beg for it."

"Please give me your cock, Sir!"

He shoves in, hard, deep, choking me on his cock, to the point my eyes are watering and I'm struggling not to gag. Now he's holding my head with both hands, fucking my face, nothing tender or loving about it.

God, he's *perfect*.

When he comes, he holds still deep inside my mouth, forcing me to swallow every drop and christening me as *His*.

As he catches his breath he finally pulls out, rubbing his softening cock all over my face. The next thing he does shocks me.

He slowly lowers himself to the floor in front of me with a pained grunt, gently cradles my head in his hands, and tenderly kisses me all over my face, including along the tracks of my tears. As he does, he whispers over and over what a good girl I am for him.

I don't even realize I'm really *crying*, at first. Not just eyes watering, but *crying*.

I am *not* a *crier*.

Not until he gathers me in his arms and gently rocks me do I realize I'm crying.

"Oh, my god," I finally manage after about fifteen minutes.

He chuckles. "So how was that?"

I sit up, awestruck. I'm staring into his eyes. This was a test, and I knew it.

I nod. "More," I beg. "Please?"

He tucks stray strands of hair behind my ears and seems to study my face for a long moment.

"Okay," he simply says. "We'll step things up. See how you handle it."

But for today, for being a good girl for him, he cuddles me right there on the floor and fingers me until I come twice all over his hand. Then he makes me suck his fingers clean before he tenderly kisses me and calls me his good girl.

I want more.

I want it *all*.

I want him, *and* Owen.

Jesus, I'm so fucked.

* * *

Carter has given me the most important rules—Owen *always* comes first, no lying to Carter, or cheating, obviously. Also, I don't tell Owen things Carter hasn't cleared me to tell him, including the things Carter and I are now doing to each other. And, of course, Carter's in charge.

Duh.

But the rule I have to focus on first is that I'm not allowed to fall in love with Carter unless I can promise him I will marry him.

Not just marry him, but *submit* to him. And that I have to admit it to him immediately if I do fall in love with him.

Short of that, Carter has promised to do nearly any- and everything I want to try, as long as I promise to keep my heart on a short damn leash and under control.

That rule's strict, but I'm cocky and think I know exactly what I'm doing and can handle this.

Carter has a long-range plan that I don't know all the details of, but he told me it's a two-part plan. The first part, which is actually the immediate goal, is him seducing Owen and collaring him. He wants to do that before the end of the semester. Carter has made no secret to me that he's bi, and that he wants Owen to belong to him. It's one of the things I had to accept and be okay with—which I am—for him to do anything else with me.

Only once that step is completed can he even begin plotting the second part, which is to get Owen, then me, elected governor.

What, exactly, our relationships are to each other when that happens remains to be seen. Because I'm not allowed to fall in love, and I'm damn sure not ready to get married yet.

Except…

It's tough. Damned tough.

I've decided I won't question Carter's methods, unless I see him do something that I feel is not ultimately in Owen's or my best interests. I understand he's going to use some unconventional and even downright underhanded tactics on Owen. Without telling me everything, he's indicated that Owen had a rough childhood, and one of the things Carter wants to do is get Owen away from the reach of his abusive mother and help rebuild his self-confidence and trust.

But in the process of doing that, Carter's first going to have to break Owen down and take control of him from Owen's mother.

And Carter warned me it might look ugly and brutal in some aspects, but to keep the final goal in mind before I judge him.

I'm *fine* with that—*helloooo*, my father is king of the ratfucks and political machinations—as long as the goal is to help Owen, to love him and take care of him, *not* harm him.

Carter has sworn to me that he will never intentionally do anything to harm Owen, but that I have to trust him and follow his lead. Including playing dumb, sometimes.

Fortunately, I'm allowed to masturbate, because I would be an unholy *bitch* if I wasn't. I know if I ever decide I want more with Carter, that would be taken off the table, which is another reason I'm trying to keep my heart corralled.

Carter's not fucking me yet, but we've managed to do nearly everything but. He keeps me on my toes and we use a texting app that deletes our messages automatically to help prevent Owen from accidentally seeing anything.

Though as our friendship with Owen deepens, I can see why Carter is doing this. Especially the more I learn about Owen's mother and the shit she put him through. Having two loving parents, and also being financially secure, I cannot fathom what Owen has endured.

Carter and I get to arguing about this in private one afternoon, when what I really wanted to do was suck his cock. We are both half-naked on my couch, and, in passing, I ask Carter to send me Owen's car insurance information so I can pay it in advance for him as a surprise gift, giving him one less potential stressor.

Carter shuts me down.

I stare at him, still not believing he's said no. "But why the hell not? Seriously, Carter, my trust probably earns that much a damn *month* in interest. I can afford it."

His expression goes stony. "You agreed to follow my plan, and to not fuck my plan. You also agreed to let *me* be in charge. Are you backing out?"

It startles me how he can flash from the playful, sexy man he was mere breaths ago to this frigid chill. "Just tell me why," I beg. "Please?"

He starts to carefully untangle his limbs from mine. "I'm sorry, Suse. I told you my rules. Either you trust me, or you don't." He stands and reaches for his T-shirt, where it'd landed on the floor.

Suse is his safeword for me, just like me using his full name is mine.

"Wait, please?"

He stops and looks at me.

I take a deep breath. "Okay, fine. I'm sorry."

He studies me for a long time, to the point I'm not sure he's staying.

"I *mean* it," he finally says. "I have my reasons. Some of them are because Owen's placed a trust in me and I can't share the info with you yet. Some of them are my own that I'm not ready to share yet. Might never be able to share. I *have* to be in complete control of this, and of Owen. *Period.*"

"May I please ask for at least a hint of *those* reasons, then, Sir? *Your* reasons? Just a hint. Anything. Help me understand. Please?"

His expression gentles a little at my use of *Sir*. He sighs, then drops his T-shirt on the coffee table and returns to the couch. He sits, pulling me into his arms, but I can see he's still trying to figure out how or what to say to me.

I wait him out.

Finally, he strokes my hair, plays with it. "I was barely your age. It's about the woman I got the vasectomy for, shit that happened to me in Germany. I'm fucked up, Suse. As if you couldn't tell already. I'm massively fucked up, forever, because of what she did to me. Think your darkest, most depraved fantasies, and then go deeper and darker. It made me who I am *now*.

"But they're the cards I was dealt, and the hand I've got to play today. That's why my most important rule is Owen comes first, then you, and me last. She always put herself first, even though she made others vulnerable to her and told them they could trust her. I might be a bastard, and evil, and twisted, but I would rather die than harm someone who's put their trust in me."

His brown gaze settles on mine. "That's who I am," he says. "That's who I'm *always* going to be. An evil, fucked up bastard who can sometimes do good things. If you let me do what I need to do, you'll have Owen to serve you and be your sweet, loving guy, and you'll have me to be Sir when you need to let go, the bastard who will match you wherever you need to him to, and who will help you in your political career without a second thought as to what has to happen. You can have it all, *both* of us, but it means you *have* to take me the way I am *now*. That means accepting my rules and my control."

Carter's a hard person, a strong person, despite how he's having to rebuild his body.

Even still, I hear whispers of terrified pleas in his words, in his heart.

Someone else might think this was bravado, or bullshit, or that I'd opened myself to a predator.

Uh, *yeah*, Carter's a predator. It's one of the things I *love* about him. I'm a predator, too, in my own way.

Like calls to like.

It makes me feel better to know I'm not the only fucked up person in the world.

I drape my arms around his neck and ruffle his hair. "Okay, Sir," I say. "Your rules, your way. But please promise me one thing."

"I'd need to hear it first."

"If something happens with his mom, and Owen's struggling, let me give you the money to take care of him. Please? Let me do this *one* thing for him. I wouldn't offer if I couldn't afford it. And I offer it with no strings attached."

He sighs, some of the tension leaving his body before he finally nods. "Deal, pet. You have my word."

I feel like I've won a huge victory. Not only is Carter trying to win Owen's trust, I'm trying to win Carter's.

To convince him that I'm not playing a game.

To get him to understand I don't want to go anywhere.

Now all I have to do is keep my heart under control.

* * *

We've known each other four weeks when Carter texts me on a Thursday morning. Owen's freaked out because they have to go over to Orlando that Saturday for dinner at Owen's mom's house. Carter and I were supposed to get together today, but he wants to eat lunch with Owen instead.

Owen's not handling this development well, and Carter wants to spend some additional time alone with him to ease him through it.

I understand and don't begrudge it. I already know I'm not going to be allowed to go to Orlando with them, because Carter wants to control the situation as much as possible.

I still make the offer when they come over that night for dinner and to do their laundry.

While Owen's a pretty emotional guy to start with, tonight he's…well, he's an absolute wreck. Carter and I exchange secret, knowing glances several times, and I understand now why Carter wants complete control over this situation and over Owen. I *get* it.

I feel protective of Owen now, too. I'd be too tempted to smack the woman, at least verbally, and possibly make the situation worse for Owen, both with her, as well as upset or stress Owen in the process.

When Saturday arrives, Carter updates me via text throughout the day, going silent during the ride over because he's driving Owen's car. I receive a quick update that they've arrived, and then…

The wait begins. I know not to text Carter while he's there, unless I literally have an emergency I need to call 911 for, because he wants his entire focus on Owen tonight.

I consider it personal growth on my part that I'm glad he wants to focus on Owen, and I don't take it personally.

I take it as further proof Carter is a man of his word, a man I can trust.

A couple of hours later, I receive a quick update.

Leaving. Will text when home. Rough time, Owen will be okay. PHT

The last is shorthand code he's set up with me—*Please Hold Texts.*

It means wait until he contacts me, don't even text a response that I received that text.

So I do what I can to make Carter's life easier—I sit and wait, glancing at the clock to calculate a rough time of arrival for them at the dorm.

It's over three hours later when he texts me.

Home. Awake?

I reply immediately.

Yes, Sir.

My phone buzzes with another text a moment later.

She's a cunt, worse than I thought, but I know what we need to do now. I'll give you details tmrw night. You still going to Tllhsee on Owen's bd wknd?

That's an odd segue, but whatever. Carter knows about my trip. I haven't told Owen yet, because Carter told me to hold on to that info, for now.

Yes, Sir. Why?

He responds shortly after.

I want the house for the wknd. I have a plan, but need privacy and 2 nights w/him.

I think about this long and hard. I've already given the men keys and alarm codes.

Then you can use the house.

:) Good girl. Tnk you. Sleep tight. See you tmrw.

Carter doesn't use emojis very often. As in rarely.
It's the texting equivalent of him stroking my hair when I'm on my knees for him.
Especially when his cock is down my throat.
The next evening, Carter motions me to follow him outside to the lanai shortly after Owen falls asleep on the couch. Between a heavy dinner, and the stress of yesterday catching up with him, our poor boy is wiped out. Owen acted subdued today, but I sensed I shouldn't mention yesterday to him unless he brings it up first.
Carter now confirms that.
"It was bad last night," he starts, speaking low and quickly, knowing as well as I do that Owen could awaken at any time. "*Really* bad."
He recounts the evening for me. To someone else, it might

sound like an exaggeration.

Except I know our Owen—and yes, I already think of him as *ours*.

Our pet.

Hey, Owen himself came up with that label, and it privately makes both me and Carter giggle in good ways.

If only he knew.

Carter and I were raised differently than Owen, even if our adult experiences differed drastically from each other. Carter was raised standing up for himself as the little brother. I was raised to be independent and speak my mind by parents who reveled in my stubborn streak, my tenacity, my unique personality.

Owen, not so much.

I *totally* get why Carter wants to use the house for Owen's birthday weekend, and why he prefers that I'm not there, although I wish I could be a fly on the wall. Carter's afraid Owen won't fully open up around me for fear of me rejecting him.

Carter is a genius, and, once again, my confidence in him is affirmed.

"So what now?" I ask when he finishes.

"Birthday weekend." A slow smile fills his face. "I'm going to bring things to a head and shift him into full-on formal sub mode."

"How are you going to do that?"

His smile widens. "Emotional lubrication."

"So, getting him drunk, then, I take it?"

He snorts. "Fuck *yeah*, getting him drunk." He glances through the sliders to make sure Owen's still asleep before pulling me in for a long hug. Carter relaxes a little more with me in private now, as if his trust is building in me, too. "I'm glad you don't think I'm evil."

"Oh, you're evil, but we're the same kind of evil. The *good* kind of evil."

His chuckle rumbles through me. "Yeah, true."

* * *

Well, I almost fuck everything up. Fortunately, Carter doesn't ding me for it later. What happens is that Carter is too busy and focused on Owen during Owen's birthday weekend to do much texting with me. Sunday, when I tell Carter I'm on my way home from Tallahassee, he texts me back and asks me to play along following my arrival.

I hope that means a breakthrough, because Carter also decided a few weeks ago that he wasn't going to fuck me unless or until we get Owen over the hump into full-on formal submissive status. We do nearly everything else *but* that.

So yes, I have a vested personal interest in this beyond the obvious.

Sue me.

When I arrive home, Carter and Owen start telling me about their weekend. I sense a change in Owen, a good one. He acts nervous, yes, but he also seems to possess a more relaxed vibe.

And I spot the collar around his neck, the lock peeking out the back, even though it's hidden under his shirt, until they show it to me.

It's after we finish getting dinner ready, and it's in the oven, where I nearly fuck it all up.

We're sitting on the couch, and Owen's going to kneel for me and show me positions.

Keep in mind, these are positions I already know by heart.

Thank god Owen is nervous, because although they haven't told me the position names yet, without thinking, I ask him to kneel in *At Ease*.

D'oh.

Carter starts talking to me, telling me about the position, then leads Owen into the next one. Only once Owen's down in *Devotion* does Carter give me one of his infamous smirks.

"*Sorry, Sir,*" I silently mouth to him.

But all is forgiven, and he indicates for me to rub Owen's head and talk to him.

And...I do.

Before they leave that evening, while Owen's in the bathroom, Carter pins me against the kitchen wall and kisses me. "You know what happens now, right, pet?"

I smile. "Fun and games?"

He grins, and it's so perfectly evil and dark that it nearly makes me come right there. "Fun and games, pet."

CHAPTER ELEVEN

Carter, the rat bastard, still hasn't taken us over that intercourse threshold yet, even though it's been over a week since Owen formally became our submissive.

Okay, a week since Owen formally became *Carter's* submissive, and I have certain…privileges with him.

Why aren't we fucking yet? Carter refers me to Owen's admission to me about his submissive needs. That Owen was nearly panicked before they "told" me, worried I'd reject him. Carter told Owen that Carter would be working with me to show me….things.

That means the bastard extraordinaire uses much of *our* alone time together for working on my "formal" training. I mean, sure, it *is* what Carter told Owen we'd be doing, so I guess we really *should* do it, instead of further misleading Owen about what we're doing. There's enough we've already concealed from him.

Like that I already know much of this stuff.

Although, as Carter points out to me, we never told Owen we weren't having sexy time together, or getting together behind his back, and that's a key point. While there are some omissions and even a few outright lies being told that I agree are in Owen's best interest right now, we haven't actually broken any rules Carter laid down for Owen in terms of Carter and myself.

That is a key distinction.

Besides, if Owen can survive Carter's training, I *know* I can do it. It's a point of pride for me to want to be able to take what I'm going to be dishing out.

Carter *does* have a valid point, though, as much as I hate to admit it. He wants to make sure we're on the same page, and wants to make sure Owen's getting consistent training. I completely agree with that. The best way to do that is to train me, too, which dovetails nicely with the narrative he's given Owen about our current activities.

Except...

The more Carter works with me—both on how to dominate Owen in only good, healthy ways, and working on my own submission—the more I realize I can no longer deny the truth.

I *am* in love with Carter, and have been, for a while. Probably since the week we first met, if I'm really honest with myself.

I'm well aware of our deal. He clearly made a point of telling me not to fall in love with him unless I can completely give myself to him.

Marry him.

But even more, *submit* to him.

Yet the heart wants what it wants.

I'm used to getting what I want, even if I have to work my ass off for it. I'd be lying if I said I didn't want Carter.

Another promise I made to him when we started this was that I'd never lie to him.

That night, after Owen's left for the dorm, as I kneel there—naked, of course—in front of Carter in *Primed*, I feel the words itching in the back of my throat and yearning to be set free.

Carter sits back on the couch and watches me. I know he's in a lot of pain tonight, which is why I'll be driving him home after we're done. Part of that is due to a bad fall he took with me at lunch yesterday, when we had one of our "struggle snuggle" sessions here at the house.

I didn't mean to knock him off the bed.

#whoopsies

He wasn't upset about it, though. The man does have a wicked good sense of humor. He even made a joke about that's why it's always best to tie a subby to the bed, to prevent them from falling out.

But tonight, he'll leave the Snot Box here, and Owen can bring him back tomorrow morning before their classes to pick it up.

Although it won't be the first time Carter's been in pain following one of our play sessions. He'll have to cover it up in the morning during his run with Owen, use his old injuries as an excuse. I mean, yes, Carter does legitimately have bad pain days from his old injuries, but wrestling with me doesn't help things any.

Then again, he keeps doing it with me, so who's *really* the masochist?

"How's my pet tonight?" he quietly asks in *that* voice.

The voice that makes my body tingle and turns me into someone I don't recognize, but who I enjoy becoming, for a while.

I don't know how to answer him without lying, and I don't want to come right out and say it. That's why it takes me a moment to muddle through it in my brain before I open my mouth.

"Preoccupied, Sir."

He leans forward, elbows on his knees, hands clasped. "You might as well tell me, pet. I knew there was something going on, even before Owen left. You've acted tense all evening."

"I love you, Sir."

"I love you, too, pet." All three of us have said that to each other now, countless times, meaning it as friends.

"I…I mean, I'm *in* love with you, Sir."

And there it is.

I refuse to break *Primed* to wipe away the tears now rolling down my cheeks, but I hear the sigh that escapes him, see the way his gaze softens a little.

"I guess it's time we had a talk our own, then, isn't it, pet?"

"I know your rule, Sir. I'm sorry."

I still haven't been instructed to move, so I hold my position and sniffle back tears, hating that I feel so weak and vulnerable.

Something I'm definitely *not* used to feeling. Not like this. Except I also know that's kind of the whole *point* of this. Carter wants to gently break me down, wants me to understand things from this end so that I can be a better Dominant to Owen. He wants me to understand what we're doing to Owen—only more drastic in Owen's case, since Owen has so many unhealthy thought patterns Carter needs to rid our sweet boy of first, deprogram what his fucking mother did to him

Except…

I'm starting to see it's also pretty addictive, feeling like this. I wonder if Owen feels addicted to me and what we do the way I'm starting to feel addicted to Carter.

Or if Owen feels like this about Carter, too.

He studies me for a long time. "You know Owen is in love with *you*, right?"

Stunned, I study his gaze, note he's smirking, and I'm completely at a loss for words.

"*Really*, pet? You couldn't tell?"

"I-I mean, I know he *likes* me, and loves me as a friend—"

He laughs. "Pet, he *belongs* to you. Totally. There is no one else in his heart. *You* are the only one on his mind in that way. He's *in* love with you. Madly, deeply. And therein lies a slight…problem."

"Problem, Sir?"

"Yes. Well, not a problem so much as a complication. I'm *in* love with Owen. I have been since the first day I met him. You know that. I also meant what I said to you about you not falling in love with me, unless you're prepared to marry and submit to me."

My throat dries up as I contemplate that. Sure, I've masturbated to fantasies of being sandwiched between the two men, especially since Carter takes great pride in using those kinds of fantasies on me, but that's one of those impossible things.

Isn't it?

He continues. "I don't want to break up the band, so to speak. Before we go any farther, I need to know—*honestly*—how you feel about Owen."

"I like him. A lot."

"Do you love him?"

I think about that long and hard. "Of course I love him. But I'm not—"

"*In* love with him, the way you are with me?"

"Correct, Sir."

"Are you physically attracted to him?"

Hooooo, boy. *Am* I. "Yes, Sir."

"To the point you could you sleep with him?"

My face heats, so even if I wanted to lie, I'd immediately be called out on it. "Yes, Sir. That wouldn't be a problem."

It'd be a few hundred fantasies made real.

Carter continues. "No, Owen doesn't know how I feel about him yet, or even that I'm bi. I never wanted to pressure him. I wanted to make sure I didn't scare him off, or pressure him in bad kind of ways. I think he will quickly learn to enjoy being with me under the right…circumstances. Especially considering how quickly he's taken to everything I've put him through so far. He hasn't asked to reciprocate with me yet, so I don't think he's quite at that point. All he wants is unconditional love, and affection, and he gets that from me. And now from you. He's eager to please when he can trust. That's why he bends over backward for us."

"Because he trusts us." I immediately feel more shame about something that happened last Friday, when I inadvertently broke one of Carter's secret rules for me about how to handle Owen.

I'd told Owen not to be stupid, when I should have used the word *silly* or *ridiculous*. One of those kinds of throwaway lines we've all used without thinking about it.

I certainly didn't think about it, at the time.

Fortunately, Owen didn't take it the wrong way. But Carter immediately put Owen in Devotion before calling me from the room to chew me out in private in the bedroom.

Carter warned me then if I repeated the error that he would take Owen, walk out, and they'd be done with me.

"And that's why you came down on me so hard when I told him not to be stupid, even though I wasn't actually calling *him* stupid."

His gaze bores into me. "*Exactly*. In addition to the *I'm in charge* and *no lying* rules, here are our revised rules moving forward, should you accept them."

Carter ticks them off on his fingers. "Owen will *always* come first. When in doubt, default to whatever must be said or done to follow *that*. Rule two, regarding you accidentally calling him stupid the other night, you *cannot* do that again. *Ever*. If you do, I will end things with you immediately. At some point in the future, if I feel he's finally moved on to where he can easily tell generic idiom from direct insult, I might lift the restriction. But I promised I'd protect him, take care of him. That means in all ways, and that means even if I'm protecting him from *you*. It's not our fault she weaponized language against him, but it *is* our responsibility to make sure we keep him safe. He's fragile right now. Maybe it's overkill on my part, but that's my rule, take it or leave it."

I sniffle back snot even as tears roll down my cheeks. "Yes, Sir."

Owen is gentle and sweet, and the thought that I could have

wounded him emotionally, even accidentally—which makes it worse, in my mind—well, it *kills* me. I'm definitely not going to be much of a sadist when it comes to Owen, I can see that now. Carter will need to take up the slack in that department.

Somehow, I don't think either of them will mind that.

"Rule three, what we're doing right now still stays secret and between us, except for what I tell Owen. Especially the sex. Rule four, you will not date anyone but me, and you're not sleeping with anyone but me, and probably Owen. This also means I now control your orgasms, the way I control his."

I can barely talk now, with hope and the *good* kind of fear suddenly filling me. "Yes, Sir."

"Rule five, you *must* be okay with something sexual developing between me and Owen, and my complete ownership of him *and* you. No jealousy over that, over what might happen between us, either in front of you, or without you present. Yes, there will be sex involved, including threesomes. Meaning the three of *us*," he adds. "Not any outside people."

A mental image of Owen bent over the bed and eating me out while he gets plowed by Carter flashes through my mind. I give up trying to form words and simply nod.

Carter the bastard extraordinaire smiles *that* smile. "Did you just think about the upside to me owning and using *both* of you, pet?"

I nod again.

"I can't guarantee he'll be okay with that, but I suspect he will, if we handle this properly. So if you and I are going to *do* this, understand that once that final line is crossed with him, there will be times I turn him loose on you to fuck your brains out for *my* amusement. It means you do what I say, it means you don't argue with me. Means I'm trusting you not to masturbate, and to follow those rules. It means I require trust and faith and honesty. Means a lot of hard work. Some of it unpleasant."

"Yes, Sir."

"It means if I sit back and tell you to blow him, or let him fuck you, you do."

The way my pulse gallops at that thought means I need to think on that some more. Not in a bad way, but trying to understand why that idea thrills me so much.

"Yes, Sir."

"Means this is permanent. That when I finally say so, you're going to marry me." His gaze softens again. "Means I can't give you children. I had a vasectomy. Perhaps some other option in the future, but children are not in my immediate plans. They'll have to wait until later, if ever."

Children!

It's not that revelation that sends a frisson of excitement through me.

It's the fact that he's talking *really* long-term.

Permanent.

"I understand, Sir," I finally say.

He drags himself off the couch with a pained grunt and fetches tissues. When he returns, he dries my tears, helps me blow my nose, but I still don't break position. After he returns to the couch, he continues.

"I don't give up my toys, pet. I'm not interested in playing around for a year and walking away. If you want me, you'll get me, but be prepared for the flip side of that. It means if I tell you to bend over, you bend over. If I order you to your knees to suck my cock, you do it, because you're mine. Before you say yes to any of this, you need to understand I'm talking for *life*. I want us all to get our law degrees, pass the bar, and then we start getting Owen ready for the spotlight through lower offices."

"And me, Sir?"

This smile is pure amusement. "Pet, do you *really* need to ask that? That's a given. You *are* ready, except for the paperwork and real-world experience part of it. This is a package deal, and I have long-term plans for the three of us."

"Meaning Owen?"

"They're centered around Owen, yes. Here's my plan." He sits forward, his elbows on his knees, and lays it all out to me.

Excitement ripples through me. It's getting harder not to break *Primed* and throw myself at him to hug him.

Daddy's going to despise Carter.

Senator Benchley Evans won't be fond of him, either.

Me?

I'm more in love with him now than I was when we started this conversation. And yes, he's absolutely a bastard extraordinaire. It's one of the reasons I love him so damn much.

When he finishes, he sits back on the couch, thighs spread wide. "Last chance. Here's the deal—take it or leave it. I'll give you a brief test period to think this through and to get a taste of what life will be like with me full-throttle.

"However, you *cannot* discuss this with Owen. You can't even tell him we've talked about this, or what we're doing. You still can't tell him we're sleeping together. You can't lie to him, but you're smart enough to find ways around the truth. Once I ask you if you're ready to make this permanent, *then* I will tell you how we handle Owen.

"If you can't follow my orders on this, or can't commit to me for life, don't even bother saying yes. Then we'll just keep doing what we're doing now and maintain the status quo, with you understanding that Owen belongs to me, and is collared to me, but at that point my physical relationship with you will end."

My pulse gallops. "And if I say yes?"

His right hand settles over his bulge and squeezes. "If you say yes, you're acknowledging that, once I give you the final choice and you accept, you *completely* belong to *me*. Not to your father, not to the GOP, not to your dreams—*me*. Doesn't mean you won't get to follow your dreams, because I believe in having happy pets."

"But what...what if Owen doesn't agree?"

He shrugs. "More importantly, what if he does? I know where your mind is, pet. On PR. That's why my plans include long-term situations. You let me worry about PR. I can't have you marrying some asshole who gets territorial and ruins all our plans. In case I wasn't clear, this is you, and me, and Owen. No one else. In return, I will give you everything I ask of you—faith, trust, honesty. But understand that you will be sharing me with Owen, and we will *always* put him first ahead of us. We will both own him, so that's how it has to be. I will put him first, then you, then myself. Just like I expect you to put him before me."

How would it be any different than what we already have, except it'd be more perfect and guarantee I'd never have to give up either man? I *love* what the three of us have.

"Why can't we tell him about us yet?"

"I can't have him pulling away from us and feeling hurt and betrayed. I need him tied so tightly to the two of us that he will do anything to stay with us. Especially to stay with you."

Carter really is a bastard extraordinaire, but if he's willing to be with me, like hell am I going to complain. "What do you get out of this, Sir?"

He smirks. "Besides the obvious?"

"Yes, Sir."

"I get to be the power behind the throne for two of the potentially most powerful future politicians in Florida. I get to have my cake and eat it, too. I will get a brilliant, gorgeous man as my willing slave, who I can bend over and fuck, and who will happily beg for more. I will also get a beautiful, sweet, intelligent woman to be my wife and slave, a woman who seems to love and crave the darker side of me. A woman I can take home and introduce to my extremely heteronormative and macho-inclined family."

Ah.

Apparently he sees the understanding hit me, because his smile widens. "Exactly. While I'm sure I can win Owen over, given time, I'm equally sure that my family would disown me in the process. Right or wrong, I love my family." His smile fades. "I'd prefer not to lose them. I've lost enough of them already."

That's right, his two brothers, who were killed in action.

"And the info about my vasectomy is a secret," he adds. "They don't know that. Owen is the only other person in my life who knows. It will potentially make our lives far less complicated at some future point if that knowledge *stays* secret, pet."

I immediately understand what he means and I nod. "Yes, Sir."

He studies me for a long moment. "None of this bothers you? The...machinations?"

My turn to smirk. "Not really, Sir. You weren't raised in my father's house. This kind of stuff, for me, is just business as usual on any day ending in *Y.* Politics 101." I snort. "Especially in Florida."

He laughs. "I guess I didn't think about it like that. I'm so used to you loving the evil things I do to you."

My smile fades. "I have a condition of my own."

Serious Carter is back. He nods for me to continue.

"You have to promise."

"I have to hear it first, pet."

"You don't do...*that* with Owen."

Some of the stuff we've already done, if it wasn't for the fact that I have a safeword, it'd be considered sexual assault to the casual observer.

Some of the stuff we've talked about doing in the future, once Carter crosses the final line and has intercourse with me, basically *is* rape, in nearly every way.

I *want* that with him.

I *want* the darkness racing through his mental halls. I love the wild gleam in his eyes when he's chasing me through the house and catches me, pins me down to fuck my mouth.

I love *everything* about it.

I love the *fear*.

I *crave* it. I crave the adrenaline spike I get, and the way my pulse races.

His brow furrows. "Do what with Owen?"

"The dark stuff. The CNC play." The thought of Owen feeling in legitimate fear for his safety, even for consensual non-consent play, *especially* from someone he trusts as much as Carter, does ugly things to my insides. "Promise me you won't ever do anything to make him feel afraid."

He takes a deep breath. "I can't make that promise, pet. I can't be sure that—"

"The stuff *we* do. I don't mean like he's afraid of breaking position and getting a cane stroke that he knows he might get. I mean he doesn't turn around in the kitchen to see you coming at him in a ski mask with a knife and threatening to cut his throat. You don't break in in the middle of the night and he wakes up to you duct-taping his hands together and cutting his clothes off. *That* kind of play."

Okay, it was a dull knife, but still…it was *haaawwwt*.

Although that'd been my favorite bra he cut off me one night. He found me another just like it, but it took him a couple of weeks.

I'm not done. "Owen's not wired like we are, Carter." Okay, I've jumped to serious. "*Carter Edward Wilson*." I still don't break position, even though I've just safeworded. "Owen doesn't thrive on fear. You *know* that. He's had enough fear in his life already. You said you saw what a cunt that woman was to him. If you're serious about putting him first, then *promise* me you'll never deliberately, or accidentally-on-purpose, try to trigger the *bad* kind of fear in him."

He studies me for a long time before he sits back and pats his lap. "Come here, Suse."

I do, sitting across his lap, my arms draped around his neck.

He still hasn't answered me, but he's staring into my eyes. "What if, in the process of negotiations, he asks me to do something like that? What if he asks me for a CNC or takedown scene?" His hand comes to rest on my thigh, but it remains still. He's not trying to distract me or seduce me. This is serious Carter now.

"Asks-asks, or you manipulate him into begging for it?"

"Asks-asks."

I try to think about that, about the way I love and thrive on this, and I honestly can't picture Owen begging for that kind of fear.

If anything, Owen would beg for peace.

"How about you promise that you won't do a scene like that with him, that will cause the bad kind of fear in him, or deliberately do anything to *try* to trigger the bad kind of fear in him, without bringing it to me first? I get to talk to him about it, and *I* get to be the one who decides if it's go or no-go. Including I get to decide if I want to be there to watch and stop it. I get to override it. And that if you find something you're doing with him is triggering bad fear in him, you promise to stop immediately and soothe him."

He studies me for at least a minute as he turns it over his mind. Finally, he nods. "Fair enough, pet. I'll agree to that rule. I will never try to deliberately trigger the bad kind of fear in him, through a scene, or otherwise, and will stop if that happens. Even if he asks, I'll bring it to you to hear, and you get the final ruling. Period. I'll even go one better, that I will always give you safeword rights if you think he's being triggered with the bad kind of fear during a scene. I'll let you safeword for him, so we can talk."

I don't know why I start crying, but he holds me close as I do. "Thank you, Carter."

He slowly and gently rocks me in his arms. "You're welcome,

Suse. Thank you for loving him."

I guess I do really love Owen as more than just a friend.

The way I love Carter.

I nestle my head on his shoulder. "I don't need a trial period," I say. "Let's get married."

He stops rocking me. "You sure?"

"I'm sure. I know we're bending the truth around Owen, but it's for good reasons. I can see how you love him. You fucking used your body as a human shield to save your guys. If I can't trust you, I shouldn't be sucking your cock, or have given you a key to my house."

I sit up and cradle his face in my hands. "I *want* this. I want *us*, the *three* of us, for life. I want *you*."

He's looking into my eyes again. Another long, quiet moment follows before he speaks. "Ask me properly, pet."

I turn and straddle his lap, my arms draped around his neck, my forehead pressed against his. His hands settle on my ass, lightly stroking.

"Sir, I want to be your wife, and I want to submit to you as your slave. I want to spend the rest of my life with you and Owen, and I want to own him with you, and I want to be owned by you."

He doesn't answer me, at first, but I hear the way his breathing changes, faster, harder. Feel the way his fingers tense on my flesh.

Then he lets go of me, unfastens his shorts, and pulls out his cock.

I'm already wet and reaching for him, rising up a little so I can settle on his cock, both of us moaning as he fists my hair and we *kiss*.

We *kiss*, and we *fuck*.

It starts out a slow, deep grind, his other hand kneading my ass as I ride him and find the perfect angle to get over. When I find it, I rock harder, working it, chasing it and needing it more than anything now.

I've never come just from a guy fucking me—*ever*.

And he knows this, because I don't lie to him. Despite the fiction we spin for Owen, I know Carter isn't lying to me. He doesn't have to. We accept each other at our darkest levels without shame.

My fingers dig into the back of his neck as I crest and fall, gasping as it bursts inside me.

"Good girl," he says against my lips. "Do it again."

And I do. After the second time, which takes longer, his hands grab my hips, fingers digging in with the good bite of pain as his gaze turns hard.

I *want* it. I want *all* of it, and all of *Him*.

"You going to be Sir's good little slut, baby?" He starts thrusting into me harder.

Oh, god, I'm going to come again. "Yes, Sir!"

"You going to like watching him watch *me* fuck you, and then watch as I make him suck the taste of your pussy off my cock?"

"Yes, Sir!"

He sucks on my bottom lip. "I can't wait to make you suck my cock while he's fucking you, baby."

Aaaaaaannnd I'm *there*. I'm *officially* a slut. His triumphant grin as he thrusts and fills me, falling still with his cock pulsing inside me, twists me around his heart.

He nuzzles my nose with his. "Marry me, Suse," he whispers, and I suspect this might be one of the rare times I get to glimpse the raw, unprotected, and vulnerable center of Carter's soul. "Please, marry me."

I press my lips to his forehead. "Yes, Carter. I'll marry you."

He sighs, his eyes falling closed as he bows his head. I hold him, playing with his hair, my face nuzzling against his head as he wraps his arms around me.

"How do you feel about Vegas?" he asks without looking up.

"Vegas?"

"Yeah."

"For the wedding?" I rub his head the same way he's rubbed mine, and Owen's.

I feel him relax even more. "Among other things."

"I've never been there."

"I guess we'll both check it off our bucket lists, then, won't we?"

I inhale, loving the smell of Him. "I guess we will, Sir. Love you."

When he lifts his head and kisses me, it's a kiss full of promises and faith and fragile, quiet trust.

Another sigh escapes him. "I love you, too, sweetheart."

And he said he can't do gentle. *Bullshit.* He can when he trusts. I've seen him be tender and gentle with Owen, and I know he trusts Owen.

I'll never give him a reason to not trust me.

CHAPTER TWELVE

Two nights later, I'm sitting sideways on my couch, my laptop balanced on my thighs, my feet in Carter's lap. Owen's at the dorm, ostensibly studying for finals.

We're supposedly working on my submission.

Technically, it's not a lie.

"Are you sure about this, Sir?" My finger hovers over my laptop's touchpad as indecision forces me to pause.

He nods. "If you're not going to pay for it, *I* will, but we're taking him to Vegas."

"No, I'll pay for it. I meant that. I'm just worried about how he's going to react."

"You let *me* worry about that. Besides, we're not telling him until the night before."

I stare at him, at first thinking he's just fucking with me. "Seriously?"

He gets *that* look. "Are you arguing with me, pet?"

Let the battle of wills begin. I'm not sure if Carter actually gets off on waiting me out. I think he does, at least a little.

Okay, maybe more than a little.

Saaaadist, *duh*.

Of *course* he gets off on waiting me out. He never has to "force" me to do anything, outside of our dark and twisted play. I do too damn good a job of forcing myself and refusing to buckle, and he knows it.

I crack first and look at my laptop screen. After I click the button to complete the purchase, I add Carter as a recipient of a confirmation e-mail with the boarding pass information.

"Okay," I say. "Three round-trip tickets to Las Vegas. Done."

He picks up his phone and checks his e-mail, then slowly nods. "Very good, pet. Thank you." He's paying for the hotel and rental car, among other things.

"How is this helping him, again?" I ask.

"I need to forcibly jolt Owen out of this last little rut he's stuck in about his mother. The timing happens to work out perfectly." He sets his phone on the coffee table and points for me to do the same with my laptop.

I do.

He starts rubbing my feet. "His father's told me a few interesting things about their divorce."

"Such as?"

"Owen says his mother took great pride in griping that his father never paid child support past the first few months or so."

"Yeah?"

"He did pay. Until Owen turned eighteen. Not only paid, but because of their prenup, it was way more than the state-mandated rate. He also told me he sent Owen birthday and holiday cards, letters, left phone messages. According to Owen, he's had very little contact with his father, all of it initiated by himself, not his father."

My eyes widen. "She's been lying to Owen?"

"Yep."

"Does he know yet?"

"Nope."

It's hard to focus with his thumbs skillfully kneading my feet. "What else has she been lying to him about?" I muse.

"A narcissist like her? God only knows."

He teases me by pausing over the pressure point in my foot that feels like agony and simultaneously makes me totally wet when he hits it. His fingers move on without torturing me tonight.

"Probably a lot," he adds. "Assume she's lied to him about everything, because it's sort of what they do. Right now, if I forced Owen to make a choice, I am not totally certain he'd choose us over her. He's still too afraid. I need to get him so enraged that it outweighs his fear and he can't help but turn his back on her for good and choose us over her." He meets my gaze. "Then, he's ours for life."

I swallow hard, nervous, but determined to see this through. "Daddy's going to want to hire a hit man for you when he finds out."

Carter smiles. "Then I suppose we'd better take out a life insurance policy on me, shouldn't we, pet?"

"How can you even joke like that?"

His smile fades. "I'm not afraid of death, sweetheart. I've seen it, dealt it. My only fear is long, slow suffering I have to endure. Death? That's easy. Surviving is difficult. Surviving is the hardest thing I've ever done."

"What if he tries to ruin your life?"

He shrugs. "Then I guess you'll be supporting me and Owen. If your father's a smart man, he'll back off. Your trust is safe, your car and house are owned by the trust. After we graduate law school, we'll put a postnup in place, if you want. But either *you* trust me, or you don't. If *you* don't trust me, say so now. I'm not getting divorced."

"What about Owen?"

"What about him?"

"Is he going to hate us after he finds out?"

"I doubt it. Another reason we need to get him so pissed off at his mother that he's done with her for good. The path of least resistance. Once I know he's moving in the direction we want him to, we'll step up his immersion. I'll be sending him home alone with you for more intensive training. If you follow my plan and do what I tell you to do the *way* I tell you to do it, he'll do what makes him feel the best—feel the *safest*—and that's choose *us*."

"It feels…" I can't finish the statement.

He arches an eyebrow at me. "Suse, if you're squeamish over *this*, honey, you have *no* business wanting to get into politics, and you damn well know it. This doesn't even rise to the level of the mildest ratfuck."

"I know." I struggle to put it into words. "I don't want to destroy his trust. He's been through so much."

"We have to break him down to build him up." He focuses on my feet again. "Only this time, we break him down with love, to remove all the bullshit from his soul, and we rebuild him strong enough to withstand anything. Rebuild him in healthy ways. If you break your leg and it heals crooked, they have to re-break it so it can heal properly."

So far, everything Carter's done has worked. I don't have any reason to doubt him. "You'll never make him leave, right?"

He sets my feet aside and climbs on top of me, staring down at me. "I love him. And I love you. If you trust me, this will work."

"How do I know you haven't been working on me like this?"

That smirk. It wets my panties—when I'm allowed to wear them—and frustrates me, all at the same time. "So what if I have? You said you wanted me. Well, you've got me. You only have to take me on my terms, and you've already agreed to them. Again, if you're backing out, tell me *now*."

I reach up and pull him down for a kiss. Something about this man absolutely drives me insane, in both good and bad ways. "I'm not backing out, but if I catch you cheating on us, I'll cut your dick off."

He smiles. "I'm rather attached to it."

"Say it," I whisper. "Please?"

His smile fades. He knows what I want to hear. He leans in to nuzzle his nose against mine. "I promise, Suse, I will *never* cheat on you and Owen. This is just the three of us. For life. If you trust me, I *will* take care of you, and we will move mountains to get you elected to whatever office you want to run for. But we do this as *three*, and we get Owen elected first. I'll *always* be yours, the way you'll always be mine. All I'm asking is for you to love Owen, too, always put him first in our lives, and stay faithful to us. I don't want to break you. I want to build you up. I want to see *both* of you succeed."

He presses his lips to mine in a slow, tender kiss that lights fires within me.

"You're such a bastard, Carter," I whisper against his mouth.

He lifts his head and smiles. "Admit it—it makes you wet."

"Yeah, it does." I reach down and palm him through the front of his shorts. "I want to suck his cock while you fuck him the first time."

His smile widens. "Oooh. My scheming little pet. Look at you go. That's *hot*. I'll turn you into a sexual sadist yet." He nibbles down my jawline, to my neck, making me shiver. "All the dirty, nasty things we're going to do to you. Make some of those raunchy books on your Kindle look downright vanilla."

My hand cups his erection. He's hard and rocks against my hand. "You've corrupted me."

He chuckles, sounding gravelly and rough and sexy. "You were corrupted long before we met, sweetheart. Don't bullshit me." He looks at me again. "That's the *real* reason you dumped Kendall, isn't it? He was too vanilla for you. Those other excuses were just that."

Fuck. It's like the bastard can read my mind sometimes.

"There's a fine line between dominant and domineering, and he was too far in the vanilla end of domineering for my tastes. Among with the other issues he had."

Wasn't like I could admit *that* to them the first day we met, though.

"I *knew* it." He nips my earlobe, and now it's me arching against his thigh, which has conveniently ended up between my legs. I start grinding against him and he shoves it hard against me.

"I jerk him off in the shower every morning," he whispers in my ear. "Sometimes, I jerk off, too. When I put you on your knees and fuck that sweet mouth of yours, I'm usually thinking about the day I finally get to fuck him."

I whimper as I hook one leg around his and really start humping his thigh.

He's far from done. "I sometimes think about him fucking your pussy while I fuck your throat. I also think about *both* of us fucking you. Let you ride Owen in your pussy while I fuck that tight ass of yours at the same time." Another nip. "Bet you'd love that, wouldn't you?"

"*Please*, Sir!"

"Please *what*, my dirty little pet? Ask me for what you want."

"I want...*that*, Sir. To suck you while he fucks me. And both of you to fuck me." The thought of both their cocks inside me at the same time is beyond erotic.

It's a fantasy come true, and soooo damn close, nearly within my grasp.

His breath feels warm in my ear. "I *love* choking you on my cock. I love knowing I can turn you into a needy little slut, and you can't stop yourself. I love watching you drool, and making your eyes water. I can't wait until we tell your father I'm banging you every night, and that you belong to *me*."

A shudder washes through me as I nearly come right there. Before I even realize what he's doing, Carter flips me over and shoves my thighs apart. I'm only wearing a T-shirt, one of his, and he doesn't even take off his shorts. He just pushes his waistband down, and then he's inside me, fucking me while pinning my arms to the couch.

I come almost immediately.

"Oooh, there's a naughty pet who just earned a spanking," he gleefully says. "You didn't ask Sir's permission to come. Fuck, I love spanking you."

Of course he does. He loves it as much as I love being spanked by him.

There is nothing sexier than being taken like this by *Him*, rough and hard and beyond my control. Because every other aspect of Carter is exacting control, from how he talks to what he does. I can make him lose control, and he can take control of me.

Because I trust him.

I know all I have to do is say his full name and he'll stop, but to be honest?

Even when he's doing stuff to me that I don't necessarily like, I don't want him to stop.

How fucked up is *that*?

Sometimes, I even enjoy it *more* when I don't like it, because I know *he* likes it.

He slows the pace of his fucking and lets go of my left wrist just to grab my hair and yank my head back.

"I can't wait until we finally tell Owen and claim him so I can *finally* bite that gorgeous ass of yours and put marks on you." He grinds another one out of me, making him laugh. "That's two rounds of spankings you owe me, sweetheart. I felt you come. You like the thought of me sending you to class with a huge hickey on your neck, don't you, hmm? Proof someone's fucking your ass? Should meet you after your first class tomorrow morning and fuck you in the stairwell and make you walk around all day with my cum dripping out of you."

Oooooh, fuuuuuck.

I know he feels me come that time, too, and he laughs again. "Oh, my sweet, utterly fucked pet. You're such a willing slut for me. Think of how happy you're going to be with two cocks to fuck you on demand."

He flips me over again and climbs up me, pinning my arms under him, and he grabs my head.

My mouth is already open, because I play by the rules. There's that delicious, nearly crazed look in his eyes when he pushes in and starts fucking my mouth. I taste myself, briefly think for a moment that Owen's going to taste his cock exactly like this, too, and then I'm lost as I watch him pumping over me. He gags and chokes me, forces me to take him all the way to the root.

I fucking *love* it.

He treats me like an eager little slut and makes me take it all. And when he finally groans and pumps me full of *Him*, I swallow and feel just a little bit triumphant that he's using me when he could have already had Owen all to himself by now.

He came for *me*.

He finally pulls out and stretches his body on top of mine, kissing me deeply as I wrap my arms and legs around him.

He sighs. "I guess I can be nice and just give you one *really* long and hard spanking."

I laugh. "You going soft on me, Sir?"

He arches an eyebrow. "That's spoken like someone who doesn't want to be able to sit for her first class tomorrow morning."

"Sir's choice."

After a moment, he smiles. "You're learning fast, pet." He kisses me again.

"I try, Sir."

For *Him*?

I'd probably try damn near anything.

CHAPTER THIRTEEN

Of *course* Carter has a plan for Las Vegas. We fly in on Friday evening. The first goal for that night is to help Owen through dinner with his family, and talking with his dad, Gerard, which we do.

I'm in agony watching our sweet boy trying to process what his dad tells him, the truths his mom outright lied to him about for his entire life.

I'm enraged nearly beyond reason while I listen and force myself to remain calm, the concerned, loving friend, and not the woman who wants to fly into a murder-rage on her sweet boy's behalf.

When Carter takes Owen and Gerard outside to talk, he deftly plucks Owen's phone from his back pocket and hands it off to me. Probably to keep Owen from going off on his mom right then.

Carter has a plan for that, too.

First, our focus is Owen.

As I watch the three of them outside, as Owen crumples to the ground with Carter and his dad hugging him…

Owen is truly broken right now, and it fucking *kills* me.

But…

Carter is right.

The bastard extraordinaire is absolutely right.

I *get* it. Why Carter handled things the way he did with Owen.

He'd asked me to trust him, and now I can see it, *right* here. The fact that Carter exchanged knowing glances with me over Owen, who sat crying between us on his dad's couch a few minutes earlier, told me *See, I told you so.*

This is hopefully the last dark valley Carter will subject Owen to before we can truly begin the rebuilding process. Breaking him down, lovingly, to finally allow him to cut the cord with his mother without a look back. Like having to open up a wound that's refused to heal properly. It hurts, and it sucks, but it's the only way to finally clean out the infection for good.

Owen's mother infected everything in his life, up until the point we met him.

We're going to erase every trace of her from his soul and love him so hard he can't remember the bad kinds of pain.

If it was up to me, I'd call the cunt myself and tell her to fuck herself right off the tallest building in Orlando.

I know it's not up to me, though. It's up to Carter.

Carter warned me this weekend would have some fun times, but that tonight would be dark, and ugly, and every ounce of energy we had needed to be focused solely on Owen and easing him through it as best we could while not letting him gloss over any of his mother's actions, or try to explain them away, or rationalize them.

This is Owen's rock-bottom. I know next week Carter tentatively plans to let Owen come home with me—*just* me— every day after classes, and step up our personal play and sexual contact. To start rebuilding him wrapped around *us* at his core.

I hope it works. I truly do. I can't stand seeing Owen hurting like this. All I want to do is take him back to the hotel and gently make love to him. Not the animalistic play and fucking Carter and

I frequently do, but sweet and tender and uncomplicated by any requirements on Owen to do anything but enjoy it.

After hearing Gerard tell us what it was like being married to Elandra, I *reeeeeally* hope I get a chance to meet the cunt in person, one day.

I'm sure it's not a coincidence that, as Gerard recounts the divorce and what she was like, he wears a nearly identically haunted expression that I've seen Owen wear ever since we met him. It's even spookier because Owen inherited his father's beautiful green eyes.

Part of me wonders if that contributed to why Elandra decided to torture her beautiful boy.

That makes me hate her even more.

*　*　*

When Owen awakens Saturday morning sandwiched between us in our king-sized hotel bed, Carter wastes no time distracting our sweet boy from his emotional distress.

Operant conditioning.

Owen has a choice to wallow in his emotional pain, or let Carter and me basically make love to him. There's no fucking, but after the two of us get him off with our hands, Carter makes Owen eat me out for the first time.

Instead of remembering how badly he hurt last night, Owen will forever think about this weekend as reconnecting with his father, and being allowed this new first with me.

Bless his heart, he's not very good at it yet, but I don't care. He'll get better, I know he will. He more than makes up for his lack of skill with eagerness, and ends up getting me off three times before I'm done.

I know Carter's probably ready to explode himself. So is Owen, but as per their new routine, Carter will give Owen another round of relief in the shower.

I lie there feeling sated and wishing we didn't have to leave the room today. Owen looks like he's deep in subspace.

He looks *happy*.

Yeah, this is totally worth it if we can make him look like *that* right now and *keep* making him look like that.

Carter grins. "There's our good boy." He playfully rubs Owen's head. "Go get in the shower. I'll be right there. Close the door so we don't steam up the whole room, please."

"Yes, Sir." Owen climbs out of bed. I watch Carter watching Owen, and the sound of the bathroom door closing barely comes to us before Carter's on me, kissing me, shoving the waistband of his boxers down so he can fuck me.

The man's *growling*. Just the sound of that makes me start coming again before he's barely taken five strokes inside me. Thank god he's kissing me, keeping me quiet.

This is a *fuck*. Pounding, brutal, driving me into the mattress and designed to get him off as quickly as possible, because we're on the clock. Owen could open that door any second.

He shoves my hands over my head, pinning my wrists with one hand while he clamps his other hand around my throat. He only squeezes a little, just enough to remind me who's in charge, and that sends me over one last time and takes him with me with a soft, deep, satisfied grunt.

Three breaths later, he's up and moving, pulling off his boxers and wiping himself with them before discarding them into his pile of dirty clothes from last night. The shower's running now, and I watch his scarred back as he disappears into the bathroom with Owen and shuts the door.

I'm still trying to catch my breath.

Not like I have any complaints, because I just got to come more times than both of them put together, even counting what he's going to do to Owen in the shower.

I reach between my legs and slide a finger inside me, pull it out, suck the taste of *Him* and me off it.

I can't help but wonder how quickly I'll come to learn the differences between the taste of them, once Carter gets us across that final barrier.

I can't wait to find out.

* * *

Carter's wearing mirrored sunglasses today. After we drop Owen off, Carter pulls into the parking lot of a nearby shopping center to check something on his phone. We have our first task to accomplish, and then Carter said we can go check out adult shops for BDSM toys and implements after that.

After we buy a present for Owen's little brother. Because we're due back at Owen's father's house at two to have birthday cake with everyone.

"Did you decide, pet?" Carter asks.

I feel kind of silly about this. "Yes, Sir."

"And?"

I text him the link. He gets it a moment later, scrolls, reads…and starts laughing. It's a deep, rolling belly laugh I've never heard from him before.

It's a gorgeous sound. "*Really*, Suse?"

"I mean, if you don't want to—"

"Oh, no, you don't. I want to. I told you it was your choice, and I meant it. We are sooo getting the picture package, though."

I can't see his eyes, but he's smiling one of those rare smiles he has.

He's *really* enjoying this, and not in a sadistic way.

In a Carter way.

He plugs something else into his phone's GPS, and we resume our journey. Fifteen minutes later, we're standing in line in the Las Vegas clerk's office to get our marriage license.

He holds my hand the whole time. When it's our turn at the

clerk's window, we show our IDs, fill out the paperwork, sign, and he pays. We're walking now. We stop by a jewelry store next, where Carter peruses engagement rings and wedding band sets and gives me several choices to pick from that are within his budget. We'll have to hide them from Owen before we pick him up today.

"I can pay," I softly say.

He lightly smacks my ass. "You're *not* buying your own engagement and wedding rings," he says. "Pick, pet."

I feel a little guilty. Yes, of course I ran background and credit checks on him and Owen. Carter ran one on me, too. One of the things we did the other evening after I bought the plane tickets, besides fucking, was go through our finances together. I know what Carter's budget and savings are, and he knows mine.

Owen's budget is irrelevant beyond the fact that he's not in debt. We're going to take care of our boy, and that's that. Once we transition him through the next stage, Carter will take control of everything and give him a weekly allowance and extremely tight spending restrictions, at first. Once he's certain Owen has fully relaxed into the new world order and has confidence in our ability to care for him, Carter will ease those restrictions.

But he wants Owen completely dependent upon us for everything, at first, so that he can see we'll deny him nothing reasonable. I mean, if he asks for a Lamborghini or something, that's a hard no, obviously.

I've already told Carter what I want to get Owen for Christmas, and after mulling it over for a day, he agreed we'd do it together.

I want to buy Owen a car, get rid of the Subaru his mom gave him.

His last tether to her.

Every time he drives, I want him thinking about me and Carter, and us fucking him in every possible position in whatever car we get him.

Operant conditioning.

I finally pick a modest engagement ring but select a wedding band set that's toward the pricier end of the stated spectrum. Hey, Carter said to pick.

So I'm picking.

He slides the engagement ring on my left finger before we leave the store and pockets the wedding bands. Twenty minutes later, we're awaiting our turn in the wedding chapel, and Carter's already paid for the video package, photos—everything.

Now I'm beginning to wish I'd gone with a drive-through chapel option.

When it's our turn, the organist starts playing "Viva Las Vegas" as we walk to the front of the chapel—yes, we had our choice of music, too, and that's what Carter chose—and there's a fucking *grin* plastered across Carter's face as the photographer snaps our pics and another takes video while a slightly overweight Elvis wearing a white, skin-tight bedazzled jumpsuit and with muttonchops for *days* marries us.

Fuck.

Me.

I've never seen Carter grin like this before. It reaches the depths of his eyes, takes years off his face, and likely erases horrible memories from his conscious mind for a few minutes.

He's focused on the here, the now—on *me*.

I suspect I won't get to see *this* man too many times. At least, not in the beginning.

I silently make it my life's goal to try to seek *this* man out, to do whatever it takes to make him look like that whenever I can.

Thirty minutes later, we leave married.

Daddy's probably going to fucking kill him.

Benchley?

He'll *definitely* want to ruin Carter. Although I'm not sure if it'll be the news that we eloped, or the news that, when we return to Florida, we're both changing our voter registration from our respective parties to Independent, that will piss off that side of my father more.

Me?

I'm feeling both excited and the good kind of terrified, and now I can't wait to add Owen to our lives in every way. To finally be able to live together, all three of us sharing a bed every night.

Because I know we're going to succeed. At everything.

I *feel* it.

This man right here will be bedding *two* Florida governors.

And I am soooo going to enjoy the look on Daddy's *and* Benchley's faces when *I* get sworn in as Florida's governor.

CHAPTER FOURTEEN

Now — Year Four

There are many weekday mornings I awake alone in bed in the early morning hours and wonder if I'm dreaming.

Are we *really* in Tallahassee?

Did we *really* pull this off?

Because I'm living my dream, even if we've had to make serious personal adjustments along the way.

I stand in the shower this Tuesday May morning and let the spray hit me in the face to help wake me up. I know exactly where Carter is without even using our family phone tracking feature to find him.

He's with Owen.

I'm actually fine with that. I know some women might feel slighted, but I don't need Carter clinging to me every minute of the day. I need him when I need him...and then I don't. Doesn't mean I love him any less. It means I've been independent my entire life.

Of course I love my time spent on my knees in front of him— when those times happen. Lately, usually only when I ask for them to happen, because I'm busy and he knows it. We both are.

But I'm a politician with a *lot* of work to do. As we *really* crank up the re-election campaign efforts, I'm going to have even *more* work to do. It's not guaranteed that Owen will be re-elected, although his chances look damn good, if early polls can be believed.

That means Carter needs to spend time with Owen to keep him grounded and centered and focused and doing the work Owen needs to do.

I, however, am a self-starter.

On weekdays, I prefer this morning routine, without Carter's interference. Carter and Owen have always worked out together in the morning, ever since they met. It's at least one damn routine Carter can keep going for Owen to help center and ground him. I'd be a piss-poor wife and Ma'am to Owen if I denied him this.

On weekends or holidays, sure, I don't mind Carter waylaying me—and well-laying me—on my way to the shower or before we can eat breakfast.

On a busy weekday, when I have meetings starting in less than two hours? It's going to piss me off if Carter tries to go Master on me.

No one likes a pissy pet.

That's why on weekday mornings, Carter focuses his energy on his other pet, the one who legit needs him the most right now.

I would expect nothing less from Carter, and would be disappointed in him if he didn't put Owen first.

Now at night? When I have trouble shutting my brain down? Absolutely, I love Carter going into Master bastard extraordinaire mode then.

I've got a long overseas trip coming up that I'm beginning to wish I'd passed on. I leave in less than two weeks, and will be gone two weeks. I'll be traveling alone, technically. No Carter, no Owen, no Dray. Not this time.

It's for our tourism industry, so I'm traveling with Connie Drucker, head of our state's tourism commission, and her husband, Michael.

I've got a ton of work to do, in addition to campaign appearances, but Carter told me maybe it's better I take this trip now. To hard-shift my mind out of my usual routine and get me away from Tallahassee for a little while.

Especially after last Tuesday night, and what happened.

I know he's right, but I *haaate* admitting it.

See, here's the problem—unfortunately, despite Owen usually managing to fuck me over his desk—or on his couch, or over my desk, and even over Carter's desk—several times a week, in addition to the night or two every week Carter and I stop by the mansion so Owen can properly fuck me in his bed, I haven't gotten pregnant.

During the first six months of our term, I'm afraid I was apologizing to Dray a lot every four weeks when I'd discover the proof that, yet again, whatever we were doing wasn't working.

But if you look at the beautiful photo-shoot that was done of the three of us one day over at the Florida Governor's Mansion, you can't spot anything wrong, even though I'd started that morning softly crying alone in the bathroom when I realized my period had arrived.

Carter looked gorgeous, and with his arm draped around my shoulders and us looking into each other's eyes, you can't miss how we feel about each other.

Owen, on the other hand, looked fucking *hawt*. Through his office, he now receives dozens of love letters and e-mails every week. It pisses me off that Carter sets Owen up to go out for a minimum of one fairly visible "date" a month with a couple of trusted beards. They don't know Owen's ours, but the women also have their own secrets to hide and are willing to sign NDAs and stay quiet in exchange for the visibility. They usually have dinner, sometimes see a movie or play or concert, or attend some other event, and then part ways at the mansion, where the date started.

I pitch a fit and Carter cuts it back to every other month. So, during the next six months we're in office, I spend it struggling not to burst into tears anytime someone asks me about kids. Inside my brain, pet would spend those particular moments curled up in a tight ball and sobbing while, outside, Susa smiled and said one of the several ready-made answers I usually used, depending on the circumstances.

That's year one.

Year two, I spend it basically trying to ignore my monthly visitor. In whatever private times we have together, Carter and Owen start doing nothing more than cuddling with me during those particular weeks. I think Carter or Dray gives Owen a warning, because despite us not sharing a bed every night, Owen always seems to know exactly when my period starts, and always calls me in to his office for a few minutes of cuddling on his couch, my head in his lap, and his hand stroking my hair.

Did I mention how much I love my men?

Year three sees the return of Susa Evans, hardened politician. My period is irrelevant, because our agenda is in full swing, and I have more important issues on my plate, like trying to rally lawmakers on both sides of the aisle to push through legislation to help our schools and tighten background check requirements for gun purchases. I refuse to discuss my personal monthly issues with Carter or Owen. I safeword out of conversations on that topic with them on a regular basis, citing work.

Year four…

Basically, a repeat of year three, only with more bitchiness. I'm thirty-nine and, let's face it, if it hasn't happened by now, it probably won't. Unfortunately, in Momma's family, there's a history of women entering menopause in their forties, including Momma. I'm not there yet, but it's just a matter of time.

I still refuse to talk about it with Carter, and now with Owen, although I'm gentle with my sweet boy when I safeword the conversations with him. I always do it lovingly, gently, and give him a sweet kiss when I do.

Then new packages of birth control pills appear on the counter in our townhouse bathroom two weeks ago.

Enraged, I throw them away. I understand it was a silent, gentle way of Carter trying to tell me I didn't have to keep trying and doing this to myself every month. But…

Yeeeeah.

Why take something that I *obviously* don't fucking need? What a horrible, cruel reminder, every *fucking* day, that, no matter how badly I *did* want this, for me and for my men, it was something apparently outside even *my* tenacious grasp?

I'd rather have the monthly mocking by my body, thank you very much.

I might be a masochist, but I'm not *that* kind of masochist.

It was bad enough knowing I'd traded Owen's biggest dreams for mine, and that the chance to have this *one* thing was *the* one thing I couldn't give our sweet boy, or my husband.

That, in my mind, I'd failed to put my boy first the way I'd promised Carter twenty years ago that I would.

Who, to be honest, is a fucking *saint* to put up with me right now. I'm shocked Carter hadn't moved in to the mansion, or at least into Owen's townhouse next door. Even Dray's had to safeword on me a few times lately when I get bitchy.

After not talking with me about the birth control pill incident, Carter finally asked me last Tuesday evening if I wanted him to make an appointment for me in Tampa with a fertility specialist, and—

Well, I honestly don't remember much after practically screaming *Carter Edward Wilson* at him, verbally taking his head off at the kneecaps with a long, one-sided screaming diatribe, whose contents I can't even remember, while coming up off the couch and swinging at him. I'd been sitting there, reading on my tablet, scanning through the text of a new bill hitting committee that week.

At some point later, I was sobbing and realized we were both on the living room floor, and he had my hair tightly wrapped around his fist so he could keep my head pinned down. Because apparently I bit and scratched him a few times, actually breaking skin on his left arm. He was also covered with nasty bruises and scratches on both arms the next day, to the point he wore a long-sleeved shirt for his daily jog with Owen, and made sure to wear long-sleeved shirts to work every day to hide the marks.

But when my brain returns just enough to register what's going on, I find he's also sitting on me with my arms trapped against my sides, and was texting someone with his free hand.

I uselessly struggle for a few seconds before I dissolve into tears again.

Meanwhile, Carter sits there, grim-faced and silent after setting his phone aside on the coffee table.

We're still sitting there a few minutes later when I hear a car pull up outside, followed by the sound of someone entering Owen's townhouse next door, the front door slamming shut behind them.

I was still sobbing as, next door, footsteps run upstairs, the tell-tale beeps I'd rarely heard in a couple of years, unless one of us had to go next door to get something for Owen, and then the sound of footsteps running downstairs in our unit.

Only then does Carter release me. I climb into Owen's arms, wrap myself around him, and cry as we sit there and he holds me.

They told me later I apologized over and over again to him for not being able to get pregnant, while they both tried to soothe me and tell me it was okay, but I don't remember any of that.

I only remember later, after frantically riding Owen's cock, the three of us curled up together in our bed, my men on either side of me and holding me, as all three of us spent the entire night together in the same bed for the first time in over a year.

CHAPTER FIFTEEN

Two mornings ago, I awoke in Singapore. Yesterday and today, it's Kuala Lumpur. We got to see some of the region the past two days, and today is a travel day. While it's been the trip of a lifetime, it's also been a working trip, for me.

At least this morning we can sleep late, if we want to. Good thing, too, because I'm exhausted. This trip is no longer fun. Yet because of everyone who's traveling with us, including a few members of the press, I have to be "on" any time I'm not locked behind a hotel room door. Cell phones are everywhere, and even though we're not in Florida, I am not "safe."

I haven't felt good since leaving Florida, honestly. Let's add motion sickness to the list. I barely made it to the lavatory on the last flight before throwing up my breakfast. I shouldn't have been reading on a bumpy flight, but I was bored out of my mind, and I wasn't sleepy.

I also know if I tell Carter or Owen any of that they will order me to a doctor, maybe even while I'm here. I know it's probably due to my schedule being off, combined with eating or drinking something that didn't agree with me. I have a sensitive stomach, and traveling wreaks havoc with me sometimes.

Whatever it is, it'll have to wait until I'm home. I refuse to have any drama attached to my name regarding this trip. It was bad enough what I put my men through just a couple of weeks ago. I'm damn lucky Carter was able to juggle Owen's schedule the next morning so no one but his security detail knew Owen hadn't spent the night at the mansion.

It was a weakness I won't soon repeat. I'm better than that.

I also know, after all this time away from my men, that I owe them apologies, conversations.

I miss them, and maybe I'm not handling this as well as I thought I was.

Maybe I should let Carter make that appointment for me.

Or, maybe these are my karmic dues I must pay. I can't have a life so blessed in so many ways without giving up *something*, right?

Even if it is something I desperately want.

Somehow, I know I need to come to peace with never having this one thing.

So far this morning, my stomach seems to be okay. I've already taken a dose of motion sickness meds to help prevent a repeat of the tummy trouble, since weather reports mentioned storms over the waters between here and Manila. It's likely to be a bumpy flight.

I'm also wishing I'd pushed Carter to let Dray come with me. It'd be nice to have someone familiar who I could just be myself with behind a closed door. Not to mention, he's kind of earned a vacation away from my bitchy work mode.

Connie and her husband, Michael, are nice people, but they're also in their early sixties and not exactly people I can cut loose with the way I could with my men, if they were here, or even with Dray and Gregory.

Except I *get* it. Carter needs Dray's help right now, and sending the bare minimum delegates on this trip means fewer chances for the press to roast us over any spending issues. Connie's paid for her husband's trip out of her own pocket. Carter had the lawyers go through everything before okaying me accepting the trip. This is definitely a working trip, and we're keeping receipts for everything we pay for out of our own pockets, because I'm reasonably certain there will be FOIA requests hitting within minutes of our return to Florida.

There's good reason for me to be here, though. I'm hobnobbing with governors and lieutenant governors from Georgia, Tennessee, Alabama, Arkansas, Virginia, North and South Carolina, and other states in the region, as well as various other high-value state officials.

Valuable connections. Some of them who know Daddy, or know his reputation.

I've done more vital networking on this trip than I have in the past four years. When it comes time for me to run for the US Senate, I'll already have a ready-made group of people to call upon for help with campaigning and fundraising. Sure, they can't vote for me, and no one in Florida might know who the hell they are...but they can put pressure on regional and national PACs to support me.

Throw money my way.

Because once we're done with the governorship of Florida, Carter said he'll loosen his restrictions on where we get our donations, to a certain extent.

Dark money, here I come. Daddy's connections will win me a lot of cross-party funding I might not otherwise be able to obtain, along with valuable endorsements. I just need to get elected the first time. I don't care if I piss all those PACs off in the process during my first term. Once I've had one term in office, I can get myself elected to a second.

Or, by then, I look toward other career paths, like campaign consulting.

We'll see.

First, of course, is getting Owen re-elected, and then getting myself elected to two terms in Tallahassee.

I once again pack my suitcase and head downstairs a little after ten to join the others for our private late brunch. The staff will load everything into the busses that will drive us to the airport, and then the next leg of our journey begins as we're off to Manila.

Traveling used to be fun. Even campaigning isn't this exhausting, because on most nights I'm either home, or have Carter with me, or can spend a few stolen moments with Owen. I can…be *me* for part of the day.

This has been the longest stretch I've been without either or both men in…

Well, in over twenty years.

I'm sitting there surrounded by virtual strangers, halfway across the world from home, and sipping my coffee when that revelation slams into me.

Owen and Carter have been in my life for *twenty* years.

Not only have we lasted longer than a good part of the general population in terms of marriages, we're a *political* union. That's our family business. That's even harder on a relationship.

Plus we're doing it as a poly triad, and haven't killed each other yet.

That's got to be some sort of record.

I pull up our group text thread.

Eating breakfast before airport. Love and miss you both.

I don't even know what time it is in Florida. Carter's orders were to text them at any time without concern for trying to figure time differences.

Right now, I'm close to tears with homesickness. At least at home if I can't be with Owen, I know he's only a couple of blocks away at night, and we can FaceTime or Skype if he's alone.

Carter replies a moment later.

Love and miss you, too, pet. boy's already asleep. We were up early this morning, and have an even earlier day tomorrow. I'll have him reply in the morning when he wakes up. Stay safe.

I try not to feel guilty about waking Carter, even though he specifically ordered me not to worry about things like that. Hopefully it's not the middle of the night there, and he can go back to sleep. At least he's with Owen, so it means I don't need to worry as much about Carter's nightmares. I'm under orders not to worry about them, or the campaign, or anything else while I'm over here, except what I'm doing. That I'm to focus on the trip and on making connections.

But I can't help it. I miss my men. I might as well be on Mars.

I could log in to my private calendar and see where Owen and Carter will be, but that would be violating a direct order from Sir, and I can't make myself do that.

I touch the stainless steel necklace and the matching bracelet on my right wrist, jewelry Carter gave me, my day collars. In addition to our matching tattoos, it's a tangible reminder that my men are with me no matter where I go. That Owen and Carter wear mates to them—Carter, a bracelet on his left wrist, and Owen a necklace like mine worn under his shirt—makes me feel even more connected to them. Double the symbolism, we're both owned by Carter, and yet I also own Owen.

One of the things I want to do when I get home is spend a few nights just being *pet* again. I feel desperately out of touch with that part of myself.

I end up sitting with Connie and Michael and chatting with them throughout our meal. Once our guide team meets with us and goes over the itinerary for the day—a goodly chunk of which will be spent in the air—we start loading in our busses for the ride to the airport. The meds I took earlier are making me sleepy, which gives me hope that I can take a long nap once we're wheels-up. In the large, oversized purse I use for a carryon, I keep a sleep mask and neck cushion for just this kind of occasion, and it's a four-hour flight.

Note to self—remember to never say yes to one of these long junkets unless one of the guys can come with me.

This is an older and slightly smaller charter jet than the previous ones, just big enough for all of us with few empty seats, so we'll be packed in like sardines. No Wi-Fi on this flight, either. Unfortunately, Connie and Michael boarded before I did. Michael snagged a starboard-side window about eight rows behind the wing, and Connie's in the middle. But, so far, she hasn't been an annoying seat-mate. Once we're off the ground, she rarely hits the lav on these shorter flights.

Then I remember my iffy tummy during the last flight and decide perhaps the aisle is safer this time. So I suck it up, tuck my laptop bag into the overhead, stow my large carryon purse under the seat in front of me, which requires a little wedging to make it fit, and I settle in. One last check of my phone, and I don't have a text from Owen, so I shut it off and add it to my purse.

I knew I wouldn't have a reply after Michael reminds me that there's a twelve-hour difference from Florida time, and then I finally have a *d'oh* moment when I think to glance at my watch, which I never changed. I use my phone for local time, and I so rarely wear a watch anymore I honestly forget I have the damn thing on.

Still, doesn't mean I didn't hope, just a little, to see a reply.

I hate these flights, though. The ones over nothing but water. Well, for all intents and purposes nothing but water. There's the occasional scattered island chain below.

Maybe it's better I'm not *on the window this time.*

After drink and snack orders are handed out, I get as comfy as I can with my mask and my neck cushion in place, and I hope for sleep.

I do manage to doze off for a while when a jolt awakens me. More correctly, it's the nervous trills and sounds the herd packed in this sardine can have made over the jolt. I pull my mask off to find Connie and Michael holding hands, and Connie looks a little white in the face.

"Are you okay?" I ask.

Connie's jaw drops. "You mean you've *slept* through all this?"

Apparently so. "All what?"

Another jolt hits us, a good hundred-foot drop, probably, and this time it's full-on shrieks sounding through the cabin as stuff goes flying.

"*That*!" Connie says. "That was the worse one yet!"

The captain's voice, in thickly accented English, comes to us over the PA system. "Sorry about that, ladies and gentlemen. We are apparently hitting worse turbulence than was predicted. Flight attendants, please make sure the cabin is secure and return to your seats. Everyone, please remain seated with your seatbelts fastened. Thank you."

Another hard jolt bounces us. I glance out the starboard window to see tall, dark, angry banks of clouds off to our right. I'm sure the ocean is beneath us somewhere, but I can't see it with the cloud cover.

"How long ago did we take off?" I ask, tightly gripping my arm rest as another bounce rocks us.

"Almost two hours," Michael says. He checks the time on his huge-ass, ugly wristwatch, which he resets every damn time we land. "One hour, fifty minutes," he says.

I snug my seatbelt a little tighter around my mid-section and pray I don't get sick. Although what's messing with my stomach and tensing it now isn't nausea.

It's fear.

I've experienced some pretty bumpy flights in my life in all sizes of aircraft, from tiny turbo-prop commuter flights, all the way up to jumbo wide-bodies, and they're never fun. But there's a tense atmosphere now filling the cabin that doesn't feel…normal.

Not at all.

I pull my purse out enough I can shove the pillow and mask into it before I quickly kick it back under the seat. I don't want my face to get smashed into the seat-back in front of me if we take another bad bounce.

The pilot banks hard to port, which I'm assuming is north, or at least a northerly direction, because that's what makes sense, based on our destination and flight path.

That's when the plane shudders. A loud *bang* on the starboard side of the cabin makes even me scream. I'm now holding hands with Connie on my right, my other hand white-knuckling the armrest on my left.

"What the *hell* was that?" she shrieks.

"It's okay, honey," Michael says. "I'm sure that—"

His next words are ripped away—along with his right arm and part of his head—as a large chunk of something hits the side of the cabin two rows ahead of us and tears an even larger chunk about twenty feet long out of the side of the fuselage, along where the windows are. I barely notice the painful way my ears squeeze from the sudden change in pressure because I'm too busy screaming.

Which, ironically, helps my ears pop.

All around us, oxygen masks drop from the overheads like deadly puppets dancing in the air current.

This is where rational Susa and emotional pet take vastly divergent paths, my mind slowing and splitting, every millisecond a seeming forever as it happens, each heartbeat an eternity.

Susa has dropped into cold, calm, crisis-management mode, and is thinking that the engine in the wing on our side lost a part, or had some sort of catastrophic failure, and the debris hit the skin of the plane, with explosive decompression taking care of the rest when a window gave way.

Pet is screaming along with the rest of the passengers, our cries now lost over the roar of the wind and whine of the remaining, struggling engine.

Susa is remembering hundreds of pre-flight safety talks, peels my fingers off the left armrest, and somehow manages to grab the oxygen mask on the first try and push it against my face. Susa also notes how the people around her now breathe mist into the suddenly frigid air, and something about fifteen seconds or less to get the mask on before losing consciousness because of hypoxia comes to mind.

Pet is crying and terrified and thinking of my two men, and that I'll never see them again.

Susa manages to jerk my right hand free from Connie's grasp and yank the elastic band for the oxygen mask over my head and tighten it, then reaches for the one in front of Connie and has to slap her left cheek hard to make her turn enough I can force it over her nose and mouth and pull the band over her head, yanking it tight to hold it in place.

Pet is convinced we're all going to die.

Actually, Susa's pretty convinced of that, too, and wonders if it was a mistake to put on the masks. At least losing consciousness due to a lack of oxygen would mean a merciful death.

Except for that last-second awakening before impact.

Fuuuuck.

Is the automatic pilot engaged? Will we plunge nose-first in a fatal dive? Will he attempt an ocean belly-landing? Will he be able to cruise at ten thousand feet long enough to reach land? We're over open water, so it should be safe terrain to drop to where oxygen levels won't be as critical. How long will the emergency oxygen reserves last?

Did he get his own mask on in time?

Being a nerd sucks, sometimes. *This* is one of those times, all the information I absorbed about pilots and flight and airplanes when I went through that phase around age ten, when I wanted to be a commercial jet pilot. Until I discovered my best bet was to enlist in the military first and get flight training there, and decided no, thanks.

Amazing what runs through your mind when you're facing death.

All of this happens in less than fifteen seconds, because Susa is a motherfucker in a crisis, all those years of Girl Scouts and camping with Daddy—and campaigning with Daddy—and learning how not to panic now paying off.

But as Susa is struggling not to think about things like proximity to land, how rough the ocean is, and how long it's going to take to die like this, pet is desperately wishing for one last chance to speak to Owen and Carter and tell them how much I love them.

Susa is grateful they are not here right now, or Dray and Gregory. They are all safe at home, in Florida.

Because there's a damn good chance one of them would have been in Mike's seat, or I would have.

Susa also forces herself not to look over at what's left of Michael Drucker, still strapped in his seat, or think about the fact that the woman in the seat ahead of him must be dead, too, based on what little is left of her head.

Pet remembers Carter's last order via text—*Stay safe.*

Susa prays this cheap-ass charter flight has fucking life vests under the seats—and that someone has actually *checked* to make sure they're there and not expired.

Pet dives into Susa's brain for a moment and remembers the crash brace position and takes it, because even if there is an announcement on the PA, with the wind right there and roaring through the side of the fuselage, I can't hear it. I give thanks I'm wearing my sneakers and jeans, and had kept my sweater on against the cabin's chill.

Then I think about life rafts. We're far closer to the rear of the craft than we are the front, and this is where I do wish Carter was here. I risk sitting up and craning my head around into the aisle to look back. Over half of the passengers are unconscious and aren't wearing oxygen masks. I spot a terrified-looking flight attendant strapped into a rear jump seat and wearing a mask.

But there are two rear exit doors, and I know there should be life rafts there, if not the slides themselves set up to be flotation devices, depending on the model.

I face forward again. Next to me, Connie is sobbing, still holding Michael's hand.

As horrible as it sounds, maybe I shouldn't have put her mask on her. At least she'd be unconscious.

I resume my brace position and notice the woman across the aisle from me, who also wears her mask, is doing the same.

We're not banking any longer. I feel the rapid descent from the way the plane is pitching forward and how my ears are popping again. Except the entire airframe is shuddering in a way that piles an extra layer of terror on top of what I'd assumed was the maximum quota my brain and body could already process.

I thought I knew fear, terror. Not from my play with the bastard extraordinaire, either, but from that day of the school shooting. And from when Daddy collapsed with his heart attack.

Wrong.

So, *so* wrong.

I love you, I love you, I love you.

As my teeth chatter from cold and fear, I close my eyes and picture Carter and Owen's faces in my mind while I chant those three words over and over again, as if they could fly through the jagged, fatal wound killing this metal bird and into my husbands' ears.

Will they identify me by my necklace? Or my bracelet?

Will my head still be attached to my body?

Will it be my wedding rings, or the ring Owen gave me that I wear on my right hand, that identifies me?

Will it be the tattoo on my right wrist?

Will they even find my body?

Do I wish for a quick, immediate death too fast to process? Or do I want a chance to fight for my life?

I don't know. I don't know.

I don't fucking *know.*

Except those two words Carter left me with blare in my brain.

Stay safe.

My men would no doubt tell me, if they could speak to me at this moment, to fight as hard as I can.

To survive.

To come home to them.

That, however, is no longer up to me. It's up to the guy with his hands likely tightly fisted around the controls, and hopefully with a voice muffled by an oxygen mask he had time to put on as he frantically calls out a mayday and reports our coordinates to an air traffic control tower somewhere.

Hopefully, this aircraft is equipped with some sort of functional emergency GPS beacon.

Hopefully, the life rafts have EPIRBs, or equivalent devices.

Hopefully, the plane *has* fucking life rafts.

If not, we're all fucked anyway.

I breathe and close my eyes and hold on.

Hold on.

Hold.

On.

CHAPTER SIXTEEN

Susa

The world ends.

That's what it feels like.

The plane tentatively levels out for a little bit, and I lift my head from the brace position and glance around to see some passengers around us who had passed out now awakening, meaning we're likely at or under ten thousand feet.

Some of them put on their masks, some don't. All of them look as terrified as I feel.

The plane is rolling back, side to side, in a disconcerting way I don't remember feeling before on other flights, not even rough ones where the pilot has to land in heavy cross-winds. This feels like a last-ditch struggle for the life of the aircraft.

For *all* of our lives.

The shuddering starts again, bone-jarring and driving me to renewed tears.

Stay safe.

We descend again, my ears popping, the wind screaming, my teeth chattering. We're going down, and it's *not* going to be pretty.

In fact, it only takes a couple of minutes before someone's yelling something over the PA system, words that I think are,

"Brace! Brace! Brace!"

I can't really understand them, but I'm back in my brace position, and see others, who were watching me earlier, have assumed it, too.

We've flown under the clouds now. It's still damned cold, but at least it's slightly warmer than before. Looking across the aisle, to my left, through those windows, I can see grey skies above us and rain around us.

I don't want to crane my head to the right to look through the gaping hole and see how far away the water is, because I'd have to look at what's left of Mike's body to do it.

I'm no hero, like Carter. I'm a coward about some things, and I'll readily admit it.

I don't want to stare my death in the face.

I keep my eyes closed now and listen as the remaining engine throttles back. It feels like maybe they've deployed the air brakes or flaps or something.

The first hard skip off the ocean's surface as we ditch hits bone-jarringly hard and bounces us, like a stone along the water. Salty spray blows in through the hole in the fuselage, completely drenching me and Connie and everyone around us. Everyone's screaming now, including me. The water's cold, and it's rough, and I hope I can get out before I drown.

We make three more skips before we plow hard into a wave that finally grabs us and hauls us out of the sky for good, even though we're still moving due to momentum. We're no longer airborne, and we're adrift in a stormy sea that's rocking the entire cabin and will make it difficult to keep my footing.

But the pilot is a goddamned hero. He brought us down in one piece. We landed belly-down and didn't cartwheel.

The rest is up to us now.

The engine shuts off and it's eerily quiet in the seconds before people start crying, screaming, and the weird creaks and groans coming from the doomed plane's superstructure echo throughout the cabin.

I tear my seatbelt off and stand, flipping my seat cushion to find…

No life vest in the empty spot that should hold it.

Motherfucker.

I grab Connie's seatbelt, rip it off her, and yank her to her feet by her arm. She's got a life vest under her seat, and I put it on her and jerk the waist belt tight around her. A glance back at the rows immediately behind us show several more people dead or dying in the window seats in those rows.

A flash of guilt I don't have time for washes through me over giving thanks Mike got the window seat after all.

Grabbing my purse from under the seat—no, it wasn't stupid reflexes, believe me—I shamelessly shove my way into the aisle, dragging Connie along with me as we follow the red lights along the floor in the darkened cabin toward the aft exits. We're moving faster than most. But we pass an empty seat, and I flip the seat cushion to find a life vest.

Thank fucking god!

I pull it on, find Connie's arm behind me, and keep dragging her.

Along the way, I check two other empty aisle seats and grab those life vests, too.

Ahead of us, at the rear exits, the flight attendants already have both doors open and the slides deployed, although in this case, they're not so much slides as they are crappy pool floaties.

But I nearly weep with joy to see, through the windows on either side, inflated life rafts tethered to the aircraft.

I aim for starboard, where we were already, and glance up at the rear of the cabin to see an overhead bin with first aid and other informational signage on it.

Wrenching it open, I grab everything I can put my hands on

and shove some items at Connie. On our way past the rear galley alcove, I rip open the drawer marked *Water* and scoop out as many bottles as I can shove in my purse.

We're going to need them.

Now, more stunned people are moving, but water is sloshing in through the doors. Too many people are stupidly trying to head forward instead of aft, but that's to our benefit, I suppose. We're going down quickly, and it's not exactly smooth seas out there. I shove Connie out the door ahead of me, and she lands face-first on the slide, losing the items I'd handed her. I follow her out, jumping and landing on my ass. Dropping what's in my arms, I immediately grab the tether line for the life raft to drag it toward us. More passengers are making their way out now.

I yank the inflation cords on her vest, then on mine.

"Move your ass, Connie!" I scream over the storm. "Get in! *Now!*" I grab what I'd scavenged from the plane and heave everything into the raft, saving my purse for last, then grab the shit I'd handed her and throw it in, too. There's a mounting ladder on the side, and she finally heads for it. I clamber in after her.

Two men who emerged behind us help two other women into the raft before they climb in, too. A third man stumbles out of the door, lands face-first on the slide, and then tries to make it to us. We manage to grab him by the hands and haul him in.

He's not wearing a vest.

I'd shoved the extras I found into my purse but opt to hold on to them.

For now.

But...it's *bad*. The front of the plane is already mostly submerged in the rough waves. At least eight- to ten-foot seas, probably more.

And the water's not exactly bathtub-warm, combined with the wind and rain. Fortunately, it's not as cold as I first thought it was.

Wind whips around us, rain intermittently pelts us, and I take a moment to reflect.

There should be people streaming out of the exit, and they aren't. It's impossible to see through the windows as dark as it is inside the plane.

Carter would, no doubt, be grabbing people and tossing them out the doors and charging back inside the cabin to help even more. I did nothing but make a mad, nearly panicked scramble to get out.

Sure, I dragged Connie with me, but only because I knew if I didn't she would have sat there and drowned, and I couldn't have dealt with that guilt.

Mike's gone. I hate thinking like a cold-hearted bitch, but I know he loved his wife. He wouldn't want her to lose her life over his corpse. They have two married adult sons, grandchildren, a loving extended family.

Losing Mike will be hard enough on them. I can't imagine looking them in the eyes and not being able to honestly tell them I did everything possible to help save Connie.

If I even make it.

I rummage through the first-aid kit and pull out four of the five silver emergency blankets packed inside. They won't really keep us warm, but they'll keep the rain off us and maybe allow us a chance to warm up a little. I hand two over to the other women before I wrap one around Connie. Then I pull my left arm out of the sleeve of my soggy sweater, zip my purse, hang the body strap crossways over me, pull my sweater back on, and wrap my emergency blanket around me with my purse in my lap and covered by the blanket and sweater.

I have my reasons.

Mainly, those reasons being the dozen or so precious small bottles of water securely zipped inside. There's a small emergency kit attached to the inside of the raft with a couple of bottles of water in it, along with another life vest the guy missing his can wear, but no telling how long this ordeal will last.

I don't know how many people this raft can hold, but by the time the plane really flounders and it's obvious it's going under, there are only nine total in our raft—five women and four men. The line tethering us to the aircraft is about thirty feet long, putting us now well past the end of the inflated slide.

The slide on the starboard side gets cut loose by one of the flight attendants, who jumps on to it.

No one emerges from behind her.

The wind and current quickly push the slide away from the fuselage, and the raft, before we can help the people on it into the raft. Three men and two women, including the flight attendant, are clinging to it, and there's no way we'll be able to catch up to it. Two of the men in our raft desperately work to untie us so we can paddle away from the aircraft.

I try to look around, to spot the other rafts, but the one from the front entrance on the starboard side isn't visible. Either they've already cut loose and drifted away from the aircraft in the rough seas, or maybe the rafts didn't deploy, or were somehow damaged when we ditched. I can't even see the front slides now.

There are several small oars in the raft. Once we're clear of the tail section, the men manning them try to paddle us around to the other raft, but it's no use. Between the wind and the waves, we'll never be able to make it to them, either. It looks like maybe fourteen or fifteen people on that raft, and only one person, a flight attendant, on the second slide, which is also adrift now.

I wonder how many states will be planning multiple state funerals. Several governors and lieutenant governors just died, along with other state officials.

Spouses.

Hopefully I won't be adding to that number.

I wonder what Carter would arrange for mine, how Daddy would probably fight him and Owen every step of the way.

I wonder if the tragedy of losing his best friend's wife like this will help sweep Owen into a landslide re-election.

I can't help the grim smile at that thought. If nothing else, maybe my death can ensure our legacy lives another four years.

I can only hope.

When one's adrift in rough, open seas in a goddamned life raft, one is allowed to reflect like that without feeling guilty about it.

* * *

It's been maybe ten minutes since we cut loose from the plane, even though it feels like ten hours already.

But, for now, we're alive.

The men manning the paddles have given up trying to catch up with the people on either aft slide, or the aft life raft. We have some flares and other emergency supplies that I didn't spot earlier, and five other rescue packs, in addition to what Connie and I grabbed and brought with us.

No one's talking, although two of the women and two of the men are sobbing as we watch the fuselage take on water and begin its final descent. Connie's back is to it. That's probably for the best, because I watch through the wound in the starboard side of the plane as Mike's body sinks with the aircraft.

For another ten minutes by my watch we all sit there, maybe in silent prayer, maybe stunned, I don't know, when one of the women finally speaks once the plane is no longer visible.

"What...happened?" She has a soft Southern drawl that I think puts her from South Carolina.

I glance around and realize either no one else knows, or is going to speak.

Maybe they're not able to speak.

"Something ripped a hole in the starboard side of the fuselage," I say. "I think something came off or out of the starboard wing or engine. It happened after one of the hard bounces. Explosive decompression took over."

"Was it a terrorist?" she asks, wide-eyed and obviously in shock.

I shook my head. "I don't think so. I think it was stupid, bad luck and a mechanical failure."

"We need to send up flares," one of the men says, reaching for the bag.

Another stops him before I can. "Not yet," that man insists. "That's a waste right now. We need to wait until the weather clears. No one will be out looking for us yet, anyway. We're safe, for now."

But that's...debatable, and I know it. Apparently, that guy knows it, too, because I'm staring him in the eyes when his gaze meets mine. He's from Tennessee, I think. Lieutenant governor, if I remember correctly.

He was with his wife, and the governor and his wife.

None of those three people do I see in the life raft with us.

Not making a moral judgment, but I know damn well Owen and Carter wouldn't be in a life raft without me unless I was already dead.

That's when I remember seeing them sitting a row ahead of us...

Oh.

I take a deep breath. His wife probably died when Mike died.

With the rain and waves, it's impossible to see much around us. All we can do for now is hang on to the handhold lines inside the raft.

And pray.

CHAPTER SEVENTEEN

Owen

I'm struggling against building resentment as the re-election efforts kick into high gear. I know it's a necessary evil, but…

Yeah.

I resent the additional public scrutiny on me and my every waking move.

I resent the fact that it means I can't risk any late-night rendezvous with Susa for a while.

I resent it taking both of us away from Tallahassee to other parts of the state, meaning far fewer afternoon drop-ins at work, with her or Carter locking the door so the other can quickly give me what I need and crave from either of them, because we always have staff on us when we're in the office, trying to eke out as much work from us as they can.

I resent knowing we'll have another four years of this if I win, followed by another eight when Susa wins.

I resent that Susa is driving herself nearly to the point of mental breakdown, and Carter didn't call me in earlier to comfort her. That he didn't schedule time for us months ago to sit down with her, together, to gently confront her about this. She hides shit well—too damn well. Both of them do.

I know they want to protect me, but dammit, they're my husband and wife, and helpless nights like a couple of weeks ago leave me feeling like I'm not pulling my emotional weight with them.

Yet I'll still do this, all of this, because I want Susa to have my job. Because it's her dream. I *want* her to be the next governor of our state, and the easiest way to guarantee that happens is winning re-election. Our poll numbers are amazing, both for voters liking our policies and liking us personally as people. They see me and Susa as trustworthy and dependable. We have allies in lawmakers on both sides of the aisle, as well as a growing number who are switching their registration to Independent, who are responding to the poll numbers that prove the public likes and wants this centrist approach, and those lawmakers are helping us achieve it.

We make them look good, they make us look good.

This is the plan.

As much as it pains me to admit it, Carter and Susa were both right about people liking my "face." That means I can't go fucking this up. Because if I fuck it up, it means I fuck it up for *Her*.

I refuse to do that.

Susa is currently out of the country. She's on day eleven or twelve—depending on how you figure it—of a fourteen-day trip that took her to five cities in Asia as part of an official forty-person group made up of governors, lieutenant governors, and other high-ranking state officials. There's another four dozen or so family members who've paid to accompany them. It's being sponsored by an Atlanta-based organization to promote stronger business and tourism ties between a group of states in the southeastern US, and countries in the region. She awoke in Kuala Lumpur this morning. They fly to Manila later today.

Or is that tomorrow? Maybe it's technically yesterday when that happens.

I've given up trying to calculate time differences. I leave that to

Carter, because he's Carter. And because he's ordered me to focus on my job, not on Susa.

I know that's in no small part to help me not miss her quite so badly, but I still do.

At least with her out of town, it makes sense for Carter to be with me all of the time. Meaning that, for now, I'm not alone at night. While I painfully miss Susa, there is more than a small comfort to be had cuddling with Carter in bed every night. This is the longest stretch I haven't been alone in bed since taking office, and I have to say it makes me miss private life.

Despite the horrible reason I had to spend the night with them a couple of weeks ago, it was achingly sweet, too, and reminded me why I do this—because I love them.

They are my life, and I love them.

When Carter awakened me before dawn this morning, he told me about Susa's text and I texted her back, a quick *I love you*.

Then I had to hand my personal phone over to Carter to monitor after we returned from our jog, because I have a busy morning full of speaking engagements both official and campaign-related. Right now, I'm only allowed to monitor my personal phone when I'm in the office.

Because Carter damn well knows me.

I cannot afford to be checking my personal cell every thirty seconds to see if she's responded. I know Carter will let me know as soon as she replies, and I have work to do.

I had thought about going on the trip, except Carter nixed that idea with the re-election ahead of us and so much work still to do legislatively. Susa's had her fingers on the tourism issue throughout my whole term, so it made sense for her to go, along with the head of the state's tourism commission, Connie Drucker. I thought about paying out of our own pockets to send Dray and Gregory with her, but Carter nixed that idea, too. He wanted Dray here in Tallahassee, helping him with re-election planning, and

Susa concurred.

I don't argue against their plan. Not that I think I'd win that argument anyway, but I feel a little badly that Dray doesn't get this chance to travel overseas with her.

I hate that Susa's essentially alone on this trip, even though she's an adult and can take care of herself. It's *our* job to take care of her—Carter to protect her, and me to serve her.

I feel like I'm failing her. It's ironic that she thought she was failing me—yes, irrational though that thought was—by not getting pregnant.

I feel like I'm failing her, and Carter, by not getting her pregnant, even though that, too, is irrational.

Carter already had me see a doctor in Tampa and forbid me from telling Susa. He scheduled it three months ago, when I had to be there anyway for a meeting, and they took me in after-hours.

We've ruled out that it's not a problem with me. In the wake of her meltdown, Carter promises me that once Susa's back from this trip, he'll get her in at the same doctor in Tampa, go bastard extraordinaire on her, and see what we can do medically about this.

If anything.

Still, it makes me want to work that much harder, both at my job and getting re-elected, to be one less disappointment for *Her*. Again, I know that's pressure that only I am putting on myself, but there you have it. We're three people who love each other and feel responsible for the others.

Carter shepherds me through my morning. We manage to sneak alone time so he can put me down in Loyalty for five desperately needed minutes before my first appearance of the afternoon. It's a luncheon of lawmakers and other bigwigs from around the state, people focused on water quality, and we're listening to a presentation from scientists from UF about Lake O. It's being held at a large hotel downtown. The luncheon and presentation will be followed by a pool spray in the lobby, since there are so many lawmakers at the local, city, county, and state level in attendance.

I haaaate fucking pool sprays. They're barely controlled chaos, and anyone with press credentials for the event—which we usually don't get to control, unless it's an event we've put together—is able to shout out questions. Many of them are "gotcha" types of questions, even about positive topics, designed to trip me up and make me look like an idiot.

Which, considering how I'm being pulled in so many directions right now, including personally, making me look like an idiot wouldn't be too difficult to accomplish.

Fortunately, they don't have any scandals to grill me on. None that impact us in terms of they were birthed inside our administration. Today, we suspect reporters will try to get me to weigh in on a contentious special election down in Miami-Dade. It's two Democrats duking it out after a state rep died and left the office vacant when they were the incumbent and had filed to run again, so the deadline to file to run has passed. Both candidates for the special election are leveraging accusations of malfeasance at each other.

Not touching *that* with a ten-foot-pole.

During lunch, I try not to let my mind drift, to stay focused and in the moment. I'm tempted to take my work phone out and text Carter to ask if Susa's texted us yet or not.

But that wouldn't be professional, would be very risky, and would be frowned upon by my very dedicated and sadistic chief of staff.

I mean, yes, we have very safe and vanilla code questions that are absolutely boring and don't look suspicious. I can outright text Carter to ask if he's heard from Susa yet, or ask him to ask Susa to call or text me.

She's my fucking lieutenant governor. Kind of in her job description, to have work contact with me.

Although the sticking point comes from the fact that I know damn well she's out of town. But it's a...

I think.

Twelve-hour difference. And it's been a while. She's always good about texting Carter when she lands in a new city and has a connection. We specifically invested in a phone for her, personally, that would get connection all over the world. Even so, every airport now has Wi-Fi, and she can use Signal or another app to call or text Carter.

Breathe.

I try to focus on the luncheon and not look around to locate Carter. There aren't any press questions allowed inside today, but there are a couple of cameramen filming, and there are cellphones all over the place. I can't afford for anyone to catch me looking like I'm not paying attention.

I know Carter is close by, watching and listening, observing. He never leaves me, in case something happens and I need him. If I can't see him and need him, I fake cough, and he steps into my line of vision so I can let him know what I need. We have a set of pre-established cues. Sometimes I can just text him, but I have to be careful with that because of public access laws about my "official communications."

I finally survive the actual luncheon and hold back so Carter can catch up with me before heading out to the lobby for the pool spray.

I'm given an arched eyebrow. Our silent language, Sir asking if I'm okay.

I nod and we let the organizers direct me into position. Carter moves off to the side and is thumbing through his own phone when the organizer steps up to the mic to introduce me, the scientist who made the presentation, and a few other key dignitaries.

I'm not really paying much attention when I hear a bunch of phone alert tones starting to go off. Including Carter's.

And mine, as my official phone, which is tucked in the pocket of my blazer, starts going off.

Before I can get mine out of my pocket, two reporters, who are staring at their phones, both shout out questions at the same time.

"Do you have any comments about Mrs. Evans' plane disappearing?"

"Governor Taylor, will Florida be sending any assistance in the search for Mrs. Evans' plane?"

I honestly have no clue what they're talking about, and at the same time a cold, hard ball of fear congeals in my gut.

A hand clamps down on my left arm and jerks me back. I don't fight it, because I instinctively realize it's Carter. I turn, and I can't read the look on his face.

"We have to go, Owen," he softly says. "*Now.*"

CHAPTER EIGHTEEN

Carter

Over the past years, I've allowed myself to be lulled into a false sense of security. I know my two pets love me and each other as much as I love them.

Therefore, it is impossible for me to imagine any circumstance where I cannot take care of them and protect them. Even after that day at the school, where I took out the active shooter. In my mind, it was more proof that yes, I *absolutely* can protect my pets. Especially after all our years of careful planning.

Until now.

My work phone had started vibrating a couple of minutes earlier, and I'd ignored it. If I answered it every time someone called me, I'd never get anything done. I have it set right now to *do not disturb* mode. Only a few callers will make it through, anyway, in case of emergencies. But this time I look, and it's Dray.

That's when a really bad feeling sets in.

I answer it.

He sounds...

"Carter, I..." He sobs. "Susa's plane is missing."

Much like that day in the school, when I heard and recognized the first gunshots, time slows and stretches, every throb of my pulse an echoing crash in my ears.

I turn to find Owen. Dray's still talking at me on the phone, but it's already too late. Other phones are going off now, and I don't make it over to Owen before two reporters start shouting questions at him about Susa's plane going down.

I grab Owen's arm and drag him back from the reporters. I'm locked in a hell between two modes—husband, and chief of staff.

"We have to go, Owen. *Now.*"

Fortunately, I know this hotel. We've attended dozens of events here over the years, and I know the layout, have it memorized.

The man who is Owen's chief of staff breaks protocols and literally screams for the security detail to follow us as I practically drag a rightfully shocked and confused Owen out of the lobby and down a back hallway I already know from the security plans leads to an emergency exit.

Meanwhile, the man who is Owen's husband—and Susa's—is feeling helpless and desperate and confused and wants nothing more than to hold Owen and promise to try to *fix* this.

Except that would be a lie, because there isn't anything right now I *can* fix.

This is out of my hands, and I know the odds. I don't know any details.

Two of the troopers, who'd been standing along the wall near the main entrance, break into a run to follow us.

"Carter—"

"*Owen.*" I grab his shoulders and wish I could drop him onto his knees right now, but I can't. "Susa's plane went down."

I still have my phone in my hand, and Dray's yelling at me.

Chief of staff steps back into place, except, not really. Now an old and long-retired person steps forward, Sgt. Carter Wilson.

"*Dray,*" I snap at the phone. "Casualty report."

"I...I don't know. Missing. There's...there's storms in the area right now. They can't send out search and rescue yet. Pilot called a mayday, a problem with an engine, and then it dropped off radar after a few minutes.

Sgt. Wilson won't speculate—or hope. He deals with immediate facts and turns to the head of Owen's security detail. "I need a car for me. You take the governor back to his office. We need to get him out of the hotel through the back entrance. *Now.* At the office, take him in the back way and straight to his office. No press, no public. No public in his office, shut down public access to the mansion, unless it's a pre-planned event. He might want to stay at the townhouse for the next couple of days. If so, we'll need a cordon arranged to keep the public and press away. Draymond will take over for me while I'm gone. Coordinate further scheduled movements with him."

I think this guy might be former military, because he immediately shifts modes, too, responding to my clipped tones. "Yes, sir." He gets on his mic and is ordering cars be moved around, scrambling the other troopers from their current positions to join us here.

Owen's trying to get me to look at him, but I'm still on the phone. "Carter—"

I place a hand on Owen's shoulder and squeeze to silence him. "Dray, work with Julia, clear the governor's calendar today and tomorrow. Understand?"

Until I know what's going on, I need to keep Owen out of the public eye until a full statement can be drafted. "Also, get with Mike at Comms. I want you to work with him. Immediate, brief statement to be issued through Comms—'We were just made aware of the breaking news regarding Lieutenant-Governor Evans and Commissioner Drucker and her husband, and are in the process of trying to obtain more facts. Please avoid repeating speculation that has not been confirmed through official channels. We ask for the public's patience and prayers for a good outcome while we work with local officials on the ground to get the facts. While we are also aware that Mrs. Evans and Commissioner Drucker are public officials, we ask that the public please respect their families' privacies at this time, and refer all questions to this department.'

"Schedule a presser for five p.m. and have Mike run it. Add that info to the statement, along with a disclaimer to please hold all questions until then. I'll have you another statement by then. I'm sending Owen back to the office now. Do *not* put Owen in front of a camera right now, or they will never find your body. Tell Mike he'd damn well better be answering his work phone twenty-four/seven, if he wants to still have a job on the back side of this. He, or his deputy, better be answering his phone at all hours. No direct calls to the governor right now, unless it's you, Andrea, Mike, or me, or his family. Tell Julia and Andrea to refer all calls and drop-ins to Mike."

"Got it."

I hang up. When I see my phone's ringing from an Atlanta number, I instinctively know it's the firm who arranged the trip. I'm still standing there with my hand on Owen's shoulder, surrounded by troopers waiting on us to move, when I answer.

"Carter Wilson."

The man sounds weary, exhausted, like he's already made too many of these notifications. "Mr. Wilson, my name is—"

"Is this about my wife Susa's plane?"

"Yes, sir. I'm with the—"

"Company that put the tour on?"

"Um, yes, sir. I'm—"

"Fucking going to get some public condemnation from me personally when I can think straight, asshole. I'm the governor's chief of staff. Thank you for letting it leak, because me and the governor just got side-swiped with this in front of a *fucking* press pool spray. Are my wife and Commissioner Drucker and her husband alive?"

There's a pause. "I-I have no information regarding survivors yet. They haven't been able to—"

"*Where* are we being staged?"

I've thrown this guy for an obvious loop. He's been used to shell-shocked relatives demanding more info about their loved ones, I'm sure, but not...me. "Atlanta. Hartsfield-Jackson. We've already got a charter on standby and leaving at five p.m. for—"

"Text me gate and boarding info, whatever the fuck I need to get on that plane, to the following phone." I give him my personal cell number and make him read it back. "I'd *better* have that info on my phone in less than five minutes. If that plane leaves Atlanta without me and I'm not dead, I will hunt you down tonight and strangle you with your own nutsac, do you understand me?"

I hang up on him and we start moving again, with me now holding on to Owen's upper arm, both to keep him moving and to keep me upright.

I'm afraid if I stop moving for too long, I'll collapse, right here, in tears.

But Sarge's in charge to keep me vertical, for now.

Just inside the emergency exit, I stop Owen and make him look at me. "Dray's going to take over for me."

"But I need to go with you! I—"

"*Dray's* going to take over for me," I slowly repeat. "*Dray* is in charge. *You* have to stay *here*, for now. You *have* to run the state. When I have news, *then* I'll fly you out. Dray will tell you when you can comment publicly." All I want to do right now is pull him into my arms, hug him, and cry, and I can't.

Can*not*.

Because if I do that, I'll cease to function for a while, and that's a luxury I do *not* have.

I pull Owen behind a column to block us from possible public view and grab his face in my hands. "Be strong for me, boy," I whisper. "*Please*. Be strong for *Her*."

He looks shell-shocked, and I know the feeling. But he nods, giving me the long, slow blink that's our silent cue.

Yes, Sir.

I remember his personal cell is in my pocket. When I look, I see it's got several missed calls on it, too. *Dammit.*

I hand it to him, pressing his hands around it as I look into his eyes. "*Be my good boy*," I silently mouth. "*Love you.*"

He nods and silently mouths, "*Love you, too.*"

"*No* public statement from you yet," I add aloud. "Let Dray handle that. Refer everyone to Comms. I already told Dray."

I don't know how much of my conversation with Dray that Owen processed, but now I'm simultaneously feeling relieved, and feeling ashamed for that same relief, that I didn't send Dray and Gregory with Susa. This would be a tragedy compounded.

It also means I still have a trusted deputy to leave behind with my boy.

I send Owen with the security detail, one trooper staying behind with me while they're scrambling a couple of county deputies to drive lead and chase cars to go with us.

My personal phone is ringing.

Benchley.

He *never* calls me. *Ever.* I can count on both hands with fingers to spare the number of times he's called me over the past twenty years I've been married to his daughter, and all those previous times specifically had to do with campaign topics for Owen or Susa.

I answer. "I just found out," I say by way of greeting. "I have to get up to Hartsfield-Jackson. *Now.* Detail will run me home first to pack and get my passport."

He sounds choked, emotional. "I'll call and have a plane ready for you. Same company I always use, Hooper Hathaway Flight. Troopers should know the back entrance to their hangar. They'll be ready to go wheels-up when you arrive."

That nearly sends me over the edge into a crying jag, that we've banded together now, that he's supporting me without hesitation. "Thank you. I'll call you back when I'm en route."

He hangs up first.

The remaining trooper is waiting on me. "We ready?" I ask.

He nods. "Yes, Mr. Wilson."

I bite back Sarge's urge to correct him for the wrong title and follow him out the door.

*   *   *

The FHP security detail runs lights and sirens to race me home first. We're still en route there when the details about the charter waiting for me in Atlanta hit my personal cell phone. I was scrolling through news feeds that are blowing up with mostly repetitive and scant information about the missing flight. Technically, the flight is classified as missing and overdue, not crashed.

There is no land around its last reported position, and several news sites have already helpfully created graphics using the reported flight info to show its path and flight altitude.

Sarge is already grim, while the husband and Master don't want to speculate, and the chief of staff breathes through the fear clenching my gut.

I scramble and pack in under five minutes, remembering my chargers and the power converters because I have no clue where we're going or what we'll be doing. I also grab my personal laptop, and ask one of the troopers have someone deliver my work laptop and charger to the Tallahassee airport.

My work laptop—and the charter plane—is waiting for me and ready to depart for Atlanta when I arrive at the Tallahassee airport. I now know that the charter plane awaiting myself and other frantic family members from nearby states will ship us all to LAX, and from there an even larger, full-sized charter jet will carry us to Manila, and then from there…

I don't know.

Neither does the company. The initial plan is to stage us in Manila, unless further information comes to light.

I feel like shit that I didn't take the time to see if Connie and Mike have family in Tallahassee who could've taken the jet up with me, so I text Dray from my personal cell to coordinate with Benchley about transporting them on a charter to LAX, if necessary, if they can't make it to Atlanta.

And that, if I have to, I will personally reimburse Benchley later.

Dray responds with a thumbs-up emoji.

The State Department is already involved, as is the FAA, NTSB, FBI, Homeland Security, and other federal alphabet soup groups. The fact that there are literally several states in the Southeast now scrambling to figure out their line of succession for having both a missing governor *and* a missing lieutenant governor is…staggering.

Fuck. Me.

No one knows yet if this was an act of terrorism—because with that many state officials on board, it's a valid concern—or a mechanical failure of some sort.

I pray it's not terrorism, because Sarge knows their already low odds of survival go way down, if it is.

Needless to say, this is now the *only* news story in the cycle, at least for the national networks, as well as the BBC and others.

Numb functionality has set in only as an ingrained response left over from my days in the Army. I don't even want to see the video or pictures of the fucking media ambush poor Owen suffered.

Worse, I can't stay behind to help him through the aftermath, or bring him with me. He has a state to run, and I have a wife to hopefully find.

This is one of the sacrifices we make for what we do. I have to believe that my faith and trust in Dray is not misplaced, and hope he can keep my boy going for me.

I make a mental note to talk to Benchley about what he can find out regarding who led the media charge at the pool spray. I'll fucking *pay* for intel on those fuckers, if I have to.

I want their heads, but I'll settle for their jobs, or making their lives as miserable as possible. If it was one of those fuckers from FNB…

For the first time in my professional career, I seriously consider vengefully rescinding press credentials.

I find out who they are and can positively identify them? You can damn well bet I'll do it, too. I'll get their asses banned from the goddamned capitol building.

First, I need to get…*there*. Wherever it is they're taking us to personally observe the SAR ops once we leave LAX.

I have to go alone. Benchley physically can't handle overseas travel right now on his own, and I can't be responsible for him. Fortunately, he's pragmatic enough to know that.

Dray can't go, because I need him to keep Owen vertical and functional and focused on running our goddamned state. He's going to have his hands full, because my boy is rightfully going to be a fucking mess.

I'd give anything to be able to snap my fingers, right now, walk away from all we've worked for, and be curled up in Owen's arms and able to fucking cry on the flight, then hold him while he cries.

I hate flying. No matter how much I have to do it, I still hate it. I'm just better at masking my terror from others now than I used to be.

More important now than ever.

The bastard extraordinaire doesn't sweat under pressure. That's how we've been able to accomplish everything we have over the years.

Right now, the husband and Master are close to breaking. The only thing keeping me vertical is Sarge being yanked out of retirement and dusted off to help shore up the rapidly weakening chief of staff.

Hold on.

I don't want to contemplate any reality where Susa doesn't come home to us alive and well. Or, at least alive. Although Sarge grimly whispers to me that even a recovery of her body faces very low odds, especially depending on how they hit the water, and I *beg* him to shut up for a while.

Hold on.

I want to believe that the SAR teams will find her and the others and safely transport them to our waiting arms.

Or, at least *her.*

Hold on, pet. I'm coming.

I want to hope that modern technology will save her life. That there must be modern GPS technology on board to help them find them. My thumbs simultaneously rub my wedding band on my left ring finger, and the blue Doctor Who band on my right that Owen gave me, a near-match to the one he wears on his right hand, the ring I gave him the day he was sworn in as governor.

Susa also wears a similar band that Owen gave her, on her right ring finger.

I imagine she's alive and can feel my presence, my love, my strength flowing to her through that gesture. I pray that she can sense me sending her strength and determination.

I do not want to imagine any world in which Susa is not in our lives.

Hold on, Suse. Please, *hold on. Stay safe.*

During the flight to Atlanta, I compose a statement on my personal laptop, proof it, and transfer a copy to my work phone to e-mail to Dray as soon as we're on the ground in Atlanta. There is already an airport cop waiting at the charter hangar to drive me over to the other charter hangar.

Once I check in, I scroll through my phone again while I sit next to a wall outlet to help charge my phone. I have two battery packs with me but don't want to use them yet in case I don't have time to charge my phone in LA.

The story has blown up even more now, and my work phone shows I have ninety-seven missed calls, most of them not showing up in my contacts, meaning they're likely press.

Some of the shell-shocked family members sharing the flight with me don't have passports, so the State Department is already scrambling, coordinating with the US Embassy in the Philippines to get emergency passports issued.

I finally think to call my parents, who show up as a missed call on my personal phone. I have nothing to update them with, but I ask them to please not give any statements, and I give Mom Dray's work number and ask her to refer all calls for statements to him.

Which reminds me.

I call Owen's dad, and that's when I choke up and nearly break down, as I ask him to do the same, not give any statements.

I'm sure Owen's mother will use this opportunity to pop her head out of a hole like a zombie gopher to boo-hoo and make a fuss, so I text Dray's personal cell from my personal cell.

If Elandra shows up or tries to insinuate herself, shut her down with extreme prejudice. Ask Benchley for help.

I receive a thumbs-up emoji in reply seconds later.

He knows the history there, and why I ask that of him.

They give us another update before we board. No news. It's nighttime over there, and several countries are sending military ships to the area, plus fishing and commercial vessels have been diverted to look, but it's stormy. They can't put planes in the air yet. Even the US military is diverting a couple of ships that have helicopters on board to assist.

Thankfully, this flight doesn't have Wi-Fi, meaning I'm forced to go radio silent and can't torture myself or drain my devices by endlessly scrolling through news stories that don't have any more information than what officials have already given us.

I don't speak to anyone once we're in the air and heading to LAX. I…can't. I'm too close to the edge, everything frayed, and the last thing Owen needs is his chief of staff coming unglued on shaky cell phone footage sold to TMZ or some other vultures.

Like FNB.

Fuckers.

CHAPTER NINETEEN

Susa

I quickly recognize rescue isn't coming soon, maybe not even tomorrow. It's too stormy, and we are literally half a globe outside the range of the Coasties. I'm sure whatever regional search and rescue personnel they have in this part of the world are probably highly trained and good at their jobs, but this is a damn big ocean, and we're *literally* a tiny speck in the middle of it.

As light wanes and darkness falls, the storm rages around us and we hold on for our lives and huddle together for warmth under the emergency blankets from the kits. We're all silent, reality dawning on us. We can't afford the luxury of grief right now, or expend energy on something as trivial as idle chatter.

Or tears.

Not when we're still not out of the woods. We're alive—for now. Make no mistake, we're all well aware how quickly that status can change to our detriment.

What's not helping is I now remember why I hate boats. I'm seasick, and quickly puke up my stomach's contents. This is not good for a number of reasons, the most important one being dehydration.

If I can't keep water down, I'm dead in a couple of days.

If this fucking storm doesn't kill me first.

At least I'm not the only one who's sick. Two of the men also puke, although not as much as I do.

No one seems to be related to anyone else, or even know anyone else very well beyond having met them on the trip, besides me and Connie. I find that...disconcerting. Okay, Tennessee guy, I get that maybe his wife died with Mike.

But what happened to everyone else? I got Connie out of the aircraft with me. Did no one stick together?

It's something I silently note and store away without even realizing it until later. I am a political creature and used to noting odds, trends, weaknesses and strengths. It's what I was born and raised and trained to do, and it's what makes me a damn good attorney and even better politician.

Meanwhile, we endure.

Fear is still there, in my gut, but exhaustion and stress have temporarily shoved that to the side in the wake of the adrenaline crash that hits me. Before now? I thought I knew fear. The day I received the call from Momma that Daddy had collapsed, I felt afraid.

That knowledge of fear was pushed to the side the day I received the call about Carter and Owen being at the school during the active shooter incident. That was pure terror pulsing through me then, even after I'd talked to them on the phone, terror that wouldn't abate until I'd raced through our front door that night and found my two bozos drunk and well-fucked and splashing around in our tub full of my bubble bath.

To be fair, after what they'd survived, they'd earned the right to fuck, and to drain the bottle of Jack Daniel's I nearly broke my neck on when I ran into the bathroom and tripped over where they'd left their clothes strewn all over the floor.

I wish they hadn't used a full bottle of my damn bubble bath, though, although I'll never gripe about that.

Then there were all the times I willingly, even happily, let the sadist make me afraid during our games, games we haven't been able to play except on the rarest of occasions when at home in Brandon for fear of accidentally triggering a SWAT response if the wrong person overhears a scream.

That fear now feels stale and bland in comparison, where before I used to savor it like the finest wine rolling over my tongue.

This new, numb dread trying to take over my soul is a thousand times worse than the day of the school shooting. Now that we're in the water and not in danger of falling out of the sky, it gently slips into my mind and wants to tell me I should have left our oxygen masks off. It warmly smiles with foul, rotting teeth as it reminds me about dehydration and drowning and hypothermia. It chuckles as it helpfully replays Quint's speech to me from *Jaws*, where he explains why he'll never again put on a life vest.

In counterpoint to that, I can hear Carter's voice sharp and clear in my mind.

Stay safe.

My thumbs rub the bands I wear on my left and right ring fingers, one from Carter, one from Owen. I force myself not to cry, because I know damn well shedding tears is a luxury my puking body cannot afford right now.

* * *

The rain abates in the early morning hours. My watch is set to Florida time, and my phone is most likely wet, even in my purse. If it's not, I don't dare pull it out and risk ruining it, just in case I can figure out how to maybe use it later. Regardless, I have no clue what the hell time it really is. Once the sky begins to lighten a little, although it's still thickly cloudy and windy, I know it's probably at least six in the morning.

I glance at my watch, which says it's 7:01 p.m. in Florida, so I leave it set there and mentally swap the p.m. to a.m. for us. I don't know if that's accurate, but it's something. Close enough, I guess.

None of us have slept, but now two of the men are debating the use of the flare gun again—flare gun guy, and someone not the man from Tennessee. Flare Shooter Wannabe's opinion is he wants to use it before it gets too light. The other, more rational man argues to wait.

"Shut up!" They both look at me and I realize I said it out loud.

More correctly, I snapped it.

Okay, then. "We *can't* use the flare gun now," I say. "Either of you guys from Florida?"

They both shake their heads.

"Either of you have a working knowledge of water rescues?"

They shake their heads.

"Do you *see* any fucking boats, or *hear* any fucking aircraft?"

They shake their heads.

"Then why the *hell* do you want to *waste* our flares?" My shrill voice echoes off the inside of the raft. "Wait until you hear aircraft. Hell, wait until aircraft can *see* us." I point up. "We have a low ceiling right now. No damn vis."

Everyone looks up and finally seems to note the cloud cover. I might not be much of a boater, but I've observed marine SAR ops, both practice and for real, in the course of my official duties.

We're a state mostly surrounded by water, duh. We have Coast Guard stations. They have photo ops, and we usually have idiots who go out ahead of storms in boats that can't handle the seas and need to be plucked to safety.

I'd kill to see one of those mechanical orange and white birds in the sky right now.

"Can't they track us by satellite?" Flare Shooter Wannabe asks.

"Unless you smuggled an EPIRB up your ass, buddy, that'd be a hard no."

Tennessee guy laughs. His sad, blue-eyed smirk reminds me a little of Carter's amused expression.

Well, shoot. Guess I'm probably going to get labeled the Florida Bitch. I belatedly realize I'm channeling Carter.

Sure, a near-panicked, much snarkier Carter, but if I make it through this, I'm sure he'd be proud of me for telling him that later. "Because I don't see a rescue beacon anywhere, unless one's hidden in one of those packs," I add.

Motherfucking charter company better prepare for one fucking *hell* of a nasty one-star Yelp review from my ass.

The others finally seem to note the packs and start to search them for anything that might be helpful.

Tennessee guy tries to get up on his knees and look over the side of the raft, but we're still bouncing around in pretty rough swells.

"It's ten-to-twelve foot seas out there, easy," I wearily say, another round of nausea trying to make me dry-heave. "Or more. You won't see anything until it's lighter. Stay down and don't risk falling out or swamping us."

He slumps down again. "You're from Florida?"

I nod. "Susa."

"George. Tennessee."

I look at the other guy who challenged FSW and took the flare kit away from him. "Allen. North Carolina." Sounds like it, too, that nasally, round kind of soft twang.

FSW looks even more disgruntled than the rest of us. "Pat. Georgia." But he doesn't "sound Georgia," so I bet he's a transplant from somewhere else.

Collin from Arkansas rounds out the male contingent. Sarah was, in fact, from South Carolina.

Yay, me.

I'll take Regional Southern Accents for two hundred, Alex.

Lisa is from Alabama, although I can tell that as soon as she opens her mouth. And Ivy is from Virginia. At thirty-nine, I am by far the youngest person in the raft. George is probably the second-youngest, maybe his mid to late forties.

We're intermittently pelted by spats of rain, but it's not the hard, driving rain of yesterday. It's still windy, gusty, the water choppy, but I think the seas are starting to calm a little. We definitely aren't getting thrown around as much as we were before.

It's enough the taller men can take turns trying to spot any signs of land, or a boat. We can hear the wind and the water against the sides of the raft, but no man-made sounds that don't originate from one of us.

There's no signs of the other life rafts, or the slides. They don't spot any debris from the wreck, either.

It's nearly nine o'clock in the morning, according to my watch, when George suggests we inventory our water and other supplies.

During the night, under the cover of darkness, I slipped two bottles of water out of my purse, and I now hand them over. One I've taken a few sips from, and had Connie take a couple of sips. She looks practically catatonic now and I hope I can keep her alive.

Fuck, I hope I can keep *me* alive.

"We need to be careful with our water," George says. "We could be out here a couple of days."

If we're *lucky*, but I don't say that.

I'm sure there are some who will think I'm a shitty human being for hiding the water I have, but here's the thing—I don't fucking care what they think.

My last order was to stay safe.

I'm going to have a difficult enough problem with that as it is, under the current circumstances.

If there were kids in our life raft, totally different situation.

But these are adults, and my orders were to stay safe.

It might be the last thing I ever do, but I'm damn sure going to try.

CHAPTER TWENTY

It rains off and on for the next two days. We use the mylar emergency blankets to help hold and catch rainwater to replenish the empty water bottles, and we alternate drinking that with drinking fresh water, because there's a little salt spray in what we capture. We hope there's less chance of it making us sick if we do that.

At least it leaves us hopeful we might not die, if we can keep this up. We're all hungry, but it's not the biggest worry, for most of us.

Seasickness is mine. I'm trying to limit my sipping water to the evening and overnight hours, when my nausea abates a little and I can keep it down.

God, I fucking *haaaaate* boats. Daddy learned early on that I didn't do well in them, after my first canoeing experience, delayed due to that guy killing himself during what was supposed to be my first canoe trip, ended up with me puking all over him an hour into our trip.

That was the last time Daddy ever took me canoeing.

Future attempts I made to go on boats, even large ones, never end well. I am apparently allergic to anything but pool rafts. I usually have to dose myself with a crap-ton of seasick meds to function on a boat, but they practically knock me out, so it defeats the purpose.

Ironic, because I love shows like *Deadliest Catch*.

Pat, however, admits to us at sundown after our first full day adrift that he's a severe insulin-dependent diabetic. His condition rapidly deteriorates over the next twelve hours, until he falls into a coma around sundown on the third day.

Day four dawns with us staring at Pat's lifeless body, where it lays on the other side of the life raft as morning's light reveals his passing. He lasted longer than I thought he would, because I was ready to murder him less than an hour into this, when he wanted to shoot our flares.

I didn't *really* want him dead, though. Maybe he's with his wife, who died a row or two behind Mike.

I feel shitty for thinking this, but at least Pat didn't waste any of our damn flares. We haven't fired any of them yet.

"What do we do?" Sarah whispers as she stares at his body.

"He can't hear you," I say, and George dryly chuckles, which earns us both a glare from Sarah. The two of us, George and me, have sort of banded together as co-leaders of this hellish little survival cruise. We're both snarky. At forty-four, he is the second-youngest in the raft. He's also the lieutenant governor of Tennessee, which doesn't work the same as in Florida. He's actually the Speaker of the Senate, who is by default, in their state, their lieutenant governor.

Technically, he might currently be the *actual* governor of Tennessee, but whether or not the other man escaped the aircraft and survived is still up in the air, so to speak. That man, and his wife, insisted on heading toward the forward exits instead of aft, despite George trying to get them to come with him.

It was George's wife, Ellen, who perished in the window seat a row directly ahead of Mike.

I notice he wears a woman's wedding band and engagement ring on his left pinky, in addition to the wedding band on his left ring finger. I'm reasonably certain he took them off his wife's body before escaping the cabin. I saw him sadly staring at a necklace he pulled from his pocket yesterday, before he kissed the charm on it and then tucked it back into his pocket.

I'm not sure I'd be doing as good as he is, or even as good as Connie is, if I'd just lost Owen or Carter.

Or, god help me, both of them.

"We should wrap him in one of those blankets and leave him there," Ivy finally says.

"Like a baked potato?" George mutters, making *me* chuckle.

We fist bump, ignoring Ivy and Sarah's disapproving frowns. Lisa *tsks* at me.

"We're adrift in a goddamned life raft in the middle of the *fucking* ocean," I snap at her. "If you think I'm *not* going to make jokes, then just jump your happy little ass out and swim for it and pick another life raft. Be my guest." I look around. "Oh, wait—"

Connie lays a hand on my arm. "Susa," she implores, "*please*."

It's the first words she's spoken in over a day.

I sigh. "*Fine*. We should search him, find out if he has a wallet, keep anything like that, take his jewelry, and give him a water burial."

"Why take his jewelry?" Ivy asks, giving me a suspicious glare.

"If he's got family who wants it."

Ivy blinks. "Oh."

"What? You think I want to steal his wedding band and hustle my ass down to a pawn shop? *Look around!*" I sit up on my knees and hold my arms out, sweeping them in a circle. "We're in the *middle* of a *fucking ocean!*" I scream, close to snapping.

"You don't have to be *rude*," Sarah scolds.

Yep. I can see it now. When we get out of here, evvvvvveryone will hear about the Florida biatch. I'm sure Kevin Markos will *love* to nod sympathetically and *tsk-tsk* with them as he gets them to recount how the mean woman yelled at them.

If we get out of here.

Please let us get out of here.

"Susa's right," George says. "He's going to decompose."

Ivy wrinkles her nose. "That's disrespectful."

"It's *biology*," George says. "And as he decomposes, it puts *us* at risk of diseases."

He moves to do exactly what I suggested—stripping the body. I help. A few minutes later, we've recovered his wallet, passport, $22.48 in cash from his pockets, sugar-free breath mints—the rat bastard was holding out on us—his wedding ring, watch, a dead cell phone, and one of those small souvenir pocketknives, with *Pat* emblazoned on it, likely purchased at our last stop. Since we were on charter flights, they weren't dinging us for little shit like that.

"We might need that," I whisper, and George nods and pockets it. The rest of the stuff, except for the breath mints, we put in one of the zipper cases for the rescue packs. The mints go into the community pot, which isn't much.

"What about his clothes?" Allen asks.

I might regret this later, but I shake my head. "I don't want them. Does anyone else need something?"

They shake their heads.

I share a glance with George and we realize it's time.

"Don't tell my voters, but I'm a hard-core atheist," he whispers, nearly cracking me up. "You want to say something?"

"I'm not...anything," I admit. "But I can wing it." I clear my throat. Maybe it'll help rehab my rep for later. "Heavenly spirit, we release Pat to you, and hope his soul has found its way to whatever eternal reward he believed in. Please let him go in peace, and...blessings. Or whatever." I admit I sort of stumbled at the end, not knowing what else to say. "Amen," I add.

Soft *amens* from the others echo through the raft. Then George and I roll Pat out of the raft through a dip in the side where a mounting ladder is. There, his body slips into the water with a gentle *splash*.

As we watch Pat's body slowly disappear, sinking below the surface, George sighs and catches my eye. "We're gonna need a bigger boat," he whispers...

And I *cackle*. Making him smile, at least.

Whelp, there went my rehabbed rep.

Carter and Owen would be laughing with me.

That thought nearly drives me insane with grief, so I remain there for a moment, kneeling at the raft's side and staring at where Pat disappeared under the surface. I dig my nails into my palms and ride it out, the pain helping bring me back to myself as I raise my gaze and look out over the endless expanse of ocean.

Stay.

Safe.

* * *

We lose Ivy in the pre-dawn hours of day five. The sixty-four year old doesn't tell us she has a heart condition until a few hours after Pat's burial at sea. She also doesn't have her medication with her. She admits she's been having chest pains off and on since we hit the raft, but they're getting worse now, including her jaw and shoulder now hurting, burning like they're on fire.

The heart attack doesn't kill her immediately, unfortunately. She suffers for hours as we try to comfort her, listen to her sob and grieve for her husband, who was the governor of Virginia. She lost sight of him in the cabin, had gotten separated from him when he shoved her into the center aisle first and she ended up being carried aft by the press of other passengers. She doesn't know if he made it out.

We promise her we'll talk to him, tell him, and their children and grandchildren, everything she tells us.

It's almost a relief when she finally lapses into a coma and an eerie silence fills the raft, broken only by the sound of the wind and water lapping against the inflated sides.

I keep two fingers on her throat, checking her pulse. When I find she has none, reflexively I move to start CPR, but it's George who stops me by reaching over and gently grabbing my arm as he slowly and grimly shakes his head.

He's right, of course. Even if I could resuscitate her, how do we keep her alive?

It's kinder this way.

Since George and I are the two youngest and most physically fit, and we've sort of taken over and taken charge, we're now also apparently the official body-deal-withers. I mean, we're not undertakers or morticians, right?

Do they have a title for this shit?

All I know is that another good reason to remove bodies quickly, besides risk of disease, is that they're not a grisly reminder of what likely awaits the rest of us.

Or, god fucking help me, yes, I thought this, we won't be tempted to *eat* them.

Heavy is the head that wears the fucking crown, I suppose.

As George and I roll her body over the side after removing her jewelry and saying a brief prayer, I start recalculating the remaining water supply in my purse and on the raft. I can't help it. As George and I exchange a glance, I know he's thinking the same thing I am.

Who's next?

CHAPTER TWENTY-ONE

Carter

The next few days pass in an exhaustion-blurred haze. Less than twenty-four hours after this shit-storm hits my life, we've landed in Manila. We're put up in a decent hotel there, with the press strictly corralled and kept away from us.

Our main representative is a guy named Ocampo, a local official who does his best to strike a tone between cautiously hopeful and grimly realistic.

The seas are rough, and persistent cloud cover from typhoon systems training through the area are hampering aerial search efforts. But the using the plane's last known location, triangulated with its rate of descent and direction of travel, they put boats in the area and map out a grid to search. Forty-eight hours after the plane disappears from radar, they discover and home in on the black box's ping, and locate the wreckage in two hundred feet of water.

It's still too rough to mount a recovery operation, though.

Meanwhile, nineteen bodies are recovered, including that of the pilot and co-pilot—none of them Susa, Connie, or Mike.

All of them drowned, half of them wearing life vests.

From that, and the lack of trauma on their bodies, it means they likely escaped the cabin after the plane ditched, but before it sank, and they drowned later.

I don't know if that makes me feel better or worse.

Late on day three, a life raft is located with eighteen survivors. My brief flash of hope is cruelly extinguished when I learn Susa's not among the survivors. It was from the forward port-side exit, and none of the survivors recall seeing Connie, Mike, or Susa. Also, four more bodies are discovered.

Not them.

Day four, two more bodies—not them.

Day five, two of the slides are located, one with the body of a flight attendant still on it. She'd used strips of fabric ripped from her skirt to tie her left wrist to the slide.

The other slide is empty.

Day six, two more bodies.

Followed by a body a day—still not them—being recovered until day nine.

Day nine, a second life raft is located by an Australian naval vessel. The life raft is overturned and empty.

Day ten, the seas finally settle enough they can get an ROV down to the wreckage, where more bodies are spotted inside.

Including Mike's.

I ask officials to let me break the news to Mike and Connie's two sons, who have made their way to Manila with help from Benchley. The men had gone to bed for the night when Mike's identity is confirmed by me. I recognize his clothes and watch from family pictures I've seen over the past couple of days. It looks like he died in the crash, or in whatever caused the crash, because he's still belted in his seat.

There is no sign of Connie or Susa.

Day eleven begins the start of recovery operations to retrieve the black box and cockpit recorder, as well as the bodies. It's decided they'll try to float the plane, so *that* clusterfuck happens.

Two divers die when an airbag shifts and pins them under a wing, but I don't get a say in this. Other family members, including Mike's sons, want them to float the wreckage and recover the rest of the bodies and personal effects, instead of using ROVs or just trying to ID them and leave them.

I...*get* it. I do.

Along with other family members of unaccounted for passengers, I fade back and stay quiet, hoping for resolution.

I try to talk to Owen at least twice a day, his morning and my evening, and vice-versa, through video chat. I talk and text with Dray several times a day to get reports.

Dray should get a fucking raise for what he's dealing with.

If I was chief of staff for any other governor, Dray would also be getting a promotion, to my job, but I can't abandon my boy.

I won't.

As long as Owen is in office, I will be there with him.

But as we cross the two-week mark and there is no sign of Connie's or Susa's bodies...

I'm a realist.

I'm almost completely out of patience and self-control.

And my heart is...

My heart, which I thought had been completely destroyed in Germany...

That heart, which returned when I met Owen, which only healed more with Susa's love...

That heart, which I thought was full and complete?

That heart is completely broken.

CHAPTER TWENTY-TWO

Owen

Her.

It becomes my pulse, my background noise, the filter through which everything first must pass before making it to my conscious brain.

Even talking to Carter doesn't erase it.

Her.

I'm no idiot. I know even from halfway around the globe that Carter is managing me.

It's what he hasn't said to me yet that I try not to focus on.

I know the odds.

I take a screenshot of the last series of texts we exchanged with Susa and stare at it every day.

I spend hours looking at a picture of her and me that Carter took of us last Christmas. She's sitting in my lap and wearing nothing but one of my T-shirts and a red bow I'd just playfully stuck on her head, and we're sitting in front of the Christmas tree in the mansion. The smile on our faces as we stare into each other's eyes tells a story of two people very much in love.

I have the security detail stop by the townhouse every day. Ostensibly, so I can bring in the mail for Carter and Susa, but what I do when I unlock their front door and walk inside is go upstairs and press my face against *Her* pillow. And His, but mostly Hers.

I'm afraid, because I think it smells less like her now than it did, and I don't know what will happen when I can't smell her there anymore.

I've started using her shampoo every day.

Every day, after I smell her pillow, I set my phone's timer, drop into Devotion on the floor next to her side of the bed, and spend the next five minutes crying.

Once my timer goes off, I wash my face, blow my nose, use eye drops to help take some of the red out, and return downstairs so my detail can drive me to the mansion.

The troopers are professionals and never mention my red eyes or puffy nose when I emerge from Carter and Susa's townhouse.

Dray is amazing. When he realizes that I'm not eating before I arrive at or after I leave the office, he starts bringing food in for me. Sometimes smoothies, sometimes more, if I can handle it. He makes sure I'm at least taking in some calories during the day, and hounds me every bit as hard as I know Carter would, if he were there.

I give one official statement about the crash, on the first day, a statement that Carter drafted with Dray's help and signed off on before the charter from LAX took off.

It was short, concise, and I still managed to break down in tears before I finished reading it.

I don't watch the news. When I asked Dray, he said that clip, of me crying, was looped on nearly every channel for four days straight, the summation of collective grief, until the survivors were found and bumped it off the top of the charts.

I don't want this anymore.

I can't do this.

Maybe if Carter was here, yes, but I can't do this. Not like this.

Carter hasn't said it yet, but I suspect he thinks she's gone.

I know she'd want me to continue, to run for re-election, but if she's really gone…

If Carter tells me to, I will, especially if he says we have to do it for her memory.

But…

All I want to do is curl up in Carter's arms and cry.

Just…

Cry.

Especially when one of the last memories I have of us making love is from *that* night, when Carter called me to the townhouse, when she finally broke down and I had to be strong for her, holding her, trying to love the grief from her soul, letting her use my body in a different way than usual, trying to be the one to pull her soul back together when she spent so many years being the one to tie my loose parts in place.

She gave me a ring that I wear on my left ring finger. It doesn't look like a wedding band, but that's what it is, to me. Just like the ring I wear on my right finger is a wedding band from Carter. The ring she gave me is black with silver Celtic knots scrolling around it.

Inside, it simply says, *MINE.*

I hope she understands how much I love her.

I hope, if I end up giving up and leaving office early, that she forgives me, wherever she is.

I hope, despite his own grief, that Carter is strong enough to keep me living, because, honestly?

I really don't want to.

CHAPTER TWENTY-THREE

Susa

Sarah is seventy-two on the night of day eleven, when I watch her slip off her life jacket, remove her rings and necklace, and carefully ease herself through one of the cutouts where the boarding ladders are located. It's the cutout closest to where I'm sitting.

I'm the only other one awake. I've started trying to sleep during the days, under a mylar blanket, for what little shade it gives me, and staying up at night. It helps me not feel as thirsty—or miserably sick to my stomach—and I usually take a night watch. It also allows me to sneak sips of water. I'm down to four bottles in my purse. I've been sharing with Connie and George, swapping out bottles of rain water with bottles of fresh water. I don't know if they've caught on or not. If they have, they don't say anything.

We've been lucky that intermittent rains allow us to capture enough salt-tinged rain water in the mylar blankets to refill our bottles, but our luck will eventually run out. We are careful to only drink a full bottle each when we have enough collected in a blanket to refill them, and all the empties are full.

When we don't have rain, we only sip.

Sarah's husband was the lieutenant governor of South Carolina. She revealed to us yesterday that they'd diagnosed her with pancreatic cancer a month ago. Inoperable.

They hadn't even told their kids yet.

She'd remained mostly quiet throughout our ordeal, but yesterday she became a damned chatterbox. I didn't understand, at the time, why she was telling us all this now, but she started talking, and talking.

And *talking*.

This was going to be a sort of bucket-list trip for her and her husband, and she wasn't going to get treatment for her cancer. She was going to keep going until she couldn't go any longer. Once his term was up, he was going to retire from public life and spend the time with her. She refused to let him retire early.

We don't know if her husband made it or not. He shoved her out the starboard aft exit and disappeared back into the cabin to try to help someone else from their group who'd fallen in the center aisle.

She never saw him again.

He couldn't swim, and he wasn't wearing a life vest. He put the one from under his seat on her, because her seat didn't have one.

Ooooh, fucking Yelp, you just wait.

We've all had to answer the call of nature, although rarely now, because we're barely drinking and not eating, obviously. So I don't think much of what she's doing, at first, until I actually process that she's removed her jewelry and life jacket.

Sarah realizes I'm awake when I sit up. She pauses and meets my gaze, gives me a sad smile, and then disappears into the water. When I get up to look, I see her floating on her back, a peaceful smile on her face as she pushes away from the raft. She waves good-bye to me.

I'm going to call out to her, or at least raise an alarm, when I hear a voice behind me.

"Let her go," George whispers.

I turn and see he hasn't moved from where he was sitting next to me, but his eyes are barely open. We're all sunburned and squinting and having problems with our skin cracking, drying out. The men, including George, are all sporting scruffy beards now.

I probably look like a wookie.

"But—"

He shakes his head. "Let her go."

We're now down to six.

In my mind, I recalculate our water supply.

* * *

I'm sneaking a swallow of water the night of day thirteen when I finally process I'm hearing...*something*.

It's...

It sounds like *waves*, but it doesn't sound the same as what we've been hearing against the sides of the raft.

My mind is puzzling this over for the better part of an hour when enough brain cells finally band together to smack me upside the head. I rise, trip, and fall flat on my face, waking everyone up when I scramble to my feet and start looking around the outside of the raft.

In the distance, thanks to the moonless night, I spot the soft bioluminescent glow of waves breaking against a shoreline.

My hoarse, wordless scream gets George up on his feet. All I can do is point and scream. We've all seen daytime mirages— another reason I opt to try to sleep through the days—but George also starts wordlessly screaming and stumbles as he dives for two of the paddles, handing me one. We start paddling like crazy motherfuckers, now with Allen and Collin both trying to help.

It takes us nearly an hour, but we finally hear scraping beneath us as we bottom out in the shallows. George is laugh-sobbing as he falls out of the cutout and stands, showing he's in water that's not even waist deep on him. We're all wordlessly sobbing as Allen and Collin both clamber out and help George drag the raft out of the water.

I nearly face-plant when I try to get out, and George has to catch me and help me out, but...

It's fucking *land*.

I don't know if it can rightfully be called an *island*, because it can't be more than three thousand square feet, if that.

But it's not.

Fucking.

Ocean.

The six of us sit there, crying and holding each other in the dark.

* * *

I must have used up what little energy I had left, between the paddling and trying to get out of the raft, because as my watch shows it's 5:30 in the morning, I realize now that I can't stand. My body still wobbles like I'm on the raft, and my knees won't support me. I have to crawl or drag myself across the ground.

George, Allen, Collin, and Connie have all scoured the tiny spit of land in the dim light for everything possible we can use. There's various plastic debris, some random metal, pieces of styrofoam fishing buoys, and other crap. There's some tufts of grasses at the highest point of our current residence, which is maybe ten feet above the water, if that, but that's all in terms of vegetation on the mostly rocky land. We must have arrived at high tide, because the water eventually starts to recede, giving us a few more yards of real estate all the way around.

I catch sight of something moving near me in the pre-dawn gloom. Reflexively, I grab a paddle and smack the fucking *crap* out of the moving thing, hearing a sickening and yet satisfying *crunch* as I do.

Turns out it's a crab.

Motherfucker.

I let out another wordless scream that probably sounds more psychotic than celebratory as I point to my smashed prize.

It takes the men less than five minutes to grab paddles of their own and start searching for more of the little fuckers, where they're mostly hiding among the piles of seaweed left bundled at the high-tide line. Connie and Lisa are nearly as bad off as I am, Lisa sitting there and silently watching, Connie aimlessly standing in one spot with another paddle, but not much help as she looks around her at the ground.

We end up with fifteen. They're less than four inches across, most way smaller, but George uses Pat's pocketknife to start splitting them open and divvying them up. While my stomach rebels, I manage to keep a couple of bites down but hand the rest of mine off to Connie when I realize if I risk any more, it's just going to come up again. I need to preserve the water in my stomach.

She looks like she's going to argue with me before she sighs, takes it, and eats it.

* * *

Once it's fully daylight, the men carefully drag the raft all the way on shore. We don't want to lose it. We're not out of the woods by any stretch of the imagination, but we're still alive.

#notdeadyet

I can barely talk now, thanks to screaming and my swollen, cracked lips, but George, at least, can understand me. I manage to tell him about an episode of *Mythbusters*, where they dug a hole in beach sand, stuck a container in the bottom, and used a plastic tarp over the top to condense water.

They find one patch of ground above the high-tide line that might work. George and Collin use scraps of metal they scavenged to start digging, and three hours later, they have made a bowl in the bottom of the hole with one of the mylar blankets folded to catch the most water, and weighed another blanket around its edges over the top of the hole. I'm afraid to use one of the bottles to catch the water, even with the top cut off, for fear that we might position it in the wrong place. We can't see inside with the top blanket over the hole.

By the end of the day, we've collected almost a full bottle's worth of water.

It's...something.

We set it to the side.

Now, it's me and George both sitting up and taking night watch.

The crabs return.

I'm the first one to spot that, and George grabs a paddle and starts whacking, waking Allen and Collin in the process.

We end up with twenty this time, and I manage to keep two down, and give one of mine to Connie.

I still can't walk, though. I'm too weak.

* * *

By the early morning hours of day nineteen, I'm unable to keep much down. George and I had fallen asleep. We awaken to find Lisa sitting in the surf, laughing, and drinking sea water cupped in her hands. When he tries to grab her, she fights him, until he finally stumbles back and gives up.

He doesn't have the energy to expend to try to save her.

Allen and Collin try to talk to her, and she ignores them.

Connie sits there watching and cries.

I'm not...doing so hot. We're really rationing water like crazy now, because we haven't seen rain in two days.

Lisa is the first lady of Alabama, and fifty-nine years old.

She eventually crawls out of the surf and collapses facedown on the ground.

George and Allen get her rolled over and, with Collin's help, drag her up past the high-tide line.

She never regains consciousness. I keep an eye on my watch and George checks her pulse every thirty minutes.

Somewhere between five-thirty and six that evening, she dies.

I don't even try to eat any crab that night, and make the others take my share, especially George, since he moved around the most today. My secret purse stash of water is long gone, and without any rain, our little makeshift water catcher won't keep up with demand.

We have maybe three days of water left.

* * *

By late afternoon of day twenty, I haven't been able to stand in six days. Seven?

I don't know now.

George stays close to me, and any time he sees me try to move toward the water, he forces me back to the raft.

Now, he sits against the outside of the raft with me propped against him, always keeping an arm around me so he can feel me if I move. He tries to keep me shaded as much as possible.

I've started talking. Connie's asleep inside the raft with Collin. Allen is sitting on the other side of the island, keeping watch.

Now I understand why Sarah started talking.

Because I know soon I won't be talking anymore.

"Carter lost two brothers," I say to George. "Pete and Tom. They were both killed in action." I squint as I stare out over the dark, velvety water in the waning light. "We tried so hard to have kids, me and Owen."

"Carter," George says.

"Huh?"

"You said you and Owen tried to have kids. Owen's your friend. Carter's your husband."

I nod. "I'm dead anyway."

"Stop talking like that. Something could happen."

I turn my head. "It's the three of us," I say. "It's not just me and Carter. It's Owen, too." I snort. "I own him."

"Susa, honey, maybe you should try to sleep. Save your strength."

I shake my head and I struggle not to cry. "I'm never going to see my guys again. We've been together since college. Like *Fifty Shades*? We were ahead of the bell curve."

"Um, oh."

"That's what I mean by I own him. He's mine, and we both belong to Carter, my husband."

George holds a bottle of water to my lips. "Take a sip, Susa."

I try to push his hand away. "You shouldn't waste any more water on me."

He gently pulls my hand away. I don't have the strength to fight him. "You let *me* decide that. Sip, girl. *Now*."

For a moment, he reminds me so much of Carter that I do as he says.

I feel better in the evenings and at night. I can keep water down at night, and he knows that. He tries to get me to drink more at night.

"I had a meltdown a couple of weeks ago," I admit. "I mean, before the trip."

"What kind of meltdown?"

"Because we can't have kids. Four years we've tried now. Carter can't have kids, but Owen can, so Carter had me and Owen trying. I guess I've been getting more upset about it, even though I thought I was doing okay. Then Carter went behind my back to my doctor and got my prescription for birth control pills refilled, and left them for me on the bathroom counter. I chucked them."

"Why?"

"Because fuck it, why take them if I can't get pregnant? I think it was his way of trying to tell me that it was okay, that I didn't have to keep trying, if I didn't want to. That was before the meltdown. Like, days, or something. Maybe weeks. I don't even remember now."

Thinking's hard. Really hard. But I want this all said so maybe he can tell my guys for me. "Then he tried to talk to me about seeing a fertility specialist, if I really wanted to keep trying, and…" I feel shame about this now. "I snapped."

"Snapped?"

"I don't even remember most of it. I came up off the couch swinging and he had to pin me down and text Owen to come over and help calm me down."

"Ah. You are *feisty*."

"Yeah. Sort of." I sigh. "Tell them I'm sorry, please? I'm sorry I didn't listen to them and let them take me to a doctor. That I'm sorry I was so stubborn."

He adjusts the shade of the mylar blanket over me. "It'll be getting dark soon," he says. "About another hour. You'll feel better then, sweetie."

I wonder how many more sunsets I'll see. "If they rescue you…" I don't want to cry and waste the precious few swallows of water I had. "Please tell Carter and Owen I love them. And that I'm sorry for my meltdown."

"You'll tell them yourself, girl."

I finally squint and try to focus on him. Hard to recognize him now with the beard, but his blue eyes peer back at me from his sunburned face. "I'm not going to make it," I tell him. I know beyond him is Lisa's body. "Don't let me start drinking salt water," I beg. "Please? You have my permission to smack me with a paddle." I giggle. "Just not on my ass. I like that too much."

He smiles. I think. Hard to tell as blurry everything looks. "You talk an awful lot for a girl who's convinced she's dying."

"You sound awfully cocky for a guy stuck on Gilligan's Island.

Look how that worked out for them."

"They got off."

I snort. "Oh, that *wasn't* a double-entendre? Sorry."

He laughs. "No, really. They were rescued. There was a movie."

"Yeah, but they ended back on the island. I think that was the plot for *Lost*, too. Metaphor for Hell." I gasp. "Shit!"

"What?"

"I think I *literally* just came up with the perfect analogy, and I'll never get to tell anyone else about it." I fight the urge to pout. "Tell Carter I said the whole cycle of *Gilligan's Island* is basically the uselessness of existence. Futility. Failure."

"That's…deep."

"I never had kids to watch it with. We never got to have kids."

He holds my hand and does a passable British accent. "We're not dead yet."

I gasp. "You've been holding out on me! You like Monty Python. You rat bastard."

I almost start crying again when I think of Carter.

He chuckles. "My wife hates Monty Python." He sadly sighs. "Hated," he whispers.

Fuck. "I'm sorry." He's been so strong, not talking much about losing his wife. His kids lost their mom, might lose him, too.

Here I am, whining, when I have two perfectly good and safe husbands waiting for me at home.

At least they won't be alone. They'll have each other.

He squeezes my hand. "Thank god the kids didn't come with us. I almost bought them tickets, but my brother was going to Alaska for three weeks and offered to take them all with him. Ellen wanted them to go with him so we could have some time alone."

Kids. "How many kids again?" I know this already from our talks, but once I die, he might not have anyone to talk to, depending on how long the others survive. I feel guilty I'm going to be abandoning him.

"Two boys and a girl. Nineteen, seventeen, and fifteen."

I squeeze his hand. "Sorry."

He looks at me. "Trade you a kid for a husband?" He smiles.

I think. Hard to tell with the scruff on his face.

"I don't know. You a Top or a bottom?"

"Oooh, me? Totally a Top. Ellen liked when I blindfolded her and tied her to the bed. That's as kinky as we ever got as far as sex, because that's also how we ended up with three kids."

"Yeah, well, that'll do it. What else did you guys do?"

"Had to get sneaky because of three kids. But she was...mine."

Ah. Maybe that's why we clicked so well. "I'm sorry."

"Thank you." His hand finds mine and squeezes, stays there, and I don't mind.

"You took her rings," I softly say. "And was that her day collar? The necklace?"

He sounds choked up. 'Yeah."

"My bracelet," I say. "And my necklace. Please make sure they get back to them. And my rings." I indicate my right ring. "Owen gave me that one. He's our husband, even if we can't tell anyone."

"They're lucky guys. I'm sure they're worried to death about you right now. Make sure you drink when I tell you to, or I'll tell them you were a bad girl and they *won't* spank you."

"Ah, you rat bastard. And here I thought we were friends." I sigh. I want to sit up, but I can't. I don't have the strength to do anything but lean against him. "How much water is left?"

"Allen's working on another pit." George shifts position and helps me sit up, leaning against him. "We'll be okay."

I make a noise. "Did I actually pray for it to *stop* raining at one point?"

"Yeah. How stupid were we?"

"I'm from Florida. You'd think I'd know better. Take the rain when it comes and be grateful for it." We sit in silence until sunset.

Our backs are to it, because we've gotten used to sitting with our backs to the sun whenever possible. "Turn me around," I softly ask. "Please? So I can see it?"

He does. I can barely hold my head up. "Feel free to eat me when I die," I offer. "I should have some ass meat left. Maybe my boobs. Tell Carter and Owen I gave you permission."

George chuckles. "I can see why you need two men to corral you if you're this spunky when you're convinced you're almost dead. You must have put a hurting on Carter the night you swung on him."

"I did. I got bitey, too. He had to wear long sleeves to hide the marks."

"Lucky man."

"Oooh, the governor of Tennessee is making a pass at me. I think."

He chuckles. "Lieutenant governor."

"Nope. You probably got a promotion."

"He might have made it."

"Nah. Battlefield promotion." I manage to raise my hand enough to sort of salute him. "Lucky bastard, *sir*," I tease.

Aaaannnd, once again, I'm thinking about Carter. About his words to me that night back in college, when I asked to be his and he proposed to me.

My smile fades. "Dying's easy," I say. "Surviving's harder."

I don't think I ever *truly* appreciated what he meant that night.

I do now.

"You're not going to die, *girl*. I don't give you permission to do that."

He's trying so hard. I can't help it. I'm crying, but it's mostly dry crying because I'm so dehydrated. "Please tell them," I whisper. "Tell my guys I love them. Tell Carter I tried. That I tried to stay safe. That was his last order to me, to stay safe. Please tell him I tried."

He shifts me again, holding me. "Shhh. It's okay, sweetie. I'm *not* leaving you behind. We'll both make it, I promise."

"Tell them I want them to get married," I whisper. I don't know why I'm bothering to whisper, but oh, well. "Tell them to please be happy. I want them to be happy together. And tell Daddy I'm sorry I didn't get to be governor."

"I'd vote for you." He kisses the top of my head and stays there like that, his face in my hair, his breath warm against my scalp. It reminds me of the early days with Carter.

I hope I'm reminding him of good times with Ellen. I don't begrudge him this at all.

Helloooo, *dying*.

We might be getting more rain soon, though. The wind has picked up a little today, and it looks stormy off to the southeast.

Probably not soon enough to help me, but maybe Connie will make it.

Hopefully George will make it. Those kids deserve to have their dad back.

I bet he's going to be a kick-ass governor.

I'm staring out at the horizon as it turns a deep, beautiful purple, and I know my time is short because I'm seeing little lights bobbing around.

"I see angels," I say. "Well, I'm fucked."

He snorts. "You're still alive, honey."

I go full-on Monty Python. "No, I'll be stone-cold in a moment." I snort. "Stone crabs. I'll be stone crab in a moment."

"Nah. You've got to tell me all sorts of raunchy shit to pass on to your guys. You can't leave me hanging like that. I'm a widower now. I need stories for my tell-all book I'll write when I'm eighty to embarrass the hell out of my kids. Ellen would want me to do that."

I'm still seeing angels. "If I'm so alive, Dom Smart-ass, why am I seeing *them*?" I manage to point.

George finally lifts his face from my head and then promptly lets out a scream. He lunges over the side of the raft, dropping me in the process. I fall back, painfully hitting the ground.

He's still screaming, sobbing, and seconds later, I hear a *phwomp* and a painfully bright light arcs up, up, up, streams of light doubling and tripling in my vision.

Now the others are all screaming, and another *phwomp*, another light.

George returns and helps me sit up, keeping one arm around me so I don't fall over again. He's sobbing and laughing and sobbing and laughing and sobbing and...

You get the idea.

Then he shoots off another flare with his other hand, wordlessly screaming before he kisses my cheek and starts screaming again.

I squint reeeeallly hard.

The angel lights change course, from where they were slowly tracking across the horizon, and start heading our way.

CHAPTER TWENTY-FOUR

Carter

I know there's not really anything I can "do" but sit and wait and hope for news.

Any news.

Except the bitch of it is that I'm a realist. My military training comes back to me despite me trying to will the knowledge from my brain. Three days without fresh water, max.

It's been three fucking *weeks*.

I hate being a realist.

The SAR ops has been scaled back, and is now being considered a recovery mission. The black box was recovered, and Mike's body was found strapped into a starboard seat on the wing.

Susa and Connie's bodies were not in the cabin, nor were they among any of the bodies recovered so far.

That means nothing, of course.

Two of the life rafts, and one of the slides, are unaccounted for. The one overturned life raft that was found doesn't give me much hope. No one knows which life raft it was. The eighteen survivors plucked from the life raft say they lost sight of everyone else in the storm in the immediate aftermath of the ditching.

It's not looking promising, no matter how I ask Owen to please breathe and focus on work and to not give up hope.

Maybe that's cruel of me to say to him, to not give up hope, but I'd rather be with my boy when I finally acknowledge the inevitable.

Be there to hold him.

I *know* I need to book my return flight to Florida, but I can't yet make myself acknowledge the finality of that decision.

Of returning empty-handed.

Of returning…*alone*.

Of facing my boy and having to admit to him—and everyone else—that she's *really* gone.

Hypothermia. Drowning.

Did she die of exposure? Did she drown adrift in open water? Did sharks attack her before or after she died?

Did she drown trapped in the aircraft and her body washed free?

Was she aware of what was happening?

Was she scared and screaming for us as the plane went down?

Part of me hopes she died instantly and unaware in the initial engine failure and cabin decompression. That she was dead before the plane even ditched.

Except the fact that she wasn't found strapped into a seat would tend to discount that theory. The seatbelts on the two other seats in Mike's row were intact, unbuckled. They weren't ripped or torn from their anchors, meaning either the seats were vacant—unlikely—or their occupants unfastened their seatbelts at some point and were not belted in when things went to hell.

The seat cushions were displaced and no life vests founds. Again, that means nothing. Not really.

Another option I don't want to contemplate and will never mention to Owen or anyone else—that maybe they *hadn't* been wearing their seatbelts when it happened, and they were both sucked out of the plane during the initial event.

It is a grim possibility one of the NTSB investigators confirmed when I confronted him about it in private, *needing* to know if it was possible despite not wanting to know.

If that happened, their bodies could have ended up anywhere, and likely will never be recovered.

Likely hit the water like sacks of concrete and disintegrated. The plane was at thirty-two thousand feet when the event happened.

Like I said, that's not a possibility I really want to think about, for a lot of reasons.

Part of me who doesn't even believe in god prays my pet didn't suffer, didn't know, wasn't in agony.

Wasn't afraid.

Part of me hopes that, if she wasn't wearing her seatbelt, she took a nap, like she's wont to do on longer flights. That she didn't have time to don her oxygen mask, and was killed so quickly that she never even knew what happened.

A *very* large part of me hopes that.

#realistssuck

I will *never* share these thoughts with Owen, or with anyone else. My boy wants to hope they'll find her and Connie both, alive, some sort of movie miracle. That maybe they washed up on an island and they'll pluck them off it with a pet volleyball and some FedEx packages, or some shit like that.

I know how hard this is on Owen, being alone and in Florida, and it makes my heart ache even more. I feel like I've failed both my pets. I couldn't protect one, and I'm not there to console the other.

Me? I compartmentalize. I *have* to. It's the *only* way I can function at this point. It's a skill I learned after losing Tom and Pete, and my friends. A skill I honed to fine precision during my time in-country, especially after I was wounded and my two best friends were killed, another gravely injured.

Otherwise, it'd be too damn tempting to find a gorgeous beach somewhere, watch a sunset, and suck-start a pistol.

Except…I can't.

Owen.

I can't do that to him. I can't leave him alone. That'd be cruel beyond measure, and I've failed enough already as a husband and Master.

Everyone here has been kind and bending over backward for us. They ruled out terrorism, since it was a charter flight. Based on the cockpit recordings and black box data, it looks like a stupid, catastrophic mechanical or structural failure with the starboard engine, probably triggered by the severe turbulence they encountered.

Fricking random bad luck.

I want to rage and scream but I keep that locked deep inside me. I keep my expression as neutral as possible and nod when talked to, carefully choosing every word I say before I say it. Despite all the US and foreign government wonks here now from various alphabet-soup agencies, somehow *I* have become the de facto spokesperson for what's left of the group of family members.

The stoic husband, the decorated war vet, the chief of staff.

The widower-apparent.

Part of me starts to think maybe I should ask Owen if he wants to pull out of the race. No one would blame us if he did. We can quietly return to Tampa at the end of his term, grieve, and eventually get married. Maybe go to Vegas, to the same chapel where I married Susa. Exchange the same vows.

Try to love as much pain as we can from each other's souls.

Part of me knows if I did that, if there was any truth to the theories about ghosts, that Susa would mercilessly haunt us for giving up politics after working so damn hard to achieve as much as we have.

I know her. I know my sweet, vicious little pet. She'd be screaming at me to capitalize on this, use it, mercilessly *leverage* it into a slam-dunk victory. Milk every ounce of sympathy we can from it.

I *know* she would.

But...to be honest? Even the bastard extraordinaire has his limits. I don't have the heart to do that, I don't think. Not unless Owen tells me that's what he wants, to honor her like that by staying in and continuing to work for re-election.

If he does? Then absolutely, that's what we'll do.

Otherwise...

I don't know anymore. The plan has...dissolved.

I feel like a significant part of *me* has dissolved.

I'm not sleeping more than an hour or two at a time. My nightmares plague me—both the old ones of Germany, and that day in the desert, as well as new ones.

Of Susa screaming and reaching for me, her hand slipping out of mine every time before she's pulled into an abyss where I can hear her screaming and can't reach her.

Can't save her.

Can't keep her safe and protect her, the way I promised I would.

I cannot make myself admit that I'll never again stare into her blue eyes. Don't want to admit I'll never hear her sweet moans as I make her come.

Refuse to admit that my heart breaks even more knowing the three of us will never become parents.

That it's Owen's most secret dream, and one I can no longer make come true for him, shatters my already shredded heart into a million jagged pieces.

* * *

It's the middle of the night when my personal phone rings. I don't recognize the number, but I groggily answer anyway because I'm not sure who I gave this number to over the past three weeks. I've gotten used to hanging up on reporters.

"Carter Wilson."

At first, I have difficulty understanding the caller and his accent when the man hurriedly introduces himself. It's more my exhaustion and just-awakened state than his thickly accented English.

Yet it's his next words that send a jolt of adrenaline pinballing through my system.

"I have positive news about your wife, Mr. Wilson. She has been recovered, and is being transported now with others."

At first I think the man is fucking with me. As much as I'm desperate to at least recover Susa's body to bring her home so Owen and I can have her cremated and keep her with us in some small way, I know the chances of them ever finding her or the other fifty-plus passengers who are still unaccounted for is slim to none, at this point. Not this long out. I only hope she died quickly and didn't suffer.

I hope she died knowing how much we desperately loved her.

That there will never be another woman in our lives.

I close my eyes and struggle to process the caller's words, what he's saying not quite piercing through my exploding grief. I don't know why he thinks his news is worthy of the label "positive," but whatever. I'm sure his English is way better than my Filipino, or whatever language he grew up speaking here, so I probably have zero room to talk.

"I'm sorry, I can't understand you," I say, finally interrupting his increasingly agitated monologue. I'm still hung up on his first sentence after he introduced himself. "Can you *please* start over and repeat what the first thing was you said?"

"Susannah Evans. Your wife. She and others are being

transported by boat to Bandar Seri Begawan. They arrive, maybe six hours, maybe seven."

I'm too ragged and raw. I close my eyes, the sob escaping me. Closure, at least, can happen now. Owen and I will always grieve her.

Now how to break the news to my boy?

"Thank you," I manage to choke out. "What do we have to do now? To claim her body?"

I've been expecting this, but not really thinking I'd have it, especially three weeks out. I figured we'd be planning a public memorial for her with nothing but pictures to celebrate her life, and—

"She asked for you."

I'm not sure if my heart's actually stopped or not.

"What?" I'm thinking this idiot obviously doesn't know English as well as he thinks he does, and how cruel of him to fuck with me like this.

"She *ask* for you," he insists.

I finally force myself to sit up, feet on the floor, my body protesting as I do. I rub my forehead against the massive headache I'm almost hoping is an aneurysm so it damn well kills me right fucking *now*.

"Look, *dude*, I don't know what you're trying to say, but—"

"She is *alive*. They find her and others *alive*. Your wife, Susannah Evans."

"*What*?" I know I scream it, but I'm wide awake now, adrenaline spiking my pulse in a way it hasn't since that day in the desert so many years ago before the car bomb forced my life into an unanticipated direction. Or the day at the school, when I had to be a soldier again.

I'm standing now, with no memory of even getting out of bed. "What do you mean she's *alive*?"

"*Alive*. She and four others. Please, pack quickly. We send bus to hotel for you and other families within hour. We will fly you there. Please, wait downstairs in meeting room. Mr. Ocampo to arrive shortly to talk details. He is en route."

"Okay." I can't think. "Okay. Alive? Okay. Wait, alive? *Really*? Are-are you sure it's *her*?"

I will absolutely fucking track down and rage-murder this fucker with my goddamned bare fucking hands if it fucking turns out he's fucking wrong about her fucking identity and it's someone else.

Fuck.

"Yes! Susannah Evans. They are on fishing vessel. Rescued off island. Please, hurry, Mr. Wilson. Mr. Ocampo asks no press yet. *No* press. Please. He talk to families first."

"I...thank you. Thank you, I will. Thank you!"

The line goes dead and I'm still holding my phone to my ear, trying to...process.

Alive?

She's alive!

I slump onto the bed and my hands are trembling so badly I can't manage to get my goddamned phone to open my contacts. I finally have to use voice commands to ask Siri to call Owen's personal cell phone for me.

My whole body is shaking. When Owen answers, I'm already crying. Now, hearing the sound of his voice, I completely crumple.

Sobbing.

Poor Owen probably assumes the worse when he hears my voice, but before he can ask me anything, I'm babbling. "Where are you? *Right* now. Where are you?"

"Sir?" He sounds confused by my question, so I clarify, the bastard extraordinaire making a brief appearance.

"*Where* the *fuck* are you, *boy*?" I scream.

"I'm in my offi—"

"Alone?"

"Yes, S—"

"Alive." I choke up saying it. "She's *alive*. They found her alive! They just called me and told me to pack, that they're going to fly us to where they are. They found five people alive, and she's one of them!"

I know it's the stress, but I start giggling when I hear his choked sobs.

"A-alive? Are you *sure*?"

"The guy said he is. Also said not to notify any press yet. I honestly don't know where the fuck he said they're taking them, they're on a fishing boat or something. Rescued off an island. I've got to get packed and meet everyone downstairs. Ocampo's on his way over to talk to us. It's the middle of the night here, and he woke me up." I'm babbling again, and I know it.

Alive!

CHAPTER TWENTY-FIVE

Owen

Thank god I'm in my office with the door closed when I receive Carter's call. From the way Carter had been crying when I answered, I was absolutely certain this was *not* the news he was going to drop on me.

For once in my entire life, it's never felt so fucking good to be so goddamned wrong about something.

"Can I tell Benchley and Michelle?" I manage to choke out.

"Yeah, but tell them no press."

"Can we fly out and join you?"

"Not yet. I don't know what kind of shape she's in, or when she'll be able to travel. I-I...I don't even know... I mean, I have no fucking clue where they're taking her, or where they're taking us to meet them. I don't want any press near her yet."

I have to ask it. "Are you *sure* it's her?"

"The guy insisted it's her."

I *still* don't want to hope. We've had our hopes crushed so many times already. "I'll wait to call Benchley then."

"I don't want him hearing it from the news, though, Owen. In case it fucking leaks. Go over there, *right* now, and talk to them. Tell them *exactly* what I've told you, and that I'll be in contact as *soon* as I know more. I promise. Keep your phone charged. Personal phone."

I'm still struggling to process...*this*. "Yes, Sir. I will."

That's going to be dicey, though. The press are all over me, between the re-election and now *this*. Well, not this, about the search for her. Every goddamned pool spray, at least two or three reporters are still asking me about her, or if there's any progress, even though we've requested they limit those questions to the official daily briefing, or contact Comms directly about it.

Once word leaks out that Susa's alive, it'll be in*fucking*sane.

"Emphasize to him *not* to tell the press," Carter adds. "No fucking FYIs, no fucking scoops, no fucking hints. He can't call friends or other family members yet, either. *Nothing*. Full radio silence. I don't know if they've notified all the families yet, or how many are still here. I don't know what kind of shape she's in. I mean, he said he's sure it's her, and that she's asking for me, but I don't know for sure, you know?"

"Yes, Sir." I'm still crying and suspect I will be for a while. "Please tell her I love her."

"You fucking bet I will, buddy. I *promise*, as *soon* as I have eyes on her, I'll call you on your personal cell. Keep it on you."

"Yes, Sir. Thank you."

"I need to go, Owen. I love you."

"I love you, too, Sir."

"Be my good boy," he says. "Do what I tell you. Right now. *Go*."

"Yes, Sir." I set the phone down on my desk, put my head down, and allow myself five minutes to quietly sob.

Then I head for my private bathroom to wash my face and clean up. I'm still...in shock.

Fuck the state, fuck the election. I want to fly there *now*, charter a jet, and *go*.

But...

I'm his good boy.

And *Hers*.

So I'll do as I'm told, for now.

I grab the bottle of eye drops from the medicine cabinet and dump in more than is recommended, hoping it'll relieve the redness there. Dray stocked up for me, to help me look reasonably presentable.

Only once I'm sure I can talk without crying, or looking like shit and alerting the press, I summon Dray to my office without telling him why.

Not that it would trigger any suspicions in him for that. With Carter gone, and Susa...not here, Dray has been stepping in for Carter to help me keep the state running.

Dray has no interest in running for office himself. Like Carter, he appreciates where the power truly flows to and from, and wants to be tapped directly into it without the aggravation of being the public face all the time. The secret lightning rod and force of nature.

I'm standing behind my desk, looking out the window with my back to the door, when he arrives a few minutes later. I don't turn when he closes the door behind him.

"Governor?"

"Lock it," I softly say.

"Why?"

"*Please.*"

I hear the lock softly snap, like I've heard it snap so many countless times when Carter or Susa want privacy with me.

But in this case, it's not Susa or Carter. And it's not because we need the privacy for sex.

When I turn, I guess I look worse than I thought, because Dray's eyes widen.

"Sir? Are you all right?"

"Carter just called," I said, bursting into tears again despite hating that I can't be stronger. "He thinks they've found her alive."

"What?" he gasps, rushing over to me.

The story spills out of me. "Can you call Michelle, please? Make sure they're home, don't say why. Lie, if you have to. Then, if they are home, please handle getting the detail ready to get me out of here. Back entrance. Tell them I need to leave, *now*, and can't be seen leaving."

He looks…stunned. Like I feel. "Sure, yeah, of course, Governor."

I grab his arm. "*No* press. *No* leaks. Carter was emphatic about that. We're not sure it's her, not really. But I can't have her parents hearing a rumor from the news."

He hugs me tightly, a soft sob escaping him. I hug him back, sympathizing completely.

"Shit, we need to get ourselves together or people will think that she's dead," he says.

"I know." A choked laugh burps free from me. "She's gonna fucking *kill* us if we fall apart now."

"I know, *right*?" Dray pulls away, sniffling, and grabs a tissue from the box on my desk. "May I use your bathroom, sir?"

"Yeah, of course. Eye drops are in the medicine cabinet."

He laughs. "Thanks."

A few minutes later, the state troopers have cleared the back corridor and stairs, and I'm running, not even bothering to put my jacket on. For once, my detail is having to hoof it to keep up with *me*.

Dray's close on my heels, his laptop and planner in hand, and juggling three different phones, including my official one. I've got a death grip on my personal cell, my charger cord shoved in my pants pocket.

Two minutes later, we're in the back seat of a black Tahoe and speeding through Tallahassee streets.

Benchley's well-protected house, sitting fenced-in on five

acres, the house itself nestled within a thick surrounding border of trees, and with a long driveway behind a locked gate, will provide us a modicum of privacy. Since I've made a point of stopping by at least three times a week since this nightmare began, hopefully anyone staking them out won't think anything of it. Michelle already has the front door open when Dray and I rush in past her.

"Owen, what's going on?" she asks.

"Where's Benchley?" I only want to tell this once, and feel myself already starting to cry again.

Her face goes white. "They found her body?" she whispers.

"Benchley?" I roar, heading toward the room he uses as his home office.

Dray drapes an arm around Michelle and herds her along with us. Benchley is standing, heading for his office door, when I rush through it.

"Carter just called me." I completely lose it as I relate as verbatim as I can what Carter told me. Michelle goes to her husband, their arms wrapped around each other and looking more frail than I can ever remember.

Dray's holding me now as I finish choking it out. "*No* press. He was emphatic about that. No press, no leaks. Radio silence until he says otherwise."

Benchley is nodding, his eyes wide, crying as hard as his wife now is. "When can we leave? I'll charter a jet."

"I don't know. As soon as Carter tells me. I don't even know where we'd meet them yet, or when."

"Fuck *when*, I want to fly over there *now*," Benchley insists.

"We *can't*," I insist. Maybe it's selfish of me, and I don't fucking care, but *I* want to hug her and put eyes on her before Benchley and Michelle do.

Fuck it. She's *my* wife. Maybe not in name, or publicly, but I want *this* thing. This *one* damn thing.

They can hog her for as long as they want *after*, but I *need* to hold her *first*. Because it'll probably be the only moment I get to have alone with her for weeks and weeks, considering the press coverage, the campaign—all of that.

I need to know she's alive, and I *need* to tell my Ma'am how much I love her.

"Like I said," I continue, "I don't even *know* where we'd be going. Carter didn't understand what the guy said about location. I got the impression they're flying them to wherever it is."

"My passport isn't current," Michelle sadly says, saving me further argument. "I meant to renew it and totally forgot. It expired last month." I know damn well Benchley won't travel overseas without her.

"Well, we need to find out where they'll arrive in the States," he says. "We'll charter a flight for them, if we have to. We'll catch a jet out there. All of us."

This I don't argue with. I doubt they can fly straight through to Florida from overseas. Most likely, they'll touch down in LA or Dallas first. Or maybe Hawaii. I don't know.

But, again, any plans made right now are nothing more than what-ifs, everything contingent upon when she actually comes *home*.

If it's truly her.

And who knows the when, because I'm sure there's going to be a hospital stay in her future.

I don't plan to stay much longer. In fact, I'm about ready to have Dray signal to the security detail that we're going to leave when my personal cell rings.

It's Carter.

I answer. "Carter, Dray and I are with Michelle, and Benchley, at their home. You're on speakerphone." That means, hopefully, he'll remember to watch what he says.

He sounds choked up. "They're flying us to the capital city in Brunei, then driving us to the nearby port where the boat's going to dock, unless the boat gets there first and they take them to the hospital. If so, they'll take us straight there. It's…it's *her*. I'm *sure* it's her. They showed me a crappy cell phone pic the boat's crew sent, but it's *her*."

"Where the fuck is Brunei?" Benchley asks.

"Borneo." We hear a ragged laugh. "There *will* be shipwreck jokes later, once we get her home. Fucking *Borneo*."

I want to drop to my knees in *Devotion*.

I want to start sobbing with relief.

I settle for closing my eyes and rubbing my forehead with my left hand, my phone tightly clutched in my right. "Connie?" I ask, because we need to know.

We already know about Mike.

"I don't know," he says. "The crew told authorities two women, but the picture I saw only showed her. I guess there are a lot of typhoons in the area and their connection isn't good. The military doesn't want to risk picking them with a chopper and getting them hurt. It's a huge commercial fishing vessel, not some little dive boat, so they didn't want to risk trying to transfer them to a military vessel. They dropped two medics and medical supplies by helo to the fishing vessel. They're dehydrated and starving, but they're alive. I don't know anything beyond that."

Thank god for Dray. When Benchley's knees give out, he's there, helping get him into a chair.

I'm damn sure not worth any help. I'd been standing there with my eyes closed. Dray's already got him by the time I register Michelle's panicked gasp when Benchley starts to collapse.

"What happened?" Carter asks.

"Benchley's not—"

"I'm *fine*!" the man barks. "Don't you *dare* fucking call 911." He jabs his finger at Dray, who already has his phone out. "I want to be on a fucking plane *right* now!"

"Stay *there*," Carter says, sounding stern. "I need to let doctors evaluate her first. If you want to be helpful, find me *the* best hospital close to where she will be. Do I let them take her to Manila, or get her stabilized and fly her to Honolulu, or back to Singapore, or Australia, or where? I don't know anything about this region. If you *really* want to help her, find *that* out for me."

Dray's now tapping info into his phone. "Brunei?" he asks.

"Indonesia region, yeah. These fuckers are going to pay for whatever it takes to transport her, so I don't care where it is as long as it's reasonably close."

"Fly her back here to fucking *Florida*, Carter," Benchley orders.

"Well, obviously. But if she needs to spend a week or two in a hospital, or longer, and she's stable enough to transport first, I want to transport her to the best place."

"On it," Dray says, his thumbs flying over his phone. "Give me an hour."

"You can have about four, at least. Meanwhile, prepare to clear Owen's schedule to fly him out here. Don't say anything to anyone yet, just start planning the logistics. Owen, make sure you have your passport."

"Yes, Sir." I can't help it, it's automatic, and hopefully everyone is so frazzled right now it'll pass unnoticed by Benchley and Michelle.

"Okay, I need to go. I'll call you all back once I'm there. *No* press."

Then, he's gone.

Dray and I hug each other as we cry, and I don't give a fucking shit if Benchley Evans is watching me cry.

She's *alive*.

CHAPTER TWENTY-SIX

Susa

I fucking *hate* boats.

Did I mention that?

It doesn't matter that it's a big fucking boat, I'm getting massively seasick again.

It's bad enough I'm starving and dehydrated and I'm so sunburned I feel like a piece of beef jerky. Trying to keep anything down in the stormy seas is nearly impossible, even though this vessel is so big that its motions feel more like a gently rocking hammock than what we endured in the life raft while being tossed around in the storm.

The men in the launch who rescued us didn't speak a word of English, and I didn't fucking care, because apparently "starving, crying woman" translates well into any language.

Lucky me.

I have to be carried, and I even remembered to grab my purse.

They get us all into the launch. I reach for George and they let me lie there with my head in his lap. Connie leans against his other side, and like that we all start crying as Allen and Collin lean on each other where they're sitting on the other side of the launch.

They also recover Lisa's body.

George holds on to me so I don't roll around. I really need to remember to tell Carter to send him a bottle of something good to drink for taking care of me and not letting me give up.

Somehow, I don't think either of my men are going to mind or feel jealous.

I do, however, feel sad for George, that he'll now have to process his grief. At least he's got three kids to focus on, and they'll need him, I'm sure.

They transport us back to their huge-ass fishing vessel. I mean, this ain't no goddamned *USS Minnow*, this is a fucking *ship*. One that looks even bigger than the ones I've seen on *Deadliest Catch*. I don't know what kind of fish they catch, but I don't care, either.

Honestly? They could be clubbing baby seals with Flipper at this point, and serving them in blue whale soup in a shark fin bowl, and I wouldn't give a flying fuck, as long as they plucked our asses off that goddamned rock.

I'd even settle for a crab boat.

The captain's English, while passible, isn't great. He tells us the military—whose, I have no clue—is flying out a medic team they'll drop to us. There is another storm approaching, and they're afraid that if they try to transfer us to a helicopter, or to another vessel, bad things could happen.

Sorry, I've been in one plane crash, and technically shipwrecked. I'd rather not add a helicopter crash to round out the hat trick.

The medics eventually arrive. Meanwhile, the others can sip water and electrolyte solutions and keep it down, but I can't. I'm puking again.

I can tell from the medics' tones and concerned expressions that they are more worried about my condition than they are the other four. I can't understand the medics. I don't know what they're speaking. It's definitely not Spanish, so I'm pretty well fucked. The vessel captain's English isn't very good when it comes to medical terminology. The others have IVs, too, but the medics have a hard time getting one started in me, at first. They finally get one started, and they pump fluids and medications into me through it. They bring me ice chips to suck, but the cold is too painful in my parched mouth.

Someone thinks to wet a clean wash cloth, and I can suck on that. We're told we have to be very careful not to drink or eat too much right now, because it could literally kill us. Something pings my mind, and I remember reading about that once, a long time ago, but then again, maybe not. My brain is pretty well scrambled at this point.

A barely used tube of lip balm is scrounged from somewhere, and Connie and I are bogarting it, even though we do allow George, Allen, and Collin to use it.

Maybe I died and *this* is Hell?

Over the next twelve hours or so, they question us, get our names, realize who we are and where we came from, and I beg for someone to please tell Carter and Owen I'm alive. My stomach eventually settles. Whatever they're pumping into my IV is making me sleepy. They've got all five of us crammed in a very small and primitive sick bay space that reminds me of an old fifties TV show set.

They've helped us change into used but clean plain T-shirts and sweat pants, but I want a damn shower, I want to wash my hair.

I want to shave my fucking legs and armpits and the kitty, and fuck anyone who says that isn't very feminist of me.

I want the comforts of home, dammit. Barring that, I want to at least feel human again.

Meanwhile, I'll just lie here, since I can't even fucking *walk*.

I also want to talk to Carter and Owen, but I fuck if I can remember Carter's cell number right now, or Owen's. I'm lucky I can remember my own date of birth and Social Security number.

Honestly?

I literally thought I was *dead*. I'm certain after another day on the island that I would have been. I'm still not sure I'm going to make it right now, if I'm not too far gone already. Maybe I even would have started drinking sea water like Lisa did.

I know they took her body somewhere else on the ship. I feel badly for her family and hope I don't have to face them any time soon. I can't yet.

At least Connie's alive. I couldn't help Mike, but at least I kept Connie alive.

It's...something.

I drift in and out of consciousness. I'm even more certain I'm the worst of all of us from the way the two medics look concerned when they frequently check my vitals and study the portable monitor I'm now hooked to with leads that run under my shirt, which feels like it's about twenty sizes too big, even though the tag said it's a medium.

Not a weight-loss diet I'd recommend to anyone. I wonder how long it'll take me to regain weight, or what the hell I'll be able to wear in the meantime. I'll look like shit for the pressers, and—

Jesusfuck, Susa. Can the politician please *take a goddamned* break?

No.

The ship takes a roll and I barely manage to get my head over the side of the bunk before I puke in the bucket they've thoughtfully provided for me.

Hey, I'm not dry-heaving anymore, although the foul-tasting yellow liquid I puke up is almost worse.

"Just kill me now," I beg once I've been given some water to rinse my mouth out and one of the medics gently towels my face with a damp cloth. "Please?"

The next bunk over, Connie weakly laughs where she's sitting up. "I guess there are no cruises in your future?"

"Fuck you, honey. I didn't make you drink your own pee, and I discovered crabs, so don't bust my balls."

"I will *never* eat another goddamned crab again in my life."

"A-fucking-men," George says, with agreeing mumbles from Allen and Collin.

Connie laughs again, and at least this *one* thing I can hold on to that I've done in my life.

I've brought her home with me.

Well, I've brought her to rescuers. What happens now is out of my hands, but at least I did *this* damn thing.

George is on my other side and sits up, turns, and puts his feet on the floor so he can lean in and drop his voice. "Told you you weren't dying, *girl*."

I think I stick my tongue out at him, but with my lips so bad off, and my tongue kind of swollen, it's hard to tell.

He laughs, so I guess I did.

"Hey, *Sir*," I say, then don't know how to proceed from there. I waggle a finger at him. "No tell-all book before eighty," I warn.

He laughs. "What book?"

Then he winks and reaches over to pat my shoulder.

I guess we're going to play it that way. Fine with me.

I'm sure Susa the politician will be cringing later and beating herself up for what I admitted to him during our ordeal, but for now the politician is just fucking happy to be on her way back to civilization.

One of the crewmen opens the door to talk to the captain, who's stayed there to translate for us. He turns to us. "We are almost to port. We must wait for high tide. They will bring a tug to guide us in to the dock, and some of your families will meet us when we land."

My eyes are so swollen, my face sunburned, but I cry anyway. I hope Carter *and* Owen are there. I selfishly hope my parents aren't, because as much as I want to see Momma and Daddy, I *need* my men.

Desperately.

I'm sure Carter's done a great job pretending to be strong for Owen, but he's going to need me as much as Owen does. That's just how this works. We each rely on the others in different ways.

At least, I *hope* he's done a great job pretending to be strong for Owen.

Then again, maybe they won't be there. Maybe they'll need to get to me from Florida. I honestly wouldn't hold it against them if they aren't here, because, hell, it's been three fucking weeks. They probably thought I was dead.

I thought I was dead.

And I'm sure I look like shit.

I definitely smell bad.

I wouldn't even hold it against them if they've already held memorial services for me. As long as they used decent pictures of me.

If they used crappy pictures, I *will* fucking kill *both* of them.

* * *

I think I should be excused for passing out again. When I awaken, the world is moving. I feel it and briefly freak out, panicked that I'm back on the goddamned life raft.

I open my eyes long enough to see I'm being carried out of the sick bay on a stretcher before I close my eyes again. They're taking me out first, apparently, but the movement and staring up at the ceiling makes me dizzy and makes my stomach roll.

In the distance, I hear a man screaming.

Sounds sort of like a familiar man screaming.

"*Motherfucker*, let me on this *goddamned* boat right *fucking* now!"

Oh, hey, that's my husband.

I force my eyes open, but staring up still makes me dizzy, so I close them again. "Hope you grabbed my bucket," I say. "I think I might need it. And I'd let the screaming guy on board, if I were you. As long as he's my husband. Because if he is my husband, he gets mean and bitey." Then I remember the crew can't speak English, but I hear a chuckle and see the captain walking with us. He translates, and the crewmen laugh.

The captain calls out to someone.

They're still carrying me when I hear more screaming, definitely what sounds like Carter-ish swearing, and then something that makes my eyes snap open.

"*Pet!*"

I hold up the arm without the IV as I start crying. I try to lift my head, but that makes me dizzy, too.

The men carrying my stretcher stop at the sound of footsteps pounding down the deck.

He's *there*.

RIGHT THERE!

Carter's leaning in, cradling my face in his hands, kissing me…

Crying. His tears fall on my face as he sobs.

If I'm dead, maybe I hit Heaven after all.

Except…

"Owen?" I croak.

"Florida. I'll get him coming here."

"Here, where?"

He's laughing and crying at the same time. "Fucking goddamned, beautiful, motherfucking *Borneo*!"

"No shit?"

He's still doing the laugh-cry thing. "No, shit, pet. You ended up in fucking Borneo."

"Please tell me Daddy's not here."

"No."

"Okay." My fingers curl around his. "Sir?"

"Yeah, pet?"

I'm so choked up I can barely talk now, so I squeeze his hand as hard as I can, which probably isn't much. "I tried to stay safe. I'm sorry."

He's sobbing. "My beautiful, perfect pet. I love you so fucking much, you have no idea. You came back to me, that's all I care about."

"Technically," I sniffle, "you've come to me."

He tearfully laughs. "Yeah, well, nobody's perfect."

* * *

The transfer to the hospital is sort of blurry, in my mind. Carter rides in the ambulance with me, holding my hand the whole way, on the phone with Owen.

That's when…

Well, let's just say I wasn't making sense, and I think I said "I love you" about a thousand times.

Then he called Daddy and Momma for me, and more babbling from me.

Yeah.

So much for my polished image.

Ask me if I give a fuck.

#noIdgaf

Carter refuses to leave my side during my evaluation, my treatment, and it's hours before they have me in a bed in ICU. Carter rolled up his sleeves and helped two very nice nurses give me a sponge bath and wash my hair with real fucking water and a wash basin, but no shower, no shaving for me yet.

I can't even walk.

In fact, they've put a catheter in me for now, so they can monitor my urine output.

I…sleep.

* * *

I drift in and out. It's about twelve hours or so later when I finally feel like I'm actually *awake*.

Carter's sprawled in a recliner next to my bed. As if he senses I'm awake, his eyes snap open and he sits up.

"Hey, sweetheart." He leans in to kiss me.

"Owen."

"He's in Florida, baby. Flying out in the morning. He wrapped up a couple of things and packed. He's going to bring you clothes and stuff."

"Did I talk to him already?"

He smiles. "You did."

I nod. "Daddy?"

"You talked to them, too."

"Coming?"

"Your mom's passport's expired. They'll meet us when we fly in, wherever that is."

I nod and lick my lips. Everything fucking hurts now.

Oh, hey, I'm not dying.

"You were right," I say.

His brow furrows. "About what?"

I sigh. "Dying's easy." I think about the sounds Lisa made as she guzzled sea water. That will probably haunt me until my dying day. "Surviving's hard."

His face...he crumples as he leans in, kissing me. "Oh, pet." He's crying again, and it breaks my heart. When he can finally speak again, his voice sounds so choked and full of emotion he can barely talk. "I'm so proud of you, baby. You have no idea how proud. I love you so fucking much. I've got you now. You can sleep and rest. I'm not leaving you. I'll take care of you, I swear."

I feel him swipe lip balm over my lips. "Can you take a few sips of stuff for me?" he asks.

I make fish lips at him—or, I try—and he tearfully laughs. But I manage a couple of pulls off the straw.

"Take me home, Sir."

"We will. You need at least a week here before they'll release you, bare minimum. Probably more. I had Dray working on that. We got a nutrition doctor from FSU on the phone to talk with the doctors here, and he did a consult. You're stable. It's better we keep you here and then just take you back to the US, rather than shuffling you around while you're still so fragile."

I nod. "Flying sucks."

I think he's laughing at first, but it sounds wrong. It's only when he leans in, his forehead against mine and his hands cupping my face, that I realize he's crying once more.

Sobbing.

With my fingers wrapped around his hand, I go back to sleep.

*   *   *

I guess it's only an hour or so this time. I startle awake at the sound of people talking.

"What's going on?"

"We're moving you to a private room," Carter says. "You're stable enough to be out of ICU, but we're worried about the press and stuff. I want you protected."

"Okay. Connie?"

"She's okay. Better off than you."

"I have a confession."

He frowns and leans in. "What?"

"I told George about you and Owen. I thought I was dying."

That time when he laughs, it sounds sweet and deep and easy. "I've already talked to Governor Forrester. He warned me that, for a woman who was convinced she was dying, you loved to quote Monty Python and talk a lot."

"Oh. So he did get a promotion. Good for him."

I mean, not good *why* he did, but...

#shutupImnotatmybest

Carter sadly nods. "Yeah. A lot of people did, pet. A *lot* of people. The hard way."

They settle me in my new room and I sip more of the crappy shit.

But hey, not puking!

Owen calls a little while later to talk to us before boarding his flight to California, and then Carter climbs in bed with me, where I cry myself to sleep.

* * *

Apparently, starvation is a bitch and a half on a body. When I awaken again, I've missed Owen's call before he boards the flight in LAX by fifteen minutes.

Carter tries calling him for me, but it goes to voice mail.

But…he's on his way.

He's coming.

And, apparently, Connie, George, Allen, Collin, and I are the center of a world-wide media storm.

A good one, but a crazy one.

Carter, thankfully, has already crafted a statement for me and issued it through the communications department.

Daddy, of course, gave a presser.

Yeah, okay, I'll give him that one.

Based on my blood work, they up how much of the nasty electrolyte shit I can drink. It's supposed to be cherry-flavored, I think, but it just tastes like sort of sweet ass.

Not even *good* ass.

But my mind feels really *clear* for the first time in days. I'm…

"Carter."

He cocks his head. "Yes, *pet*?" The eyebrow goes up.

I give him eyebrow right back, and he finally folds first with a sigh. "Yes, Suse?"

"He can't pull out."

I know damn fucking well he knows what I mean, yet I can also see from the look on his face that he considers pretending that he doesn't. Finally, "We can talk about that *later*."

"No, we talk about it *now*. I'll be back to work in a couple of weeks."

"Like *hell* you will."

"*Carter*." I fumble and finally get my finger on the button to raise the head of my bed. "We're *not* pulling out."

He stares at me, long and hard, before his shoulders slump. "Okay, pet," he softly says. "I won't let him pull out."

"*Thank* you, *Sir*."

He leans in and gently nuzzles my nose. "You sooooo owe me a fucking spanking when you're back in shape, you know that?"

I smile. "I'll even let Owen spank me, if he wants to."

* * *

A few hours later, there's a knock on the room door, and Carter speaks up. "Come in."

It's one of my doctors. Fuck if I can even remember his name, but his English sounds British, and he's kind of hot, although I'll never admit *that* to Carter.

#notstupid

I mean, Carter would probably think he's hot, too, but helllooo, just almost died.

The least I can do is not perv on hunky guys for a few weeks.

The doctor closes the door behind him, and he wears a...*weird* expression.

Carter's hand tenses around mine, but he doesn't squeeze. He's terrified to hurt me, and I get it, but I just survived a fucking ordeal and I *need* his strength right now.

So I squeeze Carter's hand, until he looks at me. I mean, I guess he's looking at me. I'm still squinting and everything's blurry. They said it'll probably be a few days before the swelling goes down in my face. Then they can evaluate my eyesight to see if there was any permanent damage.

Even if I end up with glasses after this, totally worth it, if that's the only remaining issue I have after what I endured.

"What's wrong?" Carter asks without waiting for him to speak.

I forget, Carter has his own past experience with doctors and hospitals, even though that was years ago, before we met.

"I have gone through your wife's test results, and I have some news for you that I am not sure how you will receive."

"Just tell us."

"Mrs. Evans is pregnant. We need to do further testing to tell how far along. I am surmising that, since neither you nor she revealed this to our medical team, that it is a surprise to you as well?"

I'm…stunned.

"Say that again?" Carter whispers. "*What* did you say?"

"Your wife is pregnant."

"You're *sure*?"

"I ordered the test be repeated just to be certain."

Now Carter's squeezing my hand.

"We're going to be parents!" I'm not sure if he's saying that to me or the doctor or if he says it while simply trying to drive the point home inside his own brain.

"Do you wish us to run further tests now, or wait and have them done later after she is released? I would prefer now, because we may need to modify her treatment protocols, and—"

"*Now*," he says. "Absolutely, now. But this says secret."

"Of course. Our patients' privacy is one of our top concerns."

The bastard extraordinaire is back. He jabs a finger at the guy. "No, I mean not a *single* word of this gets out. Change her name in the system or something, or create a new fictitious patient profile. Anything. This news can*not* get out."

"I will talk to the hospital administrator and see what we can do."

"You do that." I hear it in his tone—the bastard extraordinaire is *back*.

Thank god.

The doctor nods. "I will make a referral so that they send an obstetrician to evaluate her. They will likely order more tests."

"Sure. Yeah, of course. Whatever she needs."

When the doctor leaves, Carter stands and turns. He's wearing a grin. "A *baby*!"

I'm a realist. "Carter," I gently say, but he rolls right over me.

"Owen will be here in…" He calculates. "Fifteen hours." He's pacing, already planning how to break it to him.

"Carter."

"We've *got* to keep it secret for at least that long."

"Carter."

"Man, I can*not* wait to see the look—"

"*Carter*." He finally stops and stares at me, his face still filled with joy. "*Please* don't get your hopes up, or his," I gently warn. "After what I've been through, and my age…"

Fierce determination fills his face. "*Fuck* that, pet. I refuse to think anything other than we're having a baby."

I reach for him, and when he takes mine I tug on his hand to bring him closer. "Let's let the doctors tell us it's okay before we get our hopes up. *Please*?" I must be at least five weeks or so along. Owen sent me off to the airport with a load of cum in me after bending me over his desk while Carter guarded the door.

Then it was, what, a week before that, the night of my meltdown. So possibly six weeks. A week before that, maybe? I can't remember for sure past that. So possibly seven weeks.

That's still…that's *early*.

I guess it explains my vomiting, though. Maybe I wasn't as seasick as I thought I was.

But dehydration and starving, the stress and trauma, drinking less than pure water, eating what we did—I'm not getting my hopes up.

I especially don't want to get Owen's hopes up, because losing this baby will crush him.

I am hopeful, however, that even if I do lose the baby, maybe it means we can keep trying. I'd started to think it'd never happen. Honestly? I was convinced it wasn't happening. Not after, what, nearly four years of it not happening? I was hyper-focused on getting re-elected, and looking forward to my own campaign run, getting myself positioned for it.

I also hate myself for thinking if I do lose the baby that I need to make sure that gets leaked for maximum sympathy factor.

The politician is eager to climb back in the saddle.

Me?

Not so much.

Not until I have Owen in my arms and know he's okay. Yeah, I'm fucking superstitious, but the next plane crash I'm in, I want my men with me, if only to feel comforted knowing we'll be together for eternity.

I'm not looking forward to flying home. Oh, I'm looking forward to *getting* home, but flying's going to suck balls.

It's actually going to take both of my men to get me on a motherfucking airliner cruising over open water. I would have said they could knock my ass out with good drugs, but mommy's little case of indigestion makes that impossible now.

Carter leans in and his free hand gently settles over my tummy. I'm painfully aware how thin I am.

I'd *kill* for a damn Cuban sandwich. *Any* sandwich. But I'm on a very strict clear liquid diet, until they can transition me to the next stage. It would suck to survive what I did and die because I wanted a goddamned cheeseburger.

Mmmm. Cheeeeeeseburger…

He stares into my eyes for a long moment before he speaks.

"I'll only ask this once—"

"We're *not* pulling out of the race, Carter. We're fucking *doing* this." I hit the button to raise the head of my bed. "We worked too goddamned hard for this. You think I'm *not* using this to leverage us into a win? Fuck that shit. I am my father's daughter, and we are running Tallahassee for the next twelve years. If I can't pull off a win for myself after Owen's second term after all of this? Then I don't fucking *deserve* to be governor."

He studies me for a long time before finally nodding. "All right, pet," he quietly says. "But please figure out how to say that in a much gentler way to Owen when he gets here, huh?"

He's absolutely right.

The bastard smirks, and I can't help but smile. We really are perfect together, all three of us. I wish we could both marry Owen, too, but at least he's happy to be owned by us.

I'm not much of a praying kind of person, even after all this, but I do hope our baby makes it, if for no other reason than I know it will make Owen the happiest man on planet Earth, with Carter a close second.

And seeing them smile is truly one of my reasons for living.

Especially after what I just survived.

CHAPTER TWENTY-SEVEN

Owen

Where's a TARDIS when you *really* need one, huh? I think changing my clothes helped prevent me being recognized. Jeans, a T-shirt, sneakers, and my favorite Lightning baseball cap, one Carter gave to me years ago, when we were still in college.

The entire way over from the States, and then again on my flight from Manila, my right thumb rubs against the blue band on my right ring finger, the Doctor Who ring Carter gave to me the day I was sworn in as governor. My left rubs the band on my left finger, the ring Susa gave me.

Fuck my job.

I'll give it *all* up if it means we have Susa back.

Fuck the plan. Fuck everything except *Her*.

As our flight closes in on our destination, I struggle not to nervously tap my foot or do any number of annoying things to burn off my increasingly frantic energy.

A million anxiety-fueled scenarios are racing through my mind. That it turns out it really wasn't her after all, and somehow, it was a horrible mistake. Or that she's died while I was in the air, mere minutes before I go running through her hospital room door.

That I don't get to tell her in person one more time how much I love her.

Fuck the election, fuck everything else—I want my Susa, and I want her in my arms, and not another goddamned thing matters to me right now.

They can quote me on that, if they want. I don't fucking care.

Goddamned Kevin Markos can point a camera in my face and I'll happily flip him birds with both hands and tell him to happily fuck himself on a rusty pitchfork.

Without lube.

There are government officials waiting for me when I emerge from the plane after flight attendants make sure I disembark first, and they hurry me through customs and into an awaiting SUV for the drive with a police escort.

I can't even be bothered to pay attention to what is, admittedly, a beautiful country.

Nothing matters until I put eyes and lips and hands and every other body part possible on *Her*.

Carter is awaiting me when the hospital's elevator door opens on her floor, and it takes every ounce of strength I have not to burst into relieved tears to see him. He grabs me in a quick, wordless hug, then takes my hand and rushes with me down a couple of corridors, leading me to a private room, where he closes the door behind us.

The blinds are already drawn on the corridor windows, and we're alone. Susa looks at me at the sound of our entrance, and she's sunburned, her face swollen, her hair a wreck—but it's *Her*.

This is when I burst into tears and check out for a little while as I climb into bed with her, sobbing as I hold her and she whispers to me, and I tell her over and over again how much I love her, all while Carter leans in from behind me to hold both of us.

I unabashedly weep. Even if I had a thousand cameras pointed in my face I couldn't stop myself right now.

She.

Is.

Alive.

I'm lying there with her frail, gaunt frame tucked against me and her head in the crook of my arm when Carter finally speaks.

"We need to talk, buddy."

"Why?"

He changes sides, walking around the bed so he can look me in the eyes without me craning my neck around at an odd angle. He smiles as he lays a hand on my cheek and leans in, kissing me. "Susa's pregnant."

Rage washes through me. "*What*? Who fucking did it? I'll fucking kill them my-goddamned-self! I'll—"

It's Carter's rolling laughter that shuts down my anger, followed by Susa's soft giggle.

"What?" Fuck, the bastard extraordinaire can't be so goddamned callous and cruel that he's…laughing? "*Why* are you laughing? This isn't *funny*! Who raped her?"

Carter's now laughing so hard that tears are rolling down his face. He has to brace one arm on the bed to support him, because he can barely stand. He hooks the other around my head and pulls me in for a deep, confusing—to me—kiss.

"It's *yours*, dummy!" he says.

Susa clears her throat with a warning tone I know all too well.

"No, pet, in this case, it's *totally* warranted." Carter smiles at me. "She's pregnant with *our* baby. Yours, ours—*you. Dumbass.*"

He's…he's got to be fucking with me…right? It's been, what, the better part of four years since she went off the pill, and I've fucked her in nearly every position mentioned in the *Kama Sutra*, and a few that weren't, and…

"Really? I whisper.

Susa reaches up and tangles her fingers in my hair. "Want me to beat Sir for you for calling you a dumbass? I will. Just ask me."

I'm laughing even as I'm crying again. "We're going to have a *baby*?"

"That's what I've been trying to tell you, Owen," Carter snarks. "Sheesh. *That* didn't go the way I thought it would."

"But...but it's been so long, and..." I don't even know where to go from there so I let it die off into silence.

"It happened," Carter said. "Just our luck on the timing, I suppose." He sighs. "We're going to need to have a lot of tests done, watch her carefully. Don't... I don't want you to think this is a sure thing, yet. All right?"

I nod, but now I'm staring down into Susa's eyes. "I'll announce I'm going to pull out of the race when we get home, and—*OW*!"

She's grabbed my ear and is painfully twisting it, pulling me down close to her face, so close I feel her breath against my cheeks.

"*Listen* to me," she says, full-on Ma'am mode engaged. "You are *not* pulling out of that race. We're *still* running, I'm *still* your lieutenant governor, and we're going to fucking *win*. We're going to try to keep this secret until after the election. The plan is still in effect. This changes *nothing*."

"But—"

"No buts, Owen. I'm serious. We're running."

My hand settles over her tummy. She feels like a sack of bones, and that makes me heartsick on numerous levels, but within her...*our* baby.

My baby.

Even if we're the only three who will ever know the truth.

I'm going to be a dad.

Me!

I look up at Carter when she finally releases my ear. "Sir?"

He's standing there, *that* smirk on his face, and his arms crossed over his chest. "Don't look at me," he says. "I'm just the governor's chief of staff. I'm out-ranked."

But he can't hold it. The smirk turns into a full-on grin.

I stare down into her eyes. They're red and bloodshot and fucking gorgeous.

More gorgeous than anything I've ever seen.

"Yes, Mrs. Evans."

She smiles. "Good boy."

* * *

I finally get over to see Connie a few hours later. She's in far better shape than Susa. Her sons are with her, and I lean in to give her a hug.

She starts crying. "She saved me."

I haven't heard the whole story. Carter told me snippets, but I didn't even process most of it. I was too busy staring at Susa and imagining her pregnant with our baby.

"I'm so sorry about Mike."

She grabs my hand and squeezes. "She put the oxygen mask on me, and got my life vest on me, and got me out of the plane, and gave me crabs."

Her sons burst out laughing.

"Um…crabs?"

"Crabs. On the island. She was the first one to see them. She couldn't eat much, so she'd give me hers to eat."

"Oh! Crabs."

"And water. She made me drink. I…I would have died if it wasn't for her."

I gently squeeze her hand. "I'm glad you both made it. It's a miracle."

She nods. "I think I might want to resign my post, though."

I laugh. "You know workman's comp will pick this all up, right?"

She finally smiles. "You're going to win, you know. If she can get us home again, she's going to get you re-elected."

I nod. "I tried to talk her into us both quitting, and she said no."

"Probably was a *lot* more profane than that, on her part, knowing her." She smiles.

"It was."

We chat for a few minutes longer, then I go talk to Governor George Forrester. I knock on the open door and the man sitting next to the man in the bed looks up.

"Governor Forrester?" I ask.

"That's what they tell me," the guy in the bed says.

"Owen Taylor." I walk in and shake his hand. Carter's told me a little bit about what Susa went through, and the personal information she and this man exchanged.

No, I don't begrudge that he held her, comforted her.

Ordered her to drink.

At least when she was close to giving up, maybe he helped keep her alive when she wouldn't have made it otherwise.

I had to, at the very least, meet this man and shake his hand.

The other man stands. "I'll run get some coffee, George."

"Thanks," Forrester says.

The guy closes the door behind him.

I sit in the vacated chair. "My chief of staff told me we have you to thank for helping to keep our lieutenant governor going."

He sits up a little in bed. "You guys are really lucky." He meets my gaze. "She loves both of you so damn much." He tears up. "Ellen would have loved to have known her."

"I'm very sorry for your loss."

"Yeah, well, the main thing I'm thankful for is that she literally didn't know what hit her." He sadly smiles. "And I'm grateful for Susa. Once we can all think and breathe and are safely back on solid ground, you'd better believe I'm going to record some campaign ads for you guys, even if I have to form my own PAC to do it. And when she runs for governor. And whatever other office she runs for. I'll strong-arm the GOP in my state to toss money her way however I have to."

I honestly have no clue what to say. "Um…thank you."

"I know. It's weird talking politics right now, huh?"

"Yeah."

"She and I are a lot alike, I think. I was going to run for governor, once this term was up. I think my chances just got a lot better."

I chuckle. "Yeah, probably."

He drops his voice. "You're lucky men," he says again. "And no, nothing she told me that's personal will ever be repeated by me. We kind of have…" He sadly smiles. "I guess I have a lot in common with Carter."

"They told me." I shake with him again. "Thank you, Governor. And any runs you make, I'll be happy to help you out, too. And get Benchley Evans to pitch in."

"George. And that's a deal." He studies me for a long moment. "She did tell me y'all are trying to have a baby. I hope that works out for you."

I snort, rubbing the back of my neck. "We still off the record?"

He nods.

I shrug. "Nothing's for certain right now. It's still soon. But looks like maybe there's a reason she was throwing up. Only time will tell if everything's okay and it makes it."

His eyes widen, tearing up again, and he sits up to hug me, both of us crying now. "Congratulations, Dad. If anyone can pull this off, she can."

"I hope you're right."

Boy, do I.

CHAPTER TWENTY-EIGHT

Susa

It's two weeks before they feel safe discharging me and Connie. I've regained three pounds and while it's recommended I don't hit an all-you-can-eat buffet, I'm allowed to eat soft foods as I can tolerate them.

Mmmm. Pudding.

They said in another week I can progress to other things. Meanwhile, I can drink protein shakes and things like that.

Owen's slept in bed with me every night. He was going to let Carter sleep in my bed, but Carter, that soft-hearted bastard, ordered Owen to do it.

Fuck, did I mention how much I love these men of mine?

I don't know how Carter, Dray, and Daddy spun the story so it's not suspicious that Owen stayed with me that long, but they did it. I guess having Connie here helped. The public's been eating up the info released at every daily briefing, where they report how we're doing.

Hell, more people are asking about *us* than the usual legislative shit they ask about.

The politician in me is *howling* with the scent of victory in the air.

The Ma'am, wife, pet, and mother-to-be will simply be glad to get *home*.

Allen, Collin, and George left the hospital three days ago.

George stopped by one more time to say good-bye and give me a hug. He'd gotten a shave and a haircut and looked a lot better than he did when we were pulled off that rock. I know my men have talked with him several times, and there will likely be visits back and forth with all of us, campaigning for each other, and just sitting around as friends.

Because, come *on*, the man likes Monty Python. How bad can he be?

He also privately whispered *congratulations* in my ear as he hugged me, so I know either Carter or Owen spilled the beans to him.

Daddy doesn't know yet, and I'm not actually looking forward to telling him.

I'm afraid he might want to make me pull from the race, and wouldn't be shocked if he threatens to ratfuck us somehow if I refuse.

We go straight from the hospital to the airport, to an awaiting charter flight. From there to Manilla, then to LAX.

In LA, Carter and Owen roll me off the airplane and down the jetway in a wheelchair. We're taken off first, along with Connie, and surrounded by officials, but my men refuse to let anyone else help with me or our stuff. Owen's carrying our bags, and Carter's pushing me. One of Connie's sons is pushing her in another wheelchair.

We emerge from the jetway into a Customs area, where we're processed in what is probably record time before we're escorted out into a crowded terminal full of press, cameras, and people who explode into cheers and applause at our appearance.

*God*dammit, *Daddy.* I don't even have any fucking makeup on, and I look like shit.

I should have *known* he'd do this.

I mean, yeah, I *get* it. Senator Benchley Evans is nothing if not pragmatic when it comes to politics.

Still, I would have preferred a private welcome.

Carter leans in and whispers in my ear. "Sorry, pet. I asked him not to do this."

When I catch Daddy's eye before he's allowed to walk over to us, I spot his wink.

Goddammit.

It's been over seven weeks since I've seen my parents, and I don't know if it's because my perspective was forcibly shifted, or because the stress of my ordeal aged them in record time, but they both look incredibly frail compared to when I last saw them.

Owen looks about two breaths from tears. I hope Carter can figure out a way to get him alone to calm him down. Despite how aggravated I am at Daddy, I've given up trying not to cry as I hug him and Momma, even though I hate crying in public.

It's emotions, it's hormones, it's...everything.

I'd finally convinced myself dying wasn't the worse thing in the world, right before we were rescued.

Then my world shifted again when I found out surviving wasn't the best news I could receive.

It's hard to pound it through my skull that I'm going to go to sleep in my own bed in Tallahassee tonight. I know Carter won't be able to talk Owen into returning to the mansion, either. Carter won't have the heart to.

Neither will I.

Even the bastard extraordinaire has a soft spot or two hiding in there, somewhere, when it comes to his beloved pets.

Especially for *our* beloved pet.

For the first time in my life, I'm overwhelmed by the press and the crowd. I offer a tepid smile and hold up a hand. I'm sure I look like shit without makeup, and my hair's a disaster, but this story will lead every newscast in Florida tonight and tomorrow, and I guess I need to make it count before the news cycle spins on and leaves us in the dust.

"Thank you, everyone, for the well-wishes," I say. "I just want to get home and get back to work. We have a state to run."

Hopefully that will carefully straddle the line between authentic and orchestrated. I wish I'd known about this, or I'd have had Carter prepare me something to say.

He leans in and whispers in my ear. "That was perfect, sweetheart." He kisses my cheek.

I reach up and pat his hand.

Fortunately, we're able to get out of there in under ten minutes, and we're quickly moved to a private lounge area while they finish prepping the plane Daddy chartered for our flight home. They're going to load us on golf carts to drive us across the airport to where the private jet awaits us.

If Daddy has arranged for reporters to accompany us on the flight home, I'll fucking kill him, *and* Carter for not stepping in and putting his foot down about it.

Apparently, even Daddy knows when not to push me. No press. It'll be the five of us, Connie's sons and daughters-in-law, and a two-person paramedic team.

I eye them and then glare at Daddy. "We were cleared to fly and travel, Daddy."

He shrugs. "Your mother insisted. For you two, and for me."

Momma firmly nods. "Damn *right*, I did."

"They're not staying in the house with me tonight," I say, then it hits me.

Oh, fuck.

They're probably going to want to stay at their townhouse tonight so they can be with me.

I *need* alone time with Carter and Owen. I'm sure Owen

desperately needs that, too. I shift in my wheelchair to look at Daddy. "You and Momma can't stay in the townhouse tonight," I softly say. "You need to go home."

He looks like he's trying to get huffy with me. "Bullshit, we can't."

I sigh. "Daddy, I *need* to decompress. You guys can come over in the morning and stay all day, if you want, but *I'm* putting my foot down about tonight."

He glares at Carter. "Tell her no."

Carter snorts. "*You* tell her no. *I'm* going to be *yes-dearing* her to infinity. Sorry, but you're on your own, Benchley."

Thankfully, Momma intervenes. "Benchley, I think she's right. I warned you she and Carter will want to be alone."

Well, okay, let's go with *that*. I just won't tell them about Owen. Or, if they find out about him being there, I'll claim it's work-related, an excuse Daddy can't argue with.

Carter leans in to whisper in my ear. "Can Owen and I go—"

I pat his hand. "I'll wait for you."

He kisses me. I'm aware that Owen's already slipped away to the lounge's men's room, and Carter quickly follows him.

Probably won't put him on his knees there, but Carter can at least rub his head, talk to him.

Give Owen a moment to suck in a deep breath without a dozen people around him.

Especially when I know all our boy wants to do is kneel in front of me, put his head in my lap, and feel me rub his head.

*   *   *

We make it on board the chartered jet. I pick a set of three seats in the very back—making it harder for others to spy on what we're doing without being obvious, because they'd have to turn around— and Carter helps me strap in. I think Daddy's a little perturbed at me that I ask Owen to sit on my other side instead of him or

Momma, but he'll just have to suck it up.

After what I've been through, I don't think anyone has the right to tell me who to pick to be my seatmates.

I don't bother to hide the fact that I'm holding their hands, either. There's no press with us now, and Carter instructs the flight attendant to let him know if she sees anyone taking pictures of us with a camera or phone.

We have relative privacy.

As we rumble down the runway and pick up speed, I squeeze their hands, hard. Carter and Owen lean in, their heads tipped close and touching mine, as Carter whispers to both of us. I know how hard this is for our husband, considering Carter hates flying way worse than we do. That he's being so strong for us now is one more small thing in the infinite universe that is Carter's strength and love.

Although, to be honest, I pretty much despise flying now. I'll be going back to the I-75 commutes between Tallahassee and Tampa via car for the foreseeable future. If it wasn't for the fact that I don't want to spend a week in a car *now*, I'd have demanded Carter rent an SUV and drive us home to Florida.

Also, if it wasn't for the fact that we need to get Owen back to work ASAP, I would have asked Daddy to fly us into Tampa so we could go to sleep in the Brandon house tonight.

Once I have a couple of weeks to recover, I know I'll feel better, more steady, but if Owen was to kneel in front of me right now and beg me to let us retire from public life…

Despite my earlier declaration to him when he first arrived at the hospital, I might just say yes.

*   *   *

Home.

It's two a.m. Tallahassee time when our security detail pulls up in front of the townhouses. They know Owen's staying at "his" townhouse tonight, and probably will the next several nights, at least. So once Carter literally carries me inside and sets me on the sofa, the officers on duty tonight set up a cordon to keep the press out and away.

Dray and Gregory met us at the airport, along with a bunch of other people, state employees and the general public, but I told him he didn't have to come back with us to the house. It's late, and I'm exhausted, and I know he and Gregory need to get up tomorrow to work. Especially Dray, who's still doing his job and much of Carter's.

And I know Carter and Owen will sleep in a little tomorrow, even if I need to play dirty and beg them not to go jogging.

I told Daddy that he and Momma could come in for a few minutes, so their driver is waiting outside in the SUV they rode in.

"We might as well get this over with," I say to Carter. Behind him, Owen's gaze darts to me, then away, before he stands off to the side, out of the line of fire.

"Over with?" Carter asks.

"Yeah." I look at Momma and Daddy. "I'm pregnant. You breathe a word of that to anyone before the general election, and I'll ratfuck every GOP candidate I possibly can, regardless of what office they're running for."

Carter snorts.

For the first time in my life, I see Senator Benchley Evans truly at a loss for words. "You're...*pregnant*?"

I nod. "Yeah. Due in March."

Momma starts crying and hugs me.

Then Daddy frowns.

"What's wrong?" I ask.

He clears his throat and levels "a look" at me.

I level one of my own at him. "I'm *not* dropping out of the race, so don't even *think* about lecturing me to quit!"

He bursts out laughing and leans in to hug me. "I was going to lecture you *not* to drop out!"

A long, deep belly laugh rolls out of Carter, and even Owen starts to chuckle.

"Oh. Well, okay, then. Glad we understand each other, Senator." I give him a sharp nod.

That makes Momma laugh. When Daddy glares at her, she shakes her head. "Don't you start with me, Benchley. She's *your* daughter."

"Yeah, I guess she is." He hugs me again. "I'm so proud of you, sweetheart. And I love you so damn much."

"I love you, too, Daddy. But I mean it. I don't want this getting out yet. We've got more than enough juice right now to coast through the primary and the general. I don't want it rebounding on me, that people think I should be staying home and not running."

"Oh. Yeah, that's a good point. I didn't think of it like that."

I stick my tongue out at him. "I have a good idea every once in a while. So will you stop hating Carter, please?"

"I don't know. I've enjoyed having an archenemy all these years." But he walks over to Carter, and they hug. Then he hugs Owen. "I guess if she can put up with you boys for all these years, you two can't be all bad, huh?"

I feel a little twinge of fear that maybe Daddy knows more than he's letting on, but he smacks Owen on the shoulder in a friendly way. "We need to get you out and dating, son."

Owen shrugs. "I'm married to my job, Senator."

He waves it off. "Benchley, when we're alone."

"Go home, Daddy. Your meter's running."

"Okay, okay. But we'll be over in the morning."

"No earlier than nine."

For sure, I think he's going to argue with me, then he laughs again. "Nine, sweetheart." He kisses my cheek, then Momma gives me another hug and kiss, and they leave.

Owen leaves with them, goes to his townhouse, and is back in the living room in under forty-five seconds.

I don't think I've ever heard him run up those stairs so damn fast in my life.

Now that we're alone and locked in, Carter lets Owen carry me upstairs to our bedroom. Instead of bed, though, I want a damn fucking shower, in *my* shower.

We take one together, and they tenderly scrub me, help me shave everything…

And then the three of us curl up together in *our* bed, naked, with me in the center and my hands clasped around theirs and pressed against my tummy.

This is absolutely *the* most perfect moment in my life.

CHAPTER TWENTY-NINE

Now — Election night.

Tonight, we're watching general election returns in our usual suite in the downtown Tampa hotel.

Hey, why screw with what works?

Yes, I know that's superstitious, but after what I survived, I think I can be cut a little slack in that department.

Owen won his primary, but based on the number of votes he received, he likely would have won even if it was the general. There's been a huge influx of voters registering as Independent ever since my ordeal, both new voters and people changing their party affiliation.

It's left the Dems and the GOP scrambling to plug their sinking ships, Daddy chuckling over his sneaky daughter's shameless politicizing of her "ordeal," and Carter confident we'll win tonight's general election.

This has been a *crazy* four years. Especially the last several months. Okay, it's been a crazy twenty years, if you count from when I first met Carter and Owen in college.

Admittedly, surviving a plane crash and being shipwrecked adds to the crazy factor, just a smidge.

I don't know how Carter's kept my pregnancy a secret for as

long as he has, but he's done it.

Somehow, I suspect Daddy had a hand in helping with that. I wonder how many favors he's had to call in. Not much longer before I'll be really showing. The loose, flowing blouses and dresses I've been wearing will only help so far after a certain point.

At least one thing's for certain—my plucky story of survival has likely guaranteed Owen's re-election.

The fact that I only took an additional two weeks off after my return—and even then was working from home despite Carter trying to overrule me—shamed our opponents, who could easily be silenced by simply referring to the time I already "took off" due to almost dying in a plane crash and then having to fight for survival for several weeks…just to literally put myself back on the campaign trail.

And bringing Connie home with me. Even she's publicly said in interviews that if it wasn't for me, she would have died. No, I didn't ask her to say that.

Can damn sure bet I'm using it to our benefit. Yeah, I'm shameless when it comes to exploiting even the tiniest advantage. I won't deny it. I get it honestly, from Benchley, and from Carter.

The ruthless politician in me revels in the leverage my ordeal gave us, and in the state-wide fifty-point exit poll lead we're currently enjoying over our closest rival.

Doesn't mean it's a slam-dunk tonight. Never assume that until all the ballots are counted.

But even Daddy's relaxed and not stressing. If he's not stressing over election results, then it's as close to a guaranteed result as you can get without the actual votes being counted.

Owen, bless his heart, wishes we could scream from the rooftops that we're going to be parents. Maybe in a different timeline we could do that. But this is the path we've chosen, and that means there are concessions to make. Instead of a public celebration, he has to pretend not only that I'm not pregnant, but that it's not his baby.

In private, either in the mansion or in our townhouse, he spends hours happily curled up with me on the couch, with his head in my lap and his hand against my tummy.

Carter, the bastard extraordinaire, usually sits on the other end of the couch, with Owen's feet in his lap and an amused smirk on his face as he watches his two pets together. With Carter's presence, it means no questions will be asked about the three of us being together. Especially at the townhouse, because everyone thinks Owen's next door.

We're having a boy, and he is, so far, healthy and developing normally despite what I went through.

Owen's already named him Peter, after one of Carter's brothers who were killed in action.

Peter Benchley Taylor Wilson.

Taylor was my requirement.

Yeah, I know, but Daddy puffed up when we told him, sooo…

#happygrandpa

Then again, just to prove what a bastard my hubby is, he gave me a little stuffed crab toy after Connie first told our story publicly…

#gotcrabs?

My goddamned office is *overflowing* with motherfucking crabs. It's apparently my "thing" now.

I guess there are worse things to be known for.

Like dying.

George—excuse me, *Governor* Forrester—sent me a large picture that I immediately had hung in my office, a blown up print from the scene in *Monty Python and the Holy Grail*, where Eric Idle and John Cleese are arguing about taking away the not-dead-yet guy.

Only George had piles of crabs Photoshopped over the bodies in the cart and John Cleese's shoulder, and scattered all around them, and a dialogue bubble from John Cleese says, "It'll be stone crab in a moment."

I laugh to the point of tears when I unwrap it. Of *course* he found wrapping paper with crabs on it.

Even my sweet, gentle boy jumped on Carter's sadism wagon and seems to find me a new crab-themed something-or-other every dang week.

Sigh.

What I went through was almost enough to break me and make me beg to pull out and return to private life.

Almost.

Thank god I didn't. This...*thi*s is pure political *gold*. On top of all the good we've already accomplished during our first four years, I can't walk away now. We'll announce my pregnancy tomorrow morning, win or lose.

Owen isn't happy about this, but we'll make Kevin Markos our first interview. He literally gets two minutes, live, downstairs in the lobby, just him and one photojournalist walking with us out the back hallway to our waiting car, and that's *all*. And with only me and Owen, not Carter.

Markos isn't getting the scoop about me being pregnant, which is the only reason Owen agreed to let us talk to Markos in the first place.

Markos *thinks* he's getting a scoop, a foot-up by being able to have first cameras on us in the morning, ahead of our afternoon sit-down.

Heh.

One journalistic ratfuck, coming up. I'm sure it'll piss Markos off, but Carter suggested doing this, despite how Markos and FNB will likely paint a target on us as a result, because it sends a message that only took us four years to finally be able to deliver.

Fuck you and your shitty network over that goddamned live interview after the school shooting, you assholes.

Ice-cold revenge still tastes *damn* good. Daddy thinks it's a genius move, and even gave Carter an *attaboy* when we told him.

When the inevitable questions arise as to why we cut FNB out of the info about my pregnancy, Carter will take the incoming fire on that one and claim he was still half-asleep, and oh, darn, it was over so fast, and we were moving so quickly to get to our next interview, that it *totally* slipped our minds.

Whoops.

Carter and I both are going on-air during all the other scheduled sit-down interviews with Owen. If anyone comments about us withholding the news about my pregnancy until tomorrow morning, we'll shamelessly play the "Gee, I almost *died*, don't you think I deserve happiness?" card.

Four more years, and then it's *my* turn.

Owen might end up retiring for a while after he leaves office to stay home with the baby—who will almost be ready to start school by then—and that will work out better for all of us, anyway. Owen will be happy, our baby will be safe and cared for by his daddy, and it'll keep Owen off the media's radar for a while.

A friend of Daddy's approached Carter for help finding a long-term beard for his daughter, who's ten years younger than Owen. She lives with her girlfriend, who is an aspiring politician in the middle of her own bid for their county commission. Since they're both registered GOP, they figured it'd be easier for her to wait to come out.

Daddy talked to Carter about borrowing Owen, of course. It makes me more than a little jealous that Carter arranged for her and Owen to have dinner a few times in Tallahassee over the last several weeks, and tipped the press off about it every time.

When I put my foot down that she would *not* be joining us on election night, or at the inauguration and ball—if we win—I shamelessly played the "'your wife almost died" card to Carter.

Yeah, I went there.

Even the bastard extraordinaire didn't push back, finally giving me a smile and kissing me, nuzzling my nose. "Yes, dear," he said with a chuckle.

Damn, I love that man.

Election nights are *ours*. *Only* for *us*. Beard for the greater good or not, fuck that.

Owen is *ours*. I won't share him on a night I already have to share him with the entire damn state, and I think Owen and I earned this, considering everything else we'll have to pretend about.

Photo ops can wait for another night.

Tonight, I can't move anywhere that Owen's not constantly watching me, no matter who he's talking with. He turns so he can keep glancing at me without being too obvious.

At least most of the people here tonight, we can trust them. Maybe not with the deepest truths about us, but as my best friend, sure, Owen worries about me.

No one will begrudge him this tonight, or speak ill of him for it.

We actually have two hotel suites, in the same wing, sharing a common foyer area, and with a trooper standing guard. We used a wristband system, and only the people with a certain wristband can move between the suites. Everyone else has to stay in the other one. I did make an earlier appearance over on the other side, and will make one more before we head downstairs. Carter's using my health as an excuse, that he wants to take things easy on me.

No one questions him, assuming he means about my recovery from "the ordeal."

For tonight, Carter's pared down the list so that we only have ten people in this suite with us, besides immediate family and Dray and Gregory. Carter and Owen make frequent trips next door, to the other suite.

The truth is that Carter wanted Owen able to sit down on the couch next to me from time to time tonight, and be able to talk to me, to relax without worrying who was watching us. Everyone allowed in *this* suite tonight knows how close we are as friends and won't think a second thought about Owen's actions tonight, especially in light of almost losing me.

Only Dray knows the full truth, and that's only because he works for us.

If Daddy suspects anything, he hasn't said so.

*   *   *

Election returns begin flooding in when the polls close at 7 p.m. Eastern time in most of the state.

Fucking Panhandle.

Maybe one of my first actions as governor should be proposing we allow Alabama to annex part of the Panhandle and be done with it.

#justkidding

#sortof

#nojustkidding

Early voting numbers are record-breaking. Every political commentator is referencing my "survival miracle" as likely being a contributing factor.

No shit, Sherlock.

#duh

Well, at least my ordeal accomplished a second thing— everyone definitely knows *my* name, and it isn't Daddy's name that's the sub-lede in every story anymore.

It's now a variation of "her miraculous story of survival."

Voter turnout is astronomically higher than four years ago, both early voting and for today's voters. By seven-thirty, a clear picture is developing. Miami-Dade has *finally* gotten its shit together for this election, with ninety-two percent of its precincts soon reporting Owen ahead by over sixty points. Hillsborough has reported ninety-three percent of its precincts, with Owen showing a fifty-point lead that only widens with every data refresh. Orange County, which is Orlando, shows eighty-nine percent of precincts with Owen already ahead by fifty-six points and growing.

Those are the biggest concentrations of voters, which means it'll likely be gravy from this point on. We might see some chipping away at that lead, because rural areas of our state tend to trend red, but our most recent surveys showed increasing *I* and *D* voters registered in those areas, so who knows?

By seven forty-five, throughout the rest of a state as a whole, there's an overall fifty-five-percent reporting average from counts in progress, showing Owen ahead by over forty points and with an ever-widening gap.

At seven fifty-five, with eighty-five percent of the state's precincts reporting, the Democrat calls and concedes. The Republican waits until MSNBC, Fox News, and CNN all call it at eight fifteen.

FNB, those dickless fucks, wait until eight twenty-five to call it, until after Duval County—Jacksonville—reports in at ninety-nine percent counted, and Owen's handily won by over fifty-five points.

There are not enough uncounted, provisional, absentee, and overseas ballots left to count in the entire *state*—including the Panhandle—which would, even if none of the votes were cast for Owen, come close to bringing another candidate into recount territory, much less overtake Owen's lead.

Fuck you, Panhandle. Stupid time difference.

Carter puts on music. Owen's wearing a smile as he walks over to me and offers me his hand.

"Next to Me" by Imagine Dragons starts to play through a Bluetooth speaker, and I take Owen's hand. He helps me up off the couch, and we dance while Carter smiles and watches us, his arms crossed over his chest as he leans against the wall, his jacket off, sleeves rolled up, and tie loosened.

The handsome perv always does love watching his pets together.

Halfway through the song, Carter walks over. "May I cut in, Governor?"

Owen grins. "Certainly, Sir." Owen's going to hand me off to Carter, but this time, Carter take Owen's hand and pulls him in to dance, earning us laughter and applause.

Daddy walks over, smiling, and offers me his hand. "May I have this dance, Lieutenant-Governor Evans?"

"Sure, Senator Evans." As we dance, I watch Owen and Carter dancing. Carter's actually letting Owen lead, and while they're whispering to each other, I see one of those sweet smiles cross Owen's face.

I pause to slip my phone out of my pocket and snap a picture of them like this, just for me.

"Still say you should have married Owen." Daddy's smiling, though, so I know he's not really serious.

When the song ends, Carter hugs Owen, patting him on the back as he says something. Owen's reluctant to release him, and Carter stays there, the two goofballs of mine nearly making me cry, they're so sweet.

Or maybe that's pregnancy hormones hitting me.

Carter starts to step away from Owen but sees me watching, and they open their arms to me.

Of course I go to them. I always will.

With our arms around each other, we stand there, just breathing in each other's scents, feeling the warmth of the others.

Just us.

Carter moves in a little, pressing me even more firmly against Owen as he tightens his embrace of both of us.

"Mine," he whispers, kissing my forehead. Then he looks up at Owen and smiles. "So are you," he says.

Owen leans in and touches his forehead to Carter's. "Love you both," he says.

"I will kill *both* of you if you make me cry right now," I growl, which cracks them up.

I'm back on the couch a few minutes later, Owen and Carter next door, when my personal phone buzzes with a text message from Daddy.

It's two pictures, of the three of us standing there, holding each other—one before Owen leaned in close, one with his forehead and Carter's touching.

Okay, now I *am* crying.

I look over to find Daddy smiling as he tucks his phone back in his pocket. Then he grabs his glass of iced tea and salutes me with it.

The big softy. Like Carter, Senator Evans is a bastard when in politician mode, but Daddy does have a gooey center, when he tries.

We hadn't planned on going downstairs until ten-thirty at the earliest, which is what we'd told everyone.

So we wait, but with Carter sending word through Comms that we might go down earlier.

Nearly immediately, every channel starts running that update on their crawlers, or having their on-air reporters outright mention it. This race has been watched nationally, due mostly to my tale of survival, but, yes, also due to the fact that Owen's an Independent.

The three of us step into the suite's bedroom and, after Carter closes and locks the door behind us and pulls the curtains, he smiles and holds his arms open to us.

We both go, me kissing Owen first, and then Carter. Then Carter kisses Owen, and we all stand there, silent and…processing.

We did it.

We.

Fucking.

Did.

It.

Carter puts his hands on both our heads and draws us in, our foreheads all touching as he rubs our scalps.

"I love you both so fucking much," he says, his voice sounding choked. "You two are amazing, and I'm the luckiest man on the face of the planet."

It's nearly enough to make me cry, seeing the bastard extraordinaire emotional and stripped bare like this to us right now.

"Love you, both," I whisper.

"Love *you* both," Owen replies. Then he draws in a long, shaky breath and lets it out again.

Carter gently nudges me to hug Owen, and I do. "You're brilliant," I say. "You're so damned amazing, boy, and you've made me the happiest woman in the world."

Owen nuzzles his face against my neck. "I don't give a shit what anyone says or thinks," he says against my skin, "I *will* be in that delivery room."

"Of course you will," Carter assures him, his arms around both of us again. "I've already got Dray working on our schedules to keep them light close to her due date, and to keep us all in Tallahassee."

"Good." Owen deeply inhales again, and I know he's sniffing me, assuring himself I'm *really* real and not a dream.

He does that a lot lately. Carter's loosened up a little on the no-PDA rule. Of *course* it's natural for Owen to hug me, as my friend, especially after what I endured. A *lot* of people have been hugging me since my return.

We have a window of time where little things like this will not be exploited against us. I know that window will rapidly shrink at some future point, but for now, I will shamelessly enjoy it.

When we head downstairs at nine-thirty so Owen can give his victory speech, I stand between my men and hold both their hands.

It's only me, Owen, Carter, Dray, Gregory, and two troopers in the service elevator with us. We held everyone else back to follow, Carter once again citing me and my health. I'm not nearly as fragile as he portrays to the public, but we go with it.

They'll all know the truth soon enough.

When the three of us march out onto that stage together, we're still holding hands. The thunderous roar that greets us feels like a physical presence all around us, lifting us, cradling us.

We *did* it.

Carter turns his back to the audience to kiss me, then releases my hand and gives Owen a long, strong hug before he turns and, with his arm still around Owen's shoulders, waves his other arm to egg the crowd on and get them cheering even louder for Owen.

Smiling, Carter steps behind us, makes a point of putting his hands over ours, where they're still joined, and holds them up as he nudges us forward. Then he stands back to let us bask in this moment.

What a photo opp. I definitely want an enlarged and framed copy of this picture to hang on our wall.

I glance back to see Carter walking back and forth across the stage while fiercely waving both arms now, urging the crowd louder, leading chants of *TAY-LOR! TAY-LOR!* before he starts applauding us and gives us a bow from the waist.

Then he stands behind us again, the implication clear—*Fuck any of you who want to try to make something of this, because I'm behind them one-hundred-percent.*

Owen pulls me in for a hug and stares down into my eyes for a long moment. I think maybe he's actually going to kiss me, but he doesn't. A long, slow blink, our special code. In this case, I know it means *I love you.*

I blink back, give him one more hug, then I lean in closer to the microphone, clapping as I speak.

"Ladies and gentlemen, I present to you your current and future governor of the great state of Florida, *Governor Owen Taylor*!"

I don't even care who sees me crying now. I'm so fucking proud of him that I'm clapping just as hard as everyone else. Harder, even.

This fucking photo op isn't merely gold, it's platinum, and fuck you if you think I won't exploit it for every millisecond I can wring from it.

I glance over and catch Carter's eye, and he smirks, winking at me.

I wink back.

God I love that fucking bastard *so* fucking hard.

We've sacrificed so much over the years, my men doubly so. They've done this for *me*. That proves to me how much Carter loves me. He could have easily worked on Owen all those years ago, seduced him into his arms, and cut me completely out of the equation.

By now, they'd have been married a few years, maybe adopted a couple of kids, living a quiet life as attorneys.

Not…*this*.

Instead, Carter took a chance *on* me, and keeps taking chances *for* me.

Because he loves me.

Don't think I don't know how precious this thing is that we all share.

Loyalty.

Devotion.

They're not just kneeling positions. They're words that describe my husbands' hearts, even if we're the only three who can truly know that.

They're *mine*, and I love them.

It was only thinking about them that kept me from giving up during my ordeal, until the very end, when my body was close to failing me.

Carter's order to me to stay safe.

Knowing that, despite what I went through, they *still* want to support me being in politics, instead of all of us immediately returning to private life and being able to openly be spouses and parents and enjoy this compounded miracle.

We stand here tonight because they love *me*.

We stand here tonight because they support *me*.

We stand here tonight because I am the luckiest woman in the damn world.

I had been certain I'd never have a baby. I don't believe in divine intervention, but the confluence of events is almost enough to make me consider that it's possible.

Almost.

But not quite.

Because my baby isn't born yet. Maybe one day I might consider taking a more spiritual path in my life, but today is not that day.

Tomorrow's not looking so hot, either. Because I am my Daddy's daughter, and I am also Senator Benchley Evans' daughter—a politician, first and foremost.

A politician who's about to spend another four years as the lieutenant governor of the great state of Florida.

THE END

The Governor Trilogy continues in *Chief* (Book 3), *Yes, Governor* (Book 4), and *Pet* (Book 5).

ABOUT THE AUTHOR

Author Lesli Richardson, who is better-known by her more prolific wild-child Tymber Dalton pen name, lives in the Tampa Bay region of Florida with her husband (aka "The World's Best Husband™") and too many pets. She writes a wide variety of heat levels and genres, from mainstream sci-fi all the way to scorching ménage.

The USA Today Bestselling Author (as Tymber), two-time EPIC award winner, and part-time Viking shield-maiden in training loves to shoot skeet and play D&D with her friends. She's also the bestselling author of over two hundred books and counting, including *The Reluctant Dom*, *The Great Turning*, *Cross Country Chaos*, the Bleacke Shifters series, The Great Turning series, the Suncoast Society series, the Love Slave for Two series, the Triple Trouble series, the Coffeeshop Coven series, the Good Will Ghost Hunting series, the Drunk Monkeys series, and many others.

She lives in her own little world, but it's okay—they all know her there.

She loves to hear from readers! Please feel free to drop by her website and sign up for her newsletter to keep abreast of the latest news, snarkage, and releases.

Honest reviews are always welcomed. They help with a book's visibility and can boost its placement on book retailer sites. Even a few lines about what you felt reading the book will help. Thank you so much, it's greatly appreciated!

Visit my website to sign up for my newsletter, find out what's coming soon, and more!

http://www.tymberdalton.com

Made in the USA
Columbia, SC
15 October 2021